NIGHT FEAR

NIGHT FEAR

Paul Samuelson

Barnard Way Press
San Rafael, CA
2013, 2018

For information contact:
Barnard Way Press
San Rafael CA
www.barnardwaypress.com

Front cover photograph by Krivosheev Vitaly

Design, layout and typesetting by
Liquid Pictures
www.liquidpictures.com

ISBN Number: 978-1-7321924-0-9
Library of Congress Control Number: 2018904650

Barnard Way Press

Printed in the United States of America

NIGHT FEAR

Before

He lay face up in a patch of early spring snow, the young soldier, under storm gray billows crowding the night sky, and knew it was over for him. Wasn't supposed to be. Never him. It was always some stiff who seemed to be marked from day one who got it. Or one turned suddenly unlucky. He thought of that cocky PFC in his platoon who took a Mauser slug through the neck as he scooted up to gather his crap game winnings. But son of a bitch if it wasn't his turn now. Suddenly unlucky.

Not supposed to be me? Bullshit, he thought. *Probably deserved it.*

When he'd been hit it hadn't hurt, was only hard poundings on the back of his left thigh and up to his lumbar area. Within a moment the pain set in like flames burrowed deep. The icy ground numbed it somewhat. If he remained still it helped, but then he knew frostbite would set in. So he strained to slide his arms and legs in short arcs across the hard packed ground.

But soon the agony of movement brought despair, and so he stopped. He hoped the cold didn't lessen the bleeding that much so he'd quickly go to his last sleep. Warm tears streamed down from the corners of his eyes as he thought of his mother back home. *Oh, damn it, Mama…God damn it…Take care. Be safe always.* Maybe it wouldn't be so bad. He closed his eyes and waited…he waited…

Then something broke the night silence.

A stirring coming closer. Footfalls. Sounded like one man. Probably a German. That would be okay, too, if the Jerry just put a bullet in him. Quick and neat. Then what, a choir and angels and shit? Or…what? Who knew? Who the hell knew?

The pace of the footsteps slowed, and then stopped next to him.

The young soldier turned away, squeezing his eyes shut. "Just…fuckin' do it," he managed to say.

"Easy, buddy—Sergeant. You're gonna be okay."

The soldier looked up to see a thick red cross on a white armband and a face under the lip of a helmet. There was something about the medic's face, almost a sweetness in his eyes that didn't at all fit in this place. Not at all. Maybe he was already dead.

"I'm Eddie. Eddie Fulham. Gonna get you out of here, Sarge." The medic's voice had a tone of assurance. But the soldier wasn't up to being assured of anything.

The medic then hesitated, looking up. Clouds were parting to reveal the moon.

The soldier heard him mutter something. Sounded like, "He'll stay alive, damn it. Has to stay alive—he has to." Something like that. Talking to himself with a hint of panic.

He's not so sure, this medic.

Machine gun fire started in the distance. Bursts of metallic clacking. Rifle reports in answer. It was like an argument, the soldier thought, the sounds of a battle. Each side trying to force home some point or other, exchanging angry responses. What made him think of that? Maybe you think about any dumb-ass thing when you're on the way out.

Easier that way than regretting what mattered.

"Where you hit?" the medic asked him.

"Left side…back…back of my leg…and up a ways."

"You strafed?"

The soldier shook his head. "Grenade."

"Damn potato masher. From far enough away you're still intact. Good."

Good? The soldier almost smiled at that.

More gunfire out there somewhere.

The medic pulled out his shirttail, tore off a piece, putting it in the soldier's mouth. Then he slid his arms underneath him. "Bite down hard, Sarge. Like a terrier on a mean guy's ankle."

He lifted the soldier up—god*damn* it hurt—hoisted him and flopped him across his shoulders in a fireman's carry. Sweet-eyed medic was pretty strong.

Pain stabbed the soldier with each bounce as the medic held him across his back.

He saw sparkly, moonlit snow interspersed with black ground moving by under his barely conscious gaze. The sprawled body of one of his patrol…and the other. Then more barren frozen patches. It was dreamlike. The intermittent icy crystals seemed to dance with the labored cadence of the medic's trudging ahead. The soldier could feel his heartbeat, so weak. His eyelids fluttered open and closed…open and closed.

His delirium brought to mind some fairy tale fantasy, like his mother might've read to him years ago when he was nestled in her lap. He was being carried by a strong, good prince to the safety of his castle, even as attack birds kept jabbing their scissor-like beaks into him. The good prince strode on, bearing him, toward the castle somewhere ahead out there. The devil birds kept swooping down at him, their beaks snapping together, sounding like—bursts of metallic clacking. The fantasy dissipated like smoke in a gust of wind.

Then suddenly it was mostly dark. He strained to look up and saw pine trees, their dense, overlapping branches blocking the sky. A forest. Cover, sure, but the gunfire was louder. Closer now.

Even so, he heard the medic let out his breath in relief and whisper, "I'll be okay, yeah…It's like a room in here…Good. That's good."

What's he going on about?

"Just stay in here…in here till it starts to get light…I'll be okay."

He kept talking to himself, the medic. Like he was by himself. Maybe he knew that his load was only shot-up meat. *Useless now…useless…usele…*

The young soldier passed out.

1

Mig Czerniak braked to a stop behind an old pickup, so battered and scraped it looked like it had been through as much combat as he had overseas.

Other vehicles were parked in line in front of the truck. This was as close as he could get on the curve of dirt road dead-ending in a wide area cleared of mesquite and sagebrush around a weathered, clapboard-sided building.

What was now a clinic for Indian families from on and off the local Pima Reservation had once been the Safford Field bachelor officers' quarters. The BOQ had been split into sections and hauled a few miles here by wide-load flatbeds. Partitioned bunk areas for officers in flight training in Arizona during the war were now medical treatment rooms for those of a tribe too poor to afford its own doctors. His mother had made this place come to be; Mig was proud of her.

He got out of his Chevy coupe and gazed at Camelback Mountain in the distance. In a couple of hours the sun would lower behind it, spreading a glow over its hump, becoming a brilliant cap before thinning across the mountaintop in its descent, then disappearing. A nice end to the day and the desert heat. Though hot weather he could deal with, unlike cold. He couldn't much tolerate cold.

As Mig walked around to the other side of his car, he thought again, as he had all throughout the day, about the call he'd gotten early this morning from Eddie Fulham's mother. About Eddie. What had happened last Thursday. And the bastard was still out there who had done it.

Mig had asked for details about tomorrow, even felt compelled to write them down. He didn't know why at the time, since Los Angeles was so far away.

He opened the passenger door, and lifted a box from the seat. It was heavy, full of government pamphlets on hygiene and home health advice. Limping slightly, still after two years, Mig carried the box toward the clinic. He heard some kid inside start to wail as if being tortured.

When he entered the clinic the child's crying had subsided. Mig edged his way with the box past a group of Indian men and women conversing in the middle of the reception area, a couple of little kids playing peek-a-boo between their parents' legs. At the desk, the receptionist, phone to her ear as she jotted something down on a notepad, looked at the box Mig was carrying and patted the counter. He set it down there and mouthed, "Where's my mom?" She motioned with her head toward a hallway leading to the treatent rooms, and he headed that way.

He approached the first open doorway and looked inside the room to see Carmen Quinteros, a woman of graceful dignity in nurse's white, with a Pima boy of about four on her lap. A thermometer was in his mouth and his hand clutched a cherry lollipop. His cheek had a drying tearstreak. Carmen was showing him her wristwatch, speaking with a trace of Mexican accent. Cultured, highborn. "When the sweep hand—the skinny one you see moving—makes it all the way around two times, Wendell, then the thermometer comes out and that lollipop I gave you goes in. Okay?"

The boy Wendell smiled, opening his mouth. The thermometer started to slip out and she set it back under his tongue. "You need to keep your mouth closed—But be careful, like I told you, not to bite down."

"Yeah. Don't chomp on it and break it like I did once," Mig said, leaning against the doorjamb. "Remember that time?"

Carmen glanced over at him. "Quite well, *hijo*. But Wendell, here…" She gave the boy a quick hug, "…is better behaved than you were."

"Doesn't say a lot," Mig said. "Got those pamphlets from the printer. Put 'em in the front, at the desk."

"Thank you."

"De nada."

Her dark eyes took in his pale blue ones. "You look tired," she said.

"Been a long day, Mama."

"Wait out in front. I am almost done here."

He nodded and left.

After a couple of minutes, Carmen came out to reception with Wendell, who was now sucking on his lollipop. She was holding the boy's hand, his treatment chart tucked under her arm.

Mig observed as Carmen ushered Wendell over to his parents and siblings on the side of the room. She took on an expression of reassurance as she unobtrusively covered the little boy's ears while she spoke in low tones. When she finished what she had to say, Carmen smiled down at Wendell and tousled his hair. The parents started herding their kids toward the front door. She watched the family leave, and then gave the receptionist the chart to file and walked over to Mig. She was nearly as tall as her son and not quite twenty years older.

Carmen studied his eyes, the puffiness around them. "Tell me, how did you sleep last night?"

"Okay. Slept okay," he said, averting her gaze.

She put her hands on his cheeks and made him face her directly. "Be honest with me, Angel Miguel."

Saying both his first and middle names, she'd put the Archangel Michael onus on Mig, her expectation of him, as far back as he could remember. Carmen Quinteros was all about her ideals, and those of the father Mig had never known but had heard about when he was growing up. His mother had made sure of that, instilling her memories of Aaron Czerniak in their son. To mold him into the character of the man she had so loved. To put on Mig some kind of unwelcome responsibility, as he saw it.

Years ago she'd given him a snapshot of his father. Carmen had taken it out of its small silver frame and asked Mig to put it in his billfold. Every so often he would look at the photo. But it didn't mean anything to him, really. Someone he never knew with pale eyes like his. Relating to this man as having been his father was beyond his reach. Aaron had been a fighter for justice, Carmen had told him. Now back from the war, Mig had enough of fighting—for anything. Enough for three lifetimes.

"Only woke up once," he said. "That's doing better, uh?"

Carmen looked dubious. "If you didn't stay awake for the rest of the night."

He shrugged. "Needed to get up pretty soon, anyway. Early shift and all."

"There is the medication I had prescribed for you."

"Tried those pills, Mama. They give me headaches."

She seemed hurt; his pain was hers as well, he knew.

"I have concern." She smiled ruefully as she shook him gently by his arms with affection. "With all that you go through, *hijo*, you also have to put up with me."

During short periods of time when he wasn't forced to endure what haunted him, he'd try to believe that it was starting to go away. Sometimes he could almost be content, even joke around some again. If only the war wouldn't keep coming back.

The first time was during the victory parade in Phoenix that he was part of the summer before last, right after Truman announced the Japanese surrender. It was a mid-August day of joy and celebration. A day for shouting and tears of relief and closeness. Strangers bounced up and down, uncaring of their awkwardness, as they hugged and cheered of one spirit on that glorious, triumphant day. A day of gratitude for FDR, Eisenhower, and now Nimitz and MacArthur. Gratitude for all the servicemen and women, those who came back and the ones who never would. A day of being thankful to a just God. Mig noticed a young couple peel off from the crowd, he imagined to rush home, hurriedly strip off their clothes and entwine in hopes of conceiving a baby. One of the kids to be born in a perfect world. The tide of it all took over everyone, including Mig at first, on display in the parade.

Then, in the middle of a rousing Souza march, brassed out by the band just behind him, he looked out at the crowd on one side of the street and then the other side, and something deep in his gut suddenly, terribly wrenched. In that moment he knew. It was beyond what he'd ever known, but he knew.

Ghosts had followed him home.

He was sitting atop the back seat of a Cadillac convertible between a Seabee and a jovial Army Air Corps crewman. The three of them were in uniform for presentation, to be cheered and welcomed stateside. They were waving back and beaming at everyone, Mig, too, until it came—the inner avalanche of what he'd been through, the torrent of what he'd witnessed in the war.

And what he had done.

He doubled over and just shook. The Air Corps crewman noticed it first, then the Seabee. They grabbed Mig by each arm, and the Seabee, as he continued grinning and waving at the cheering crowd, commented that the paratrooper must be hung over from celebrating a little too hard last night. Mig pulled free from them, shoved the Air Corps guy nearly off the back of the car in his effort to spill over the rear door. He almost stumbled into a drum majorette before making it to the sidewalk.

A few people rushed up to him with concerned looks and reached out to help, but he shook them off. Mig saw them stare after him as he staggered down an alley. Then they turned back to the parade to continue in their reveling.

Unfeeling of any pain from his wounds, Mig slumped to sitting on the concrete among garbage cans behind a restaurant. As he waited for his breath to settle, his shaking to be over, he heard the band music starting to fade. The parade was moving on down the street, Mig cut off from anything of its spirit and hope. As the physical effects of what he'd just gone through subsided, he felt more alone than he'd been since that night before Eddie Fulham had saved his life. Alone except for the hellish memories.

And after that, when he was in their grip, Mig would almost wish that Eddie hadn't rescued him. Death would've spared him the anguish.

Now in the clinic reception area he felt Carmen's loving grip on his arms. "It will get better, *hijo*." There was strength in his mother's gaze. "I believe that. And you need to as well."

He nodded, coming as close to comfort with her support than she could realize. But she probably did know. Nothing much got by her.

"Are you busy tonight?" she asked.

Mig shook his head, not saying anything about packing a suitcase for the nearly four-hundred-mile drive he'd be taking tomorrow to Eddie's funeral. He had to go. Knew it was the right thing to do within minutes after getting the call.

"Want to come ho—over for dinner?"

"Jack gonna be there, too?"

She shook her head. "He has Rotary tonight."

"Too bad. I like Jack. He's a good guy."

"So how about it?" Carmen asked. "Dinner tonight?"

"Uh…depends," Mig teased, to lift his spirits.

"In what I have in the icebox, right? It is leftovers."

"Aw, I don't know…"

"If I get a couple of T-bones?"

"Well…"

She patted his cheek. "I might as well get some ice cream, too. Chocolate still, I assume. Speaking of that, pick up a block of ice, will you? I am low."

"Mama, for Chriss—cryin' out loud, when you gonna get yourself a refrigerator? They're mass producing 'em now."

"One of these days…"

She started away to return to her duties. Stopping and turning back to him, she said, "This week's *Collier's* is on the table, and there is the radio. I will be in a meeting until close to eight."

"Funding again?"

"Oh, of course, funding." Carmen looked heavenward. "Always funding," she said over her shoulder as she walked away.

There was some government money now, after the war, but not until she secured private sector support could Carmen get her clinic fully operational. She brought her experience as a nurse and shamed some doctors into donating their time a few hours a week. During one of her early country club appeals she met Jack

Tolafsen, successful produce rancher turned more successful when copper found on some of his acreage fetched a price considerably higher than lettuce.

Jack was looking for purpose beyond building income. It didn't take much convincing from this steely, passion-filled woman a dozen years his junior. Carmen offered him renewed meaning if he would write a few checks. There were more than a few, it turned out.

More and more battered pickups and stake beds filled with sick Indian families were showing up at the Gila River Clinic from the rez and surrounding area. Carmen needed more staff. There were fund-raisers, three times in the past year which Jack and Carmen co-hosted.

She gave her all to the clinic, like she had for Mig when he was growing up. But by the age of twenty-three that should be over and done with, he knew. The realization came back to him constantly that he was still too damaged inside his head to be fully a man. It ate at him again as he walked from the clinic back down the road to his car.

Mig had his own place to live, his job at the clothing warehouse, was self-sufficient as far as most of his needs went. His disability checks from the Army helped.

He drank beers and shot pool occasionally with some of the fellows after work, Dominic, Carl, Leroy. But during long moments he felt apart and didn't hear a lot of their banter. One or another of them would nudge him, looking over at the others, saying that Mig "was off in his own world again." Then he would smile and join back in, or seem to. They could usually handle his outbursts at work over seemingly nothing. The other guys liked Mig enough to usually overlook his quick temperedness. When he was too much to take, Bernie, their boss, would smooth things over. Bernie seemed to understand.

Mig dated some, had a woman every so often. Dom's lonely widowed sister was the usual one. But for him having sex was only mere physical release. Since he'd come back from overseas he felt dulled from meaningful human contact.

To an extent, Carmen could connect with him as no one else could. It was as if she could almost see inside him to what he'd been through. In a world so unsure for him, his mother was his lifeline. And this bothered him. He'd grown up considering it his duty to protect her. But after returning from overseas, emotionally ungrounded, he wondered how different he was now, really, from that little Indian boy Mig had seen on her lap a few minutes ago.

There was a commercial icehouse on the outskirts of town. Mig parked in front of it. He got out of his car and crossed to the entrance where a beefy man inside, wearing a full-length leather apron, started turning the sign hanging on the glass-paneled door from OPEN to CLOSED.

"Hey, want a block. That still okay?" Mig called through the door.

The icehouse proprietor opened the door and bobbed his head, grinning. "Sure. These days I'm glad to hold off closing up for a customer. Come on in."

He opened the door wider and Mig went in.

"It's for my mom. She's still got an ice box."

"Another diehard. Good for her."

The proprietor led him behind the counter to the refrigerated room in back. They passed by a sour-faced older man adjusting gauges on a panel of controls. The proprietor leaned back toward Mig and spoke low. "My father-in-law. Lives with us. Tired of puttering around at home so I let him fiddle around back here."

Then he said to the older man, "Tommy, can you get this fella a burlap sack from storage?"

The older man looked offended. "Anything wrong with sayin' please?"

"I meant please, Tommy. Please get a sack for this customer."

Muttering to himself, Tommy shuffled off to the storage room.

The proprietor removed a canvas cloth uncovering a long block of ice, made up of several blocks fused together. "S'what happens. All gets stuck together 'cause Tommy keeps fiddling with the Freon controls."

The proprietor took an ice pick and scored the gouge deeper between two of the blocks. Then he stabbed hard at the ice along the gouge, again and again.

Within seconds Mig's gaze became fixated. Then he blinked rapidly. An image took over his mind—a GI stabbing a German soldier with a bayonet, driving the blade into the jerking body, again and again.

As the proprietor raised the ice pick for another jab, Mig grabbed his arm.

"Come on, Westbrook, that's enough," Mig said as he tried to pull the proprietor back from the ice.

"Hey, whadaya—"

"It's over. He's dead," Mig said, as if trying to reason with him.

The proprietor struggled against Mig's hold on him. "Hey, easy there, fella. Come on. It's not—"

"The Kraut's dead, goddam it! He's already gone!"

Moments later, when he came out of it, Mig saw the proprietor looking at him with what seemed to be sympathy. Mig was vaguely aware of hearing "…thousand-yard stare, like Bill used to have. I remember how it was with him…"

Mig's breathing started to slow down. He shivered some, not only from the chill of the room.

"Just relax, buddy. Take it easy. Everything's gonna be alright."

Mig didn't respond, only gazed off vacantly.

Tommy shook his head, his mouth pinched like he'd been chewing on a lemon.

"He's plain fool crazy, if you ask me," he said.

"A little maybe, still," the proprietor said. "But I wouldn't judge it. My cousin came out of the first war changed for a time. This fellow's a reminder of the way Bill was some years back."

"Soldiers s'posed to be soldiers, damn it. They're bred soft nowadays."

"Tommy, you dumb old codger. If you weren't Evelyn's dad…"

"Watch what yer sayin'," the older man snapped.

"…I'd boot your wrinkled ass out."

After he left there, Mig drove a little ways out of town. The block of ice would keep for a while. He turned off the highway onto a dirt road and parked about a half a mile into the desert. He liked being out here at the end of day when the heat was easing up. Enjoyed watching the shadows of the guardian-like saguaro cacti spread east across the sand and brush, the low sun intensifying the colors of lupines and prickly poppies.

A cool breeze was coming down through the slopes of Camelback today. Mig grabbed his leather jacket from the back seat and put it around his shoulders. He sat on his running board and took in the expanse. Out here at this time of day, in this open starkness, his demons were silent.

There was a slight stirring a few feet from the front tire. A gray and pink-scaled Gila monster poked out from under a rock. It clawed its way forward, its fat tail seeming to help propel the ugly little beast. Relieved now from the heat, its lazy blink brought it fully awake, maybe looking for food. In the exact moment the lizard would gain sustenance, the life of some beetle or spider would end. Predators and the preyed upon was just nature's way. Not anything like war.

And not like what had happened to Eddie Fulham. Eddie, with his strange fear of night and the moon, victim of a hit-and-run.

Being out here in late afternoon, early evening was as close as Mig got to sanctuary. Usually not a time or place to dwell on anything but whatever felt right that could still reach him. With one shoe he made a little shallow circle in the sandy dirt, fixating on it. Then he looked out over the calmness and tried to reflect on what might still be decent in the world. He wanted to regain trust in that. Maybe in time he'd be able to lock away most all of the bad stuff. But he couldn't keep his thoughts to anything like better days right now. Not after the call he got this morning.

Eddie ... damn ...

It was nearly nine o'clock before Carmen got home from her funding meeting. Mig was sitting on the floor next to the radio, listening to the last comedic exchanges on *Fibber McGee and Molly* when she came in carrying a bag of groceries.

"*Lo siento.* Sorry, sorry I am so late. You must be starving."

He reached over and turned off the radio. "Not really, Mama. Couldn't wait."

"What do you mean? You didn't…"

He nodded slowly, looking sheepish. "Yeah, 'fraid so. Raided your leftover tuna casserole."

"You finished it?"

"Uh-huh," he said. "Was good. So were the two rellenos."

"And also the…So, you must not be hungry?"

He rubbed his belly and gave her a "not really" look.

"And the steaks in here…" She hefted the grocery bag.

"They'll keep, won't they?" He asked too innocently.

Not bothering to answer, Carmen walked to the kitchen and set the bag a bit emphatically on the counter. She saw the desert flowers Mig had picked and stuck in a glass of water. "Wildflowers. How thoughtful of you, *hijo.*" Appreciation was tinged by a frostiness in her voice. She opened a cupboard, took out a small vase, and filled it with water. She lifted the colorful, short-stemmed flowers and set them in the vase, arranging them neatly. "Do you have room for chocolate ice cream at least?"

"Oh, sure. Always got room for that."

"*Have*—not got. I should not need to correct *your* native language." She was clearly irked. "Well, the ice cream is starting to melt by now." She said. "I was hoping to freeze it some before… You brought the ice?"

"Yeah, sure."

"Thank you. I was hoping to freeze the ice cream a little while we had the steaks, but seeing that—"

"Good idea," Mig said, as he stood up. "I'll set the table." He went into the kitchen, around his mother, and opened a drawer. With seemingly deep intent he started to select silverware.

Carmen paused, and then he glanced over to see her smile to herself. "I think that if I look in the ice box, the casserole will still be there," she said. "And the rellenos as well."

He pretended he didn't hear her as he took out knives, forks, and spoons. He kept a grin contained.

She shook her head. "Stinker…"

Mig looked over at her with a son's kidding smirk. "Hand me

the napkins, Mama, will you? The cupboard right above you," he said, as if Carmen didn't know where she kept everything in her kitchen.

Because of the late hour, their dinner together was somewhat rushed. That helped keep him buttoned up about his plans for the next couple of days. He didn't want to say anything because Eddie Fulham had been a connection to the war and Mig was reluctant to talk about that, especially to his mother. Protecting her in a way. He'd call Carmen tomorrow to tell her that he'd left and why, not bring up something so unpleasant across the dinner table when they were having a nice time together.

It would wait till he was on the road the next morning.

2

A few hours west of Phoenix, Mig stopped to fuel up. The homely teenage kid on duty at the gas station pulled on the Chevy's latch release and raised the hood, blocking him from view. Good. There was something about the kid, his blotchy, pimply cheeks, yellow teeth that didn't fit in his mouth right. Grinning at nothing, his face naturally set goofy. Mig was irritated, as he could easily get, especially sitting behind the wheel for a long while with ache throbbing his backside. It was hot, which bothered him now. Must be inching up to at least ninety degrees here, even this early. The heat in this scorched town, Indio, was about like where he lived, but after this much time on the road, pain made him prickly, intolerant.

He got out, stretched, and walked away from the pumps, his limp easing as he loosened up some on the way across the station to a phone booth. He left the door open and dug in his pocket, pulled out the few coins he had, setting them on the metal shelf under the phone. He picked out a nickel and reached up to put it in the slot.

"Hey, ya know—"

A firm tap on the back of Mig's shoulder. He spun around, grabbed handfuls of T-shirt, and slammed the service station kid to the ground as change clattered on the floor, rolled out of the booth onto the hot dirt. Mig had his knee hovered over the kid's chest, ready to shove down hard and crush his ribcage. The kid's lips quivered, eyes wide as shot glass rims. His words rushed out. "Don't hurt me. Jus' wanted to tell ya—you're down a quart, mister."

Mig felt like an asshole. Again. And he was paying for it with pain from his quick, tense reflex.

As he got up with some difficulty, he said, "Sorry. I'm…I'm sorry." He reached down to help the kid to his feet, but he brushed Mig's hand away and got up shakily on his own.

"What the hell!?" the kid blurted, and then bent down and picked up Mig's dipstick and a rag mostly stiffened by dried grease. He faced his attacker, not sure how much to show righteous anger, it seemed. The kid's voice calmed a bit, maybe allowing for caution. "What the hell's with you, anyway?"

"Sometimes I get—Really sorry, I…Guess you better add some oil."

The kid fumed for a moment, dusting himself off with the rag. "We only got twenty weight."

Mig nodded, said that would be fine. The kid shook his head in silent reproach as he walked toward the station's supply rack. Mig got his spilled change off the ground. He put a nickel in the payphone slot, and dialed the operator. He gave her Carmen's number at the clinic and waited a few rings for pickup. Then the operator relayed Mig's query to his mother.

"Yes, I accept the charges," Carmen said, with some hesitation. "Of course."

Mig got on the line. " 'Morning, Mama."

"Why are you calling long distance? Where are you, anyway?"

"California."

"California?"

"Getting gas outside some little town," he said.

"I sensed last night that there was—What are you doing there? You have a job."

"I squared it with Bernie. It's okay."

"And what about night school?"

It wasn't enough that he'd finished high school when he came home. Carmen wanted him to go to college, prodded him to apply for the GI Bill for higher education the government offered to guys who'd made it back. Mig was in his second semester at Maricopa J.C., having taken courses that didn't aim in any real direction. He wasn't that interested in going back to school. In that regard, for him nothing had changed. He'd never been much of a student.

"Taking a couple days off. Something came up."

He told her about the phone call from Eddie Fulham's mother. Carmen said she understood. She expressed her condolences, also some disappointment that he didn't feel he could share this with her last night at dinner. She asked him where it was he was going in California.

"Los Angeles," he said.

"Oh, where that young actress a few months ago...Just horrible."

"Yeah, pretty bad," was all he said. The mutilated body found in a vacant lot had been headline news that shocked people all across the country. The victim was tagged The Black Dahlia, based on the title of an Alan Ladd crime movie. It sold newspapers. Civilians had only witnessed horror in the newspapers.

"It should be cooler where you are going," Carmen said.

"Won't mind that," he said, stepping outside the oven of the booth, as far as the phone cord would reach, to find some relief from the heat. There wasn't much.

"Are you alright?" Carmen asked.

"Swell. I'm fine."

"You have something to tell me," she said, not asked.

"Everything's okay," He answered, without conviction. His look followed a roadrunner dashing by the service bay, where the kid was tapping the last drops from an oilcan spout into Mig's crankcase.

"Unless you'd rather not." She chuckled. " 'None of my bee's wax,' as you used to say when you were little."

Mig kept looking at at the kid. "I, uh, did it again, Mama. Just before I called you. Lost my temper with someone."

"In what you said only, or—"

"Got physical. Let's leave it at that."

"So you hurt the man."

"No, but came close. A kid. Can't even be more than sixteen, for chrissake."

"Please do not swear with me, *hijo.*"

He always found it a little odd that his mother kept to this remnant of propriety from a religious upbringing she had all but rejected.

"I know you'll make it right with the boy, Angel Miguel."

Mig shook his head. Her use of both names was implied ethical challenge. He countered the verbal jab with a lie, one that dug at truth, he was fairly sure. "Tried to call you this morning before I left," he said. "You weren't home," he added, with a smile.

"I was…out taking a walk."

Her hesitation was a tell. "Must've been. How's Jack?"

"He's fine, as far as I know," she said, clipped.

What was never said—wouldn't be admitted—was that Carmen and the main benefactor of her clinic, Jack Tolafsen, were lovers. Mig wouldn't bring it up with his mother, put her on the spot about it, but he knew full well.

Carmen and Jack were both without mates, she ever since her husband to be, Aaron Czerniak, was murdered two months before Mig was born. Jack's wife of many years, Trudy, had awoken one morning with a slight headache, she'd said, leaned over to stroke the hair from Jack's forehead to kiss him, and asked if he'd like a cup of candy. He was puzzled at that, and she'd asked him why. Late that afternoon, Jack returned from work to find Trudy sprawled on their living room floor over the vacuum sweeper. He called to her but she didn't answer. He knelt down to hold her, to bring her to consciousness before phoning for an ambulance. And then felt her skin's coolness.

He mourned for nearly seven years, drinking himself to sleep most evenings. Then a friend talked him into attending a charity event to raise money for the new Gila River Clinic, and Jack met Carmen Quinteros. They took to each other, and within time their mutual feelings deepened. She nursed his sorrow with the years' residue of her own. In each other's arms, she furthered her healing, and he began his. They didn't talk of marriage, maybe fearing some ill-fate if they moved beyond their relationship as it was. They held to their secreted discretion. But Mig knew about it, as he was sure Jack's two daughters also knew, even if they didn't travel out to Arizona that often. Mig was glad his mother had found contentment with a great guy.

"It's a long drive you're making. How's the pain?" Carmen asked.

"Have to stop every hour or so, walk it out."

Carmen told her son she had to get back to work. They were short-staffed again, two of the nurses out sick. This was common, being confined as they were with sneezing, coughing kids. And Mig had to get on the road; he had a ways yet to go. Two to three hours, he figured. The graveside service was to be at one o'clock.

"Pay you back for the call," he said.

"Yes. But first take care of your food and rent." He heard the smile in her voice when she added, "And, of course, textbooks and tuition for night school this summer."

After he hung up, Mig looked back toward his car. The kid was spraying glass cleaner on the driver's side of the windshield. He wiped the glass thoroughly with a clean rag. Watching his diligence brought up Mig's guilt again.

The kid had finished the passenger's side of the windshield and was cleaning a side window when Mig walked up to him, offering him one of two opened bottles of Dr Pepper from inside the station office. "Don't bother. The rest of 'em are okay."

The kid accepted the bottle, took a swig, nodded thanks. There was quiet except for the kid slapping the rag nervously against his thigh.

"How hot you think it'll get today?" Mig finally asked.

"Hunnerd before noon. Then prob'ly higher."

"Can believe that, yeah. Pretty much the same where I came from, Phoenix."

"Never been over that way, New Mexico."

"Arizona. Gets hot there, too, this time of year."

"Ain't nothin' you can do," the kid said.

"Can move."

The kid looked blank at that, even as the sun was frying him from the neck up.

"Unless you're tied down somehow," Mig added.

They each took another drink in awkward silence.

"Sounds like you've lived here your whole—" He stopped himself, thrust out his hand. "I'm Mig Czerniak."

The kid hesitated, then shook Mig's hand with sweaty limpness.

"What's your name?" Mig asked.

"Leon…"

"Well, Leon, it's—"

"…Leon Jared Mabry. Called L.J. mostly."

"Nice to meet you, L.J. And, about before, I, uh…"

"S'okay." L.J. looked off. "Some guys get touchy, I s'pose, when you come up behind 'em sudden like I did."

Mig wasn't going to try to explain what he really didn't understand himself. There wasn't much left to talk about. He paid the kid, a couple of bucks extra. As he started his car and pulled out of the service bay, Mig was saddened thinking about L.J., his last name that sounded like maybe. A homely, nice kid who he imagined would spend his life slowly drying up here, never knowing anyplace but where fate had planted him and where he'd stay till he was all over. Nothing maybe about him.

Waiting for a car to pass before he got back on the road, Mig thought that L.J. might be lucky in a way. His own life seemed to have no certainty, no purpose. He turned onto the highway and continued driving toward Los Angeles.

3

For all the death that he'd seen, and some caused, Mig had never been to a funeral before. He hadn't known Eddie Fulham that well, not as well as Eddie seemed to have understood him. Mig doubted anyone really could figure out Eddie, especially as good-natured as he'd been.

He was too gratingly optimistic for many of the combat-weary. Likely for some of them, he'd be reassurance. They'd cling to whatever of that they could get. Most, though, in that last winter of the war, probably were put off by the way Eddie was. Nerves frayed from battle, they wouldn't be able to take Eddie Fulham's sweet smile, his words of encouragement. They weren't about to buy into what they considered phony good cheer from any chaplain, let alone some bandage-wrapper.

Eddie and Mig had formed a brief friendship in the field hospital near Mannheim. When Mig was on the mend enough to be free of painkillers and clear-headed, he wanted to thank the one who had picked him up out there that night and brought him to safety and kept him alive. At first, he was merely patronized about his request. Smiled down at, complimented on his appreciation, and that was it. This only pissed him off. He really did want to give specific thanks, and he kept at it until his request became shouted demand.

So Eddie Fulham, when he was back at HQ, was sent to Mig's bedside. He sat down on the floor, arms draped over his knees, his face on level with Mig's. Eddie just shrugged off the wounded soldier's thankfulness. He changed what seemed for him to be an uncomfortable subject by drawing attention to a deck of cards on the floor next to Mig's cot. Lots of solitaire, Mig had told him. What the hell else could you do when you're facedown all day besides read paperbacks and play with yourself. Eddie had smiled at this, at which Mig said, "I mean solitaire."

"Up for a little gin rummy?" Eddie had asked.

They were about evenly matched gin players, and the challenge brought Eddie back every day for over a week until he got his orders to head once more to the front lines. While playing cards they'd make small talk, share smutty jokes, jaw about sports. Eddie would tease Mig about the Brooklyn Dodgers being in a slump, Mig insisting that would end as soon as Peewee Reese got out of the Navy. Mig, who'd been taught some boxing when he was a boy, claimed to know with quickly summoned authority that Willie Pep's title was safe. No featherweight, Sal Bartolo included, could touch him. He and Eddie speculated that if Ike Williams moved up to heavyweight he might be a threat to Joe Louis.

As GIs did, Mig complained about the food, the Army in general, how piss-poor the battle campaigns had been conducted. But here he wasn't joined by Eddie, who just deflected any grousing, allowing for it, but not seeming to have any need for relief from the enervating mix of tedium and tension of war himself. Mig had been intrigued by Eddie's outlook, his positive innocence. In a way, it linked to some frayed thread of decency in a world gone to hell.

They'd sent each other penny post cards a few times since they'd been back from overseas, none in this last year. Contact between them had run out. But even so, Mig knew he owed Eddie this much, to make the drive out to L.A. and see him laid to rest.

He had a memory again in bed the night before he left Phoenix, a reminder of that time that always seemed the worst of all the yesterdays.

The eyes. The pleading eyes of a young German soldier about Mig's age. His brown stubble of beard, sparse, boyish. He was panicked, not strong enough to pull Mig's hands from around his throat, choking the last of life from him. A brief convulsion, then stillness. Then after Mig had given all he had in this effort, something in him wondered why. In a circumstance outside of war, he and the young man he had just strangled, might've tossed back beers together, traded looks with flirtatious girls down a bar in some town, plotted with each other to get them in the sack. In another circumstance maybe the German soldier's mother and Mig's mom would've found things in common, exchanged recipes, memories about each of their now grown sons, faked exasperation at their boys' joshing.

The other soldier's eyes stared through Mig, blank now. There would be no other relationship between them…Unless…Mig tore open the young man's shirtfront and grabbed the oval-shaped dog tag on a chain around his neck, broke off the half of the tag intended for ID at wherever Nazi military records were kept.

The name on the tag, Jurgen Gutfreund. Good Friend. Every now and then there would've been occasion to bring up his surname with smiles all around when this young guy, Jurgen, had done something nice for someone.

After the war was over, Mig would look up this fellow soldier's family, the Gutfreunds. He'd tell them what a brave young man Jurgen was. Too bad they'd never had that beer together, never double-dated any girls, their moms never met. But Mig never had a chance to look up the family of his young counterpart who was supposed to be his enemy. The half dog tag had been lost in Mig's transfer to the field hospital.

As Mig would drift to sleep, this memory was sometimes overlaid by a dream.

The young German's family is now there on the battlefield. They all gaze down at Mig, the killer, the murderer. He wants their understanding, their forgiveness for just doing what he had to do. But they only stare through Mig at some point of forever as if they hold some truth that he can't comprehend. Something of common decency he isn't worthy of ever knowing. Their pleading faces make him feel shame. Now they are speaking to him. Mig can tell what they are saying to him in German. "Where is Jurgen?" "What have you done to our boy?" "Please give him back to us." Their silent litany bores into Mig as the family moves toward him, imploring, closer and closer...

He had awakened in a sweat, as he always did after these dreams. And he had the shakes again. Maybe someday it all would be over, this so-called battle fatigue, as if it were just a matter of being soul-exhausted from combat rather than trapped in the horror of it. Outlasting death, moment to moment, and delivering death. But after two years back stateside it was still there, still plaguing him most nights. Even in the brightness of some days.

It was an overcast day at Rosedale Cemetery, with its acres of lawn-planted low hills, stands of shade trees and tall palms. Among the tombstones of various sizes and shapes were some that were pyramid-shaped. Mig wondered if Egyptians who'd lived in Los Angeles were buried there. The air bothered his eyes. He thought it might have something to do with the yellowish brown fringe on the horizon.

Eddie's mother, a fragile appearing woman, stood looking stricken next to her wheelchair-bound husband. He rubbed and patted her thin arm gently with his meaty, workman's hand. Eddie's father was stern looking. Mig wondered if he'd been strict with Eddie. Aside from immediate family, there were few people in attendance. Those who knew Eddie's parents, Mig guessed, and some relatives and neighbors. When Mig had gotten the call from Eddie's mom, she as much as said that she knew no other of her son's friends to notify. Mig had thought that Eddie, the way he was, would go over better now in peacetime.

Those in attendance at the burial were invited to gather at Eddie's parents' home only a few blocks east of the cemetery on West 17th Place. On the way there, Mig saw a group of young boys playing kickball. He remembered playing kick the can on a vacant lot in Brooklyn, before he and Carmen had moved to Arizona. He fixated on the boys and almost sideswiped a parked Hudson.

Eddie's mother had set out canned salmon loaf with little round hollow bones that crumbled easily when chewed, which Mig didn't much care for. Eddie's aunt brought a cherry Jello mold with marshmallows mixed in. That didn't appeal to him, either. He took a little food, just to be polite, but it felt kind of weird, feasting on this occasion. A chowdown for everyone to stave off sadness. Didn't make much sense to him. There was a green salad, a bundt cake, oatmeal and chocolate chip cookies. And coffee. Eddie's mom asked Mig if he'd like a beer instead.

"No thanks, Mrs. Fulham. Coffee's just fine."

"You sure? Eddie always liked his beer."

He would've preferred beer, but he felt out of place here and didn't want to put her out. He shook his head, smiling shyly. "Not right now. Thank you, anyway."

"Eddie always said that German beer was the best."

"He was right about that, ma'am."

Mig had never had German beer. They didn't serve it in the field hospital where he'd been laid up. What he remembered about Germany was the cold, still, after winter in the Ardennes. The goddamn cold had cut through him almost as much as the tiny shards of metal they couldn't find to dig out.

Mrs. Fulham had offered to let him stay at their house. He had thanked her, but said that he'd already checked into a hotel. That was for her and her husband's benefit. This could be one of the nights he yelled in his sleep.

"Probably a good thing I'm not staying here," he'd said. "I snore a lot."

She asked if Mig was taking advantage of the GI Bill and he'd said yes, that he was going to junior college.

"Your final exams must be coming up soon. Are you studying for them?"

He said yes, but it wasn't true. To many guys who'd come back from Europe or the Pacific, going to college might've been clear purpose, important to building a new life. They'd been in the vortex of everything inhuman, but seemed able to not look back. But at least for some of them, Mig wondered if there were times when they too had uncontrollable shakes, awaking with a start in darkness as breeze through open windows chilled their sweat. Could a hot shower wash away the terror, so they could just pick up their lunch pails and head off to work, and then to night school on their way to better paying jobs, sun-filled lives?

Were they looking brightly ahead, or desperate to forget?

Guys even younger than Mig had proposed in letters to girls back stateside they didn't even know that well. It was home one day, married the next, with a baby on the way soon thereafter. Getting to where God smiled. Ex-GIs settled in comfortably on the mortgaged side of picket fences, far away now from the kill land.

Being adrift as he was, Mig envied their sense of hopefulness. Having the nightmare of war displaced by things looking up so much. Good fortune spit-shined. After years of deprivation, money in people's pockets and products to spend it on. Cars being manufactured again. Soon there'd be affordable housing in block after block of tracts. Nationwide broadcasting of television before very long. And already, mass-produced refrigerators as he'd kidded his mother about not buying yet. As if it were important. Any of it.

"Mig..? *Mig..?*"

"Uh…Pardon, Mrs. Fulham?"

"You were—Are you alright?"

"Just drift off sometimes, ma'am. Bad habit."

"I was saying about the favor you offered to do for us…"

"You mean packing up Eddie's things."

"It would be such an imposition. After coming all the way here, and then going up to Ventura."

"Not at all, ma'am. Don't give it a thought."

There was more to Mig's offer that he wouldn't mention. He'd found out that for the last couple of months Eddie had lived not here in Los Angeles, but in a little town an hour or so up the coast. That was was where it had happened. Mig didn't place much trust in some small town police department and it's concern over the hit-and-run death of a guy nobody there would know that well. When he was up there to get Eddie's things, Mig would check in with the Ventura cops. To assess how much they were really on the job to find Eddie's killer.

"I'll bring back his things, Mrs. Fulham. I want to do it."

Eddie's mother lowered her gaze. "It *is* an imposition, but thank you. Warren's limited in what he can manage. And I'm…

It's so hard right now."

" 'Course it is, ma-am. Yeah."

"Eddie would mail us part of his paycheck every week." Her eyes welled up. "And the most lovely notes…"

Mrs. Fulham pulled a lace handkerchief from her waist pocket and dabbed at the moistness in her eyes as her sister came over to tell her that a neighbor lady had just come to the back door with a pot of freshly-made potato salad. The two women went to the kitchen to deal with the added food.

Mig wished he could leave. He didn't belong here, with people close to Eddie's family. But he'd stay at least until some of the others were leaving. Being the first to go might seem disrespectful.

"Say, young fella, could you come with me? Want to show you something."

Mig looked down to see that Eddie's father had wheeled his chair up to him. Even crippled, Warren Fulham exuded square-jawed resilience. Different from Eddie's quiet, understated strength, the father's demeanor was that of a man you didn't want to cross. From the waist up he appeared all-capable.

"Sure, Mr. Fulham."

"Warren. Call me Warren. Never was formal much. Follow me."

He led them toward a group of men and women. "S'cuse us, folks."

Those in the group parted quickly and Eddie's father wheeled out of the living room, Mig following. They went through a hallway and down to a back bedroom. Once inside it, Eddie's father reached up and flipped up the light switch near the door.

"Eddie's room," he said. "When he was growing up."

There was a bed with maple headboard and covered with an off-white spread tufted with faded green cotton puffballs. On the darkly stained wood floor was a round, multi-colored rag rug of tightly bound cloth strips. The bedspread looked to have had years of washings and the floor showed no dust, Mig noticed. The room had been well kept up after Eddie had occupied it. There was a small mirror in a brass frame on one wall, the brass recently polished. On the facing wall hung a large photo of Yosemite Valley, featuring Half Dome. Eddie's father indicated the picture.

"Went up there to Yosemite—the three of us—when Eddie was…about twelve, I guess. Was a good trip." He nodded privately in remembrance. "On his way to the camp restroom late one afternoon, he saw a bear. Never made it to the restroom. Pissed his pants, he did." He willed a smile, which gave way to sadness.

"This was Eddie's room," he said again, forgetting he already had, Mig guessed. "Mildred wanted to fix it up some. Hang more pictures. New curtains and such. But then Eddie moved out, up there to Ventura, so there wasn't much point. Seemed she always wanted to…to keep him a boy somehow. Know what I mean?"

Mig said that he knew. It was the way of some mothers. Certainly not his own.

"Was all I could do to offset her babying him."

Warren Fulham reached into a side pocket of his wheelchair and took out a small, long box He lifted the lid of the box and removed a star-shaped medal suspended from a short, striped ribbon. He gazed at it wistfully. "But he was a man now. She never could get used to that." He held up the medal. "Know what this is? 'Course you must."

"Bronze Star, sir."

"The Bronze Star…" The father gazed at it with pride. "Eddie must've done okay over there."

"He was a good soldier. Medics had the roughest of it," Mig said.

"Then he comes home an' gets run down on a lonely road one night. Doesn't seem right after him going through what he did and making it back from overseas." He held up the medal for Mig to see more closely. "After getting this, doesn't seem right."

"No, sir, it doesn't."

"Mildred, she…she can't bring herself to look at reminders of Eddie any more than can be helped. Except for keeping this room up. Almost think she expects…"

Mig thought back to the last time he'd seen Eddie in the field hospital outside Mannheim.

Mig had been face down in bed, as he had been since he got there, stitched up in several places from his left thigh and buttock to partway up his back. Several pieces of shrapnel had been removed, most of it, along with part of a kidney.

"Hey, buddy…"

Mig turned his head up to see Eddie grinning. He sat on the floor, draped his arms over his knees as usual. Then Eddie paused, reached into his pocket for a handkerchief, covering his nose with it as he sneezed. He'd done that on his last couple of visits.

"Jesus, Eddie. Bringing that cold into a hospital. And you a medic."

"Told you before, it's not a cold, just my damn allergies. They act up every spring…How ya doin'?

"No complaints," Mig answered. "Food's great and I just got laid this morning."

"Oh, sure, in the shape you're in." Eddie looked around, then leaned closer and whispered, "With that blond, Betty Grable-lookin' nurse, I bet."

"Would you believe it, Eddie? She's in love with me."

Eddie rocked back slightly and laughed. He indicated the short columns of cards in solitaire play on the floor.

"You done with that, Mig? Probably cheating your own self, anyway."

A few beds over, a man moaned in pain.

"Shuffle 'em," Mig said. "Got a feeling it's my day."

"We'll see about that. Weee'll just see…"

Ignoring the intermittent nearby moaning, they played their usual five hands of gin rummy. Best two out of three. Mig had been right; it was his day. After they set the cards aside, they went through their usual kidding back and forth about luck versus skill. Then Eddie settled into a look of concern. "How are you doing, Mig?"

"You already asked when you got here."

"I mean, all told?"

Mig shrugged. "Hurts pretty bad still. They tell me it will for who knows how long." He grinned. "Think me bein' gimpy might get attention from the ladies?"

Ignoring that, Eddie said, "Promise yourself something."

"What's that?"

"Promise you'll keep it just to your wounds. The hurt, just to your wounds."

"What the hell you talking about?"

Eddie sneezed again, apologized again. "It takes a few weeks sometimes, maybe even longer, before some GIs start to, I don't know…cave in on themselves. I've seen it. Some guys haven't even been wounded. The damn war starts eating at 'em when they're out of harm's way, about to head stateside. Who knows? Maybe even after they get home. Don't be one of those guys, Mig. That's all I'm saying."

Mig was put off, wanting to object but not knowing quite to what. "Jeez, Eddie, you think I'm not tough enough?"

Eddie reached over with a brotherly grip on Mig's shoulder.

"Problem is, you're tough on yourself."

Mig looked away, gave a snort of dismissal.

"You feel things more than some guys—most guys, Mig. Stuff gets to you."

"Never knew you were inside my head, Eddie. Should charge you rent."

"You take stuff on. Tell me I'm wrong about that."

Mig said almost too low for Eddie to hear, "Angel fuckin' Miguel…"

"Your name pronounced the Spanish way." Eddie smiled. "And so what's Spanish for Lucifer?"

"It's screw you."

They both laughed. Then Eddie sneezed twice more in rapid succession, wiped his nose. Didn't bother apologizing. "When you gettin' out of here, anyway?" he asked.

"Early next week, I think. What about you?"

"Oh, out of *here* tomorrow. Back to the mop-up. There's a few holdouts left, giving our guys trouble…Want to get your address before I leave."

"Sure," Mig said. "Hey, rumor has it you're up for a Bronze."

Eddie looked uneasy, with distance in his voice said, "Yeah, so they tell me."

" 'Gratulations."

Eddie looked away as if he wished the subject hadn't come up. "Got you to thank for it. But thanks doesn't really fit."

"If not for you, I'd still be lying face up—but under packed dirt."

"You don't understand."

"Maybe you don't feel like, you know, a hero, or anyth—"

"Hero, my ass," Eddie snapped.

"We were up on nerves, most of us. Didn't even think about whatever we did—had to do. They make heroes out of that, Eddie. Just accept it."

Eddie gripped his arms tight around his knees. "Oh, sure. Sure I will. Let 'em pin that medal on me and know it's all bullshit."

"I'm tough on *my*self?" Mig said.

Eddie shook his head slowly. "I know the real truth."

Mig reached over and held Eddie's chin to look him in the eye. "Even without getting screwed much lately, I'm glad to be alive, Eddie. Really glad about that. My vote is you earned the Bronze."

Eddie pulled away from him. "That's a crock! There was nobody else out there. I needed you with me, Mig. I needed you with me, simple as that."

"Must've been really great company."

"It was night."

"It was before I passed out. Figure it stayed that way till— what are you talking about?"

"I can't be alone outside at night. I just can't."

"It was a bad one, alright. Jerries had us—"

"*Any* night!" Eddie nearly yelled. "I can't be alone outside on clear nights—anywhere. Ever since I was a kid…the moon… by myself with the moon staring down at me. I hauled you out not to be alone out there. That's the simple truth of it."

Mig took in hearing this strange admission. "…Okay, Eddie. Whatever you say. But, you know, I'm still damn grateful."

"I wanted to get you out besides. 'Course I did."

"Nice to hear you take some credit. Swell."

"But you did me the great favor, Mig, of not being dead that night." Eddie looked away. "I'm getting the Bronze for being too scared not to snatch up any live body to be with me. To keep me safe from my stupid fear…my little kid's stupid fear."

Mig gazed down at Warren Fulham softly kneading the medal between his thick, blunt fingers. There was respect in his touch, and love. This was all he had left of his son.

"Sir, you said Eddie was run down on a lonely road at night. You mean they *found* him at night."

"Sometime near midnight, we were told."

"He'd been there since day and no one saw him?"

"Hell, no. Even a country road's got some traffic during the day. Couldn't of been more than a few minutes af…after…"

The man clenched his jaw as he fought back tears. Then he surrendered to his grief and sobbed. Mig thought about Eddie Fulham and what he'd said about his dread of being alone under the stare of the moon. Who else had been on the road with him that night when he was run down?

Eddie would not have been out there by himself.

4

As he drove north the next morning, discomfort from his wounds became insistent enough for Mig to pull over on the highway and get out of his car. He walked off the pain as best he could by the roadside. After a couple of minutes, a Model A open-cab pickup entered the highway from a dirt road and drove past Mig. After a short distance, the truck swung wide on the road shoulder, turned around, and then pulled to a stop a few yards behind Mig's car. A grizzled older man in bib overalls got out and ambled toward him.

"Hey there, youngster, you lost?"

"Just taking a stretch, that's all."

"Uh-huh. Musta' been on the road awhile."

As he came near, the old man eyed Mig up and down as if seeing what price he'd get on the open market. Then he smiled, revealing uneven, brown-stained teeth. He spat a stream of tobacco juice in the dirt.

"You're wonderin' where the turnoff is."

Mig looked puzzled. "I am?"

"Sign blew down in a howler of a wind last week. Busted it up fairly good. Ain't put another'n back up yet."

"That your job, see that it's done?"

"Naw, naw. Ain't *my* job." The old guy folded his arms as if for emphasis. "Responsibility's determined by county. This'd be Ventura County. 'Nother sign back down the road some's in L.A. County. Always been arguin' about which one's responsible for what. But this one's Ventura's."

"Well, they'll probably figure it out."

"No figurin' to do, really. Line's the line."

"The county line, you mean."

"Yup. Just a matter of getting' a crew off its butt and out here."

"I see."

"Off its lazy butt…"

He unfolded his arms and planted his hands on his hips. Leaned forward slightly, spat again. The dark brown glob landed inches from the first one.

"Well, that's government workers for you," Mig said.

"Gov'ment? How so gov'ment?"

"Ventura County government."

"Blowed down sign ain't got nothin' to do with that."

"But you sai—"

"Said it was *in* Ventura County. But the County ain't responsible. Sign company is. Foster and Kleiser. They got offices in both counties."

"I'm sure you know what you're talking about, old-timer.… Well, so long."

As Mig started to walk to his car:

"You gonna keep headin' north like your car's pointed?"

"That's the idea," Mig said as he kept walking.

"O-kaay…"

Mig stopped, turned back around. "Why'd you say it like that?"

The old man raised his thick, sprouty eyebrows and shook his head, thrusting his arms up in the air. "You already missed it.

The turnoff."

"Turnoff to where? Isn't Ventura up this road?"

"Town of, yeah. I thought you was lost. Thought you was lookin' for the lion farm that blowed-down sign woulda told ya where the turnoff was to get to."

"*Lion* farm? What's that?"

"Jungleland USA. Most folks just call it the lion farm."

Mig smiled. "They butcher 'em or just milk 'em?"

The old man chuckled, tobacco juice dripping past his thin, cracked lips. "Naw, just train 'em for Tarzan movies. Other animals, too. People like to drive up from Los Angeleez and watch the shows." He pronounced the city's name with a hard g.

"Maybe I will, too, when I'm back here in…Where are we, anyway?"

"Thousand Oaks, they call it, like it's a town. But it ain't. Just a few houses in the Conejo Valley here and 'a course the lion farm."

Mig looked around at the low, rolling hills and gnarled oak trees in the endless spread of dry, tawny grass. He recalled talk and news articles about residential tracts planned to relieve the postwar living accommodation shortage.

"Sure room for a lot of houses."

"Never happen," the old man said.

"Oh? Why's that?"

" 'Cause the Janss family—my employers, who own mosta' this land—seems they like it jus' the way it is."

"Nice work if they can hold up progress."

An especially big spit from the old man, followed by a look of disgust. "Progress? That what you call all the buildin' they're startin' to do 'round the country nowadays?"

"It's what the world calls it," Mig said.

"Not up this way, we don't. Maybe down there in, ya know…"

"Los Angeleez?"

The old man nodded firmly. "The damn war bein' over stirred up a whooole bunch 'a stuff in folks. There's too much of just about everything now, right after years of not near 'nough of it."

Mig shrugged, had no comment. He'd never considered any downside to the new good times. Not for most everyone.

"We'll be back to greed, like before the Depression," the old fellow continued. "Opportunity they like to call it, but soon enough it'll be plain damn greed. There'll be those who'll hunger after more'n they got any right to have….Sunshine'll fade to shadow, mark my words, boy."

Less than an hour later Mig arrived in Ventura. As he came into town he saw a railroad dining car that had been de-wheeled and set on a foundation. A sign identified it as a restaurant, THE SIDECAR. He wondered if people ate there to imagine they were on a train trip. And did they avoid viewing out the windows to not have to see they weren't going anywhere? A few blocks into town, down the street from Sears & Roebuck, was a Shell station, where he gassed up and asked for directions to the local newspaper.

The *Star Free Press* building was on Santa Clara Street. Mig entered a small lobby crowded with filing cabinets and heard the muffled sound of typewriters from somewhere else in the building.

He asked a matronly secretary where he could find back issues of the newspaper. She had a pleasant, plump-cheeked face that beamed with his request. They had everything on microfilm, she told him with a tone of satisfaction that made it seem archiving the paper in this way had been her idea. He was interested in a recent issue, Mig told her, from six days before.

"Oh," she said. "That recently wouldn't be on microfilm quite yet. Let me get someone who can help you."

She picked up the handset on top of a wood veneered console with a grille over a speaker in front, a row of switches below that.

"Our new Dictaphone." The secretary looked up at Mig and smiled, it seemed proudly, as if the choice of purchase had been another of her accomplishments. He smiled back at her.

She flipped one of the switches and leaned toward the machine. "Gerald…"

After a moment, a staticky voice answered. "Yeah, Dottie?"

"A young gentleman here wants to look at one of last week's issues."

"Okedoke. Be right up."

Within a few seconds a man wearing a knit cardigan sweater over a window check sport shirt entered the lobby from the back of the building. When he opened the door the clacking of multiple typewriter keys became more evident, then muted again as he closed the door behind him.

In his mid-forties and bald, except for a fringe of graying sandy hair, there was an openness about him. Had a wife, kids, was an easygoing dad, Mig figured. The man introduced himself as Jerry Caswell and indicated for Mig to follow him through a side door into a room with what appeared to be several days or a few weeks of newspaper issues, each spread open from its center and draped over long lengths of thick, wood doweling supported on steel racks.

"Now…Dottie said you wanted an issue from last week. Which one would that be, sir?"

"The twenty-ninth. Last Thursday."

"Okedoke, that would be…right about over here."

Caswell lifted one dowel, setting it aside to get to another one. He hoisted out the issue, squinted to see the date.

"No, wrong date." He set that issue back. "Must be the one

next to it."

He lifted that issue out and seemed pleased. He handed the long dowel with the newspaper to Mig and indicated a wide shelf to the side of the room. "It'll be easier if you spread it out over there."

Mig went over and set the dowel on the shelf, opening the paper. He glanced at the headlines. LABOR BILL COMPROMISE REACHED, and beneath the fold, WAR FUNDS CUT VOTED. That was sure overdue, Mig thought. He looked at the contents guide to find weather and turned to that page.

TEN PERCENT EXPECTED CHANCE OF RAIN,

OTHERWISE CLEAR. HIGHS 67-70, LOWS 54-56

Mig looked over at Caswell. "Chance of rain, but clear. Wouldn't it be cloudy?"

"You wanted a last week's issue just to check weather that's been and gone?"

"That's right."

Caswell shook his head. "New one on me."

"If rain was expected, wouldn't it be cloudy?" Mig asked again, a little more insistently.

"Well, *Expected* in a ranching community like this can have a closer meaning to, uh, hoped for. Especially since—unusually enough—we actually *did* have a little rain one day last week. A light sprinkle. Got expectations up."

"Was it clear or not? That's what I want to know."

"Who remembers?"

Mig folded the paper back up and handed the heavy dowel back to Caswell. "Thanks anyway, Jerry."

As Mig was about to exit the room, Caswell called out, "Wait.

The twenty-ninth…Can't tell you about the day, but it was clear that night." He set the dowel with newspaper back in its rack.

Mig came back to him. "You sure about that? That particular night?"

"It was last Thursday. Any rain clouds from the day before would've been gone. And June gloom hadn't set in yet."

"June gloom?"

"You're not from Southern California."

Mig shook his head.

"Most of the month of June here is kinda non-weather. Dull gray overcast. Not warm, not cold. June gloom, we call it."

"So what about that night, the twenty-ninth?"

"The next day was Friday. Normally, we like Jimmie, our son, to be off to bed by ten, ten-thirty on school nights. But it being Memorial Day last Friday, there was no school. The family'd be out that morning early anyway, to pay tribute at the cemetery before the American Legion parade, so Jimmie wouldn't be sleeping in. But Thursday was the first night the grunion were running. So what the heck if he was gonna be up way past midnight. Didn't really matter."

"What were running?"

"Grunion. Little fish. They swim in on the waves late at night, bury themselves partway in on the beach to lay their eggs. When the waves go back out, you can see 'em all silvery by flashlight, tiny heads sticking up in the wet sand. Kids like to scoop 'em up in buckets. Not much for eating. But high schoolers go down and get as many as they can, have a good time with their friends."

"What's fish got to do with the weather?"

"It seems grunion only run on clear nights." Caswell shrugged. "Drawn by moonlight, they say."

5

Caswell had given Mig directions to the police station on South Garden. He parked in front and got out of his car. Looked up at the sky, felt the air. June gloom. A month of it could bring you down, he thought.

As he closed his car door he saw a slight boy of thirteen or fourteen standing behind a lamppost, almost as if trying to hide behind it. The boy looked over at Mig, strangely it seemed. Could've been with resentment or fear. Mig couldn't tell anymore, with anyone. He sometimes imagined others looked at him the same disturbing way Jurgen Gutfreund's family did in the dream. Even kids like this one.

The boy moved away from the lamppost and hesitatingly toward the police station. When he was nearing the doors, a plainclothesman and a uniformed cop exited. The boy saw them and froze.

"Whadaya need, kid?" the uniformed cop asked.

The boy shook his head quickly. "Nothin', sir." He turned away to leave.

"Hey, what's your name?"

The boy stopped, turned back around, seeming like he'd rather be anywhere else now but here. "Lon Torgen," he said, nervous.

"Well, Lon Torgen, what can we do for you?" The uniform

winked at the other cop. "You want to report a bank robbery?"

"Or turn yourself in for one?" the plainclothesman added, looking mock stern. The two policemen glanced at each other, grinned. The boy looked up at them. To Mig he clearly seemed afraid.

"How can we help you, Lon?" the plainclothesman said, sounding sincere.

The boy looked up at them a moment longer, before turning and bolting off. The two cops shook their heads and continued walking away.

"Listens to *Gangbusters*, I bet," the uniform said. "Wanted to find out how to become a cop."

"And got cold feet," the plainclothesman put in. "Maybe he'll try the fire station now. Being a fireman's next best thing." He looked at his wristwatch. "What's that kid doing out of school, anyway?"

"Didn't you ever play hooky? Besides, he's out researching careers."

The two of them chuckled as they walked away.

When he went inside the station, Mig gave his name to the desk sergeant, spelling it for him as the officer wrote it down. He told the sergeant why he was there, only to be met with a blank, jaded look. The man's face was booze-florid and puffy. He was perched on a high stool, more like affixed to it.

"You a relative of the victim?" the desk sergeant asked.

"No, just knew him."

"Friend, then."

"Sort of."

" 'Sort of'," the sergeant repeated back with what seemed to be derision. "Friend or not? Or just a curiosity seeker?"

"We were overseas together. That good enough?"

"Well, it happened out on Highway One Twenty-six. Outside town limits." The sergeant sat back on his stool, arms straightened on the counter. Looking smug, he said, "That means it was under Sheriff's Department jurisdiction, not ours."

A burly plainclothesman in his early to mid-fifties exited one of the offices off a hallway. The desk sergeant looked down the hall toward him. "Hey, Lieutenant, guy here asking about that H and R last week. We went out on that, if I remember right."

As the plainclothesman approached, Mig sized him up. Brown gabardine suit rumpled, as if he'd slept in it. Wedding ring, married a long time, face set hard, was surly with now grown kids. The man's upper body moved from side to side, taking up wide space in the hallway. The way he walked reminded Mig of the metronome on his piano teacher's old upright during the time of Carmen's failed attempt with him and music lessons. He wondered if this heavyset cop had to gauge his way through doorways.

Looking at what he'd written down, the sergeant said, "His name's Ca-zerniak."

The plainclothesman stuck out a fat-fingered paw. "Nathaniel Prye."

As they shook hands, "Mig Czerniak. The C's silent."

Prye looked at him curiously. "What kinda name's that?"

"Polish. Could be Jewish."

"You a—of Jewish persuasion?"

"My father was. I'm just me."

"So, uh, you're here about the hit-and-run the night before Memorial Day. That right, Mick?"

"Yeah. And it's Mig. Short for Miguel."

Another curious look. "You part Mesican?"

Mig bristled at the pronunciation. "My mother's from *Mexico*. You want the rundown on both sides of my family, Lieutenant?"

Prye stiffened a little. "The hit-and-run. What's your connection?"

"I knew Eddie Fulham in the war. If it wasn't for him I wouldn't be around."

Prye softened at that, nodding.

Just then, the front door opened and two uniformed Mutt and Jeff looking cops entered, roughly ushering a skinny, bedraggled man between them. The man swung a wild-eyed imploring look from one of his captors to the other, uttering protestations of his innocence in Russian.

"Ya ne chievo ne sdelal! Ya ne vinovat! Ya ne Vinoval!!"

The taller cop on the man's left jerked the man's arm hard.

"Yeah, yeah, Igor. You were just enjoying life out in nature. We know."

As they hustled him in, Mig stepped between them and the booking desk. Speaking to the man calmly as best he could in the other man's language, he asked him why he was being arrested.

"Zachno onie tebiya, uh…*garesto…garestovuvaut? "*

The Russian man said he had done nothing, nothing.

"Ya ne chevo ne sdelal! Ao opiate proisxodit. Opiate! Nevozozhno ot nix ubeshat!"

Wide-eyed, scared, the man had said that it was happening all over again. Mig glanced at a trace of ink barely revealed on the man's wrist. He reached out and pushed up his sleeve far enough to see a series of numbers tattooed on the underside of the Russian's forearm.

The shorter of the arresting cops tried to push Mig aside, but he stood his ground to quell the situation, bring some understanding. He looked from one cop to the other, saying in a measured tone, "Ease up, officers. This man was in the camps."

"Yeah, now he's been camping where he don't belong," the

short cop said.

"One of *Hitler's* camps, damn it."

"Well, then he's used to being rounded up," the tall cop said.

The short cop followed up with, "Yeah, he should feel right at home."

Mig glared from one to the other. "You got no idea, you fuckheads!"

Both cops reached for their nightsticks, but Prye put his hands out, pulsing them in a calming gesture.

"Harlan…Bob…just do what you gotta do here."

The shorter cop said, "But, Lieutenant, this wiseass—"

"Cool down, Harlan." He looked from him to the taller cop, and then back to him, sternly. "Not gonna say it again."

The two cops deflated to steamy composure.

Mig looked at the scared Russian with sympathy. He tried to reassure him that it wasn't like in Europe during the war, that he'd be treated fairly.

"Bsie budiet potdru…podrugomu v Amerikie. Onie budut spravidlivu k tebie."

He reached out and gripped the man's shoulder, trying to emphasize that it was different here.

"Onie budut spravidlivu k tebie."

The man returned Mig's gaze, without seeming able to believe him.

Prye rolled his hand in a get on with it gesture. "Alright, fellas. Settle him in once again." The Russian looked downcast as the two cops moved him past Mig and up to the desk for the booking process.

Mig strode up to Prye. "This the best use of your men, Lieutenant? Rousting this poor guy for vagrancy?"

"Vagrancy…That'd be more simple. Dimitri Temiarov—that's

his name—is getting booked on suspicion of kidnapping a twelve-year-old girl, Peggy Beledayne.”

“Not likely he’d be up to anything like that. He’s just scared like you wouldn’t believe.”

“That’s what his sister tells us. Both of ‘em DPs—Displaced Persons. European refugees from the war. ‘Least she holds down a job. He’s another matter. Gone loopy in the head.”

“Considering what he’s been through, that’s no surprise.”

“Still, though, he’s a possible crime suspect.”

“*Crime?* That’s what’s been done to *him*. Forced to live in terror.”

“I know what you mean. But when you sneak around like a hermit in the hills outside of town, scrounging for food in restaurant trashcans, lookin’ all shifty-like and crazy, you’re suspect. That’s just the way it is….Come on back to my office.”

Mig followed Prye’s side-to-side gait down the hallway. He opened a door and extended his arm for Mig to enter first.

Prye’s office had a disheveled look, like the man himself. One of the filing cabinet drawers was open partway, files jammed in so tightly one of them stuck out above the rest. Papers were stacked sloppily in thin piles on the desk, ink stains on the blotter. A pre-war model Dictaphone with scratches above the keys was on one side of the desk.

On the other side were three photographs in oxidized silver frames: one taken by a professional of a younger Nathaniel Prye looking fondly at a young woman, pretty in a homespun way, a dusting of freckles across her nose, with a baby in each arm; another posed picture of the young woman, smiling, dressed up for a portrait; and a snapshot of two little boys, laughing on adjoining swings. Mig guessed that these were the babies four or five years later.

"You speak Russian," Prye said behind Mig as he closed the door. "How come?"

Mig turned to face him, deadpan. "All us commies do. The Party makes us."

Prye was momentarily taken aback, then realized he'd been put on. "No, really," he said.

"Picked it up in my old neighborhood. Speak enough to get by some," Mig answered. "Assigned to interview refugees at the end of the war. Know a little German, too. Yiddish."

"Yiddish…Oh, yeah, that's what—You woulda' learned that from your dad."

"He died before I was born. No, some people spoke that where I lived, too. Army just found out I pick up languages sorta' easy, so made use of that. About all I was good for at the time."

Prye studied him a moment. "You'd been wounded. Your limp…"

Mig nodded.

Prye walked around to his desk and sat down, motioning for Mig to take a seat across from him, which he did.

"About that hit-and-run…" Prye shook his head. "Not much to give you on it. Nothing, really."

"I don't think it was what it seemed to be."

Prye stirred uncomfortably in his seat. "I know how you feel. But aside from the victim being who he was to you—"

"It's not that, Lieutenant."

"Look, Mig…" Prye rested his elbows on the desk blotter, folding his fingers together, a posture of professional assuredness. "Gotta tell you, I've been doing this work for going on thirty years. Investigated more crime scenes than I can even remember."

"Maybe there's something about this one you don't remember."

"Nothing to forget. I didn't go out on this."

"And it was Sheriff's Department, anyway," Mig said. "The guy on the desk told me. Probably should be talking to them."

"You could do that…and come up with the same answer. We work together pretty close, county sheriffs and us. We went out on this that night because there'd been a three-car pileup a little ways outside Moorpark. Deputies had their hands full, so we got a call to help out."

"Who else was out there when Eddie got hit?"

"Nobody, as far as we know."

"Then there's more to find out." Prye raised his hand to object, but Mig cut him off. "I've got reason to say that, Lieutenant."

Prye took on a look of forbearance and sat back. "Look, I'm sure you think you have good reason to—"

"Okay," Mig said, "how far out of town did it happen?"

"A few miles," Prye said.

" 'A few miles.' And no car that broke down or ran out of gas?"

"None that we found."

Don't you think it's odd that a guy would be by himself late at night on foot out on a lonely country road?"

"Your friend could've been hitchhiking," Prye said. "Dropped off there."

"In the middle of nowhere?"

"Maybe there was an argument. Your friend was told to get out. Or maybe he wanted to get out." Prye shook his head with irritation. "Who the hell knows?"

"Somebody does. I'm telling you, Lieutenant, there's more to it."

Prye fidgeted in his chair. "We'll be checking out where the deceased lived in a day or so. Hit-and-run is a crime, so we'll be doing that, but, uh…I wouldn't expect anything else to shed much light on the whole thing, if I was you."

"Well, I *sure* wouldn't, if I was you."

Prye flared at that. "Youngblood, I don't need your lip."

"Only pressing where I think it's needed, that's all, Lieutenant Prye. Didn't mean any offense, really."

Prye took a moment to cool down. "We took photos at the scene, but I don't think you'd want to see 'em."

"I'm past shock. Got over that at Anzio."

Prye glanced at the framed snapshot on his desk, saddened, then looked off. "Our boys were in the Pacific, one Marines, the other a Navy pilot. Liked being near the water. They both did."

"Sorry about your loss," Mig said. "Losses."

Prye looked at him, registering some surprise. "I didn't say…"

"Didn't have to."

"Twins they were." Prye settled back in his chair, looked regretful. " Andy and Greg. Good boys." He added, as if justifying fate, "Died for their country."

Mig nodded in sympathy. But he couldn't reconcile patriotism and the killing of war with anything like the certainty he once had. A troubling thought he kept to himself.

"Lieutenant, those pictures you have…"

Prye got up and walked over to a filing cabinet. He opened a drawer and took out a thin file tabbed FULHAM. Before he closed the drawer, Mig glanced at the block print on the next file's tab: BELEDAYNE.

"Don't usually show these to folks," Prye said while he walked over to his desk with the file folder. "Should say I never do. Never have." He set the FULHAM file on his desk in front of Mig. Prye opened it.

He turned over a typed police report to reveal a black and white 8x10 glossy taken with a Graflex press camera by the photographer standing just behind Eddie Fulham's body. It was front down on the pavement, face away from camera. Prye set that photo aside to show a closer angle, framed from Eddie's shoulders to just above the top of his head. Mig leaned in to look more carefully at it.

"Sure you want to see the rest? They're kinda—"

"Want to see 'em all, Lieutenant."

Prye moved the photo away to show another close shot taken after Eddie's body had been turned over. The right side of his face was obscured by dried blood, cheekbone crushed, lip torn off to the lower gum line. The hair and skin just above Eddie's forehead was gone in scraped patches, revealing thin furrows of skull, flecks of exposed bone clean of blood stains made brighter by the flashbulb. Once sweet-eyed Eddie Fulham.

Mig felt hollow in his gut. He thought the war had put him past what he was now feeling at seeing photographic evidence of Eddie's remains, and hoped it didn't show with Prye standing next to him.

"Whoever did this…" Prye said, shaking his head. "Somewhere there's a car with a smashed-in front end. We're checking every body shop in the county, so far nothing."

"Down in Los Angeles there's probably a hundred places."

"We've thought of that. Hoping, though, whoever drove that car wasn't smart enough to think beyond what's familiar."

There was a commotion of excited muffled voices from the station lobby. Prye went to the door.

"Better find out what's goin' on." As he opened the door, "Kesselman on the desk ain't much for crisis."

He rushed out and down the hall as Mig looked at the only other two crime scene photos, different angles of Eddie's body and smashed head. He turned back to the first two pictures, the ones taken of Eddie from behind, and compared the longer shot with the closer one. He heard loud talking from out by the desk.

"God*dam* it, Nate! I just want to see him!"

"Easy, Luc. Take it easy now."

"I want to *see* the son of a bitch! See what the bastard looks like."

"You're not going back there. Just resign yourself to that."

"*Damn* it. Be reasonable!"

"I'm the only one of us who *is* at the moment, Luc."

Curious, Mig left Prye's office to check out what was going on.

When he got to the lobby, he saw the desk sergeant busying himself in paperwork as a wiry man in his late thirties was pacing back and forth, confronting Prye.

"Like you've been told," Prye said, "he's in a holding cell. There's not even any charges been filed yet, and—"

"*I'll* file the charges!"

"For what? He's only in for questioning. He didn't do anything to you."

"To my family, he did, for God's sake!"

"Without evidence we've got twenty-four hours to find out. That's how long we can hold him under the law."

"Twenty-four hours!? What could be happening with our little Peggy in all that time, huh? Twenty-four lousy hours!?"

"Simmer down, Luc. By the law, we're doing all we can."

"How can I just sit by and…and…"

"This is police business. You gotta stay out of it and let us do our job."

The other man became anguished. He slumped a little, stopped pacing. "My poor little Peggy…What's he done with her?"

"We don't know that *he's* done anything. But we'll grill him till we find out if he knows anything. You can be sure of that."

"It's the third day now…Jesus, Nate…"

"*Only* the third day, Luc. She probably just ran off again."

"Never for this long before. Never this long."

"Just let us do our job. We're working on tracking down that older cousin she's gone to the other times. We'll find her." Prye looked at his watch. "Almost three o'clock. 'Bout time for school to let out, Luc. You'd best be on your way."

The man nodded with seeming reluctance.

Prye glanced past him through the glass-paned front doors. "See you got that new truck you were talking about."

"It came in just after my other one was stolen."

"Stolen. I didn't know that," Prye said. "You report it?"

"It happened the day after Peggy went missing. It didn't seem important. Not the least damn bit."

He shuffled out the glass-paned front doors. Mig and Prye watched him get in a new white panel truck. On its side was stenciled in cheerful colors: UNCLE LUC'S ICE CREAM—*ALL FLAVORS—AND POPSICLES, TOO!* Brightly painted balloons of various sizes were festooned around the lettering.

"The missing girl's father?" Mig asked.

Prye shook his head. "Lucius Jefford. He really *is* sort of an uncle, though. Sid Beledayne's used-to-be brother-in-law."

The ice cream truck started up, backed away, and turned down the street.

"God, I hope she did just run away like the other times," Prye said. "All I need is a whole goddam circus around this."

"That your main concern, Lieutenant? How it'll look?"

Prye glared at him. "Listen, I only care about that child's safety. And I resent the *hell* out of—"

"Spoke out of turn, Lieutenant. Do a lot of that now. Forget what I…"

"Temiarov's sister, Irina," Prye said, "works over at the Sunkist packing house in town. We'll let the brother cool down, best he can, till she gets off at four. Then ask her to come in to translate when we question him. Don't know, though. She might have a problem with taking part in it." He shifted his weight, looked a little awkward. "So, uh, can you do us a favor, make yourself available?"

"Like I told you, I just get by a little in Russian. After some hospital time, I was attached to G-5. We only used pretty much basic interviewing scripts."

"We'll take what we can get."

Mig thought a moment, nodded.

"Appreciate it," Prye said. "Drop back by in an hour or so." He turned and started to metronome-walk away.

"Lieutenant…"

Prye stopped, turned back. "What? I really need to take a leak. My eyeballs are starting to float."

"Those first two pictures you showed me. The ones from behind…"

"What about 'em?"

"Something was off."

"You don't say. Didn't tell me you're a photo expert."

"Don't have to be," Mig said, "when it's obvious."

"And that would be..?"

"The back of Eddie Fulham's neck was darkened."

"A shadow, so what?"

"Same shadow in both shots?" Mig shook his head. "Don't think so, not with flashbulbs. Must've been something else."

"You trying to play cop now?"

"Seen enough death to know after the heart stops pumping,

blood pools at the lowest part of a body, shows through the skin. If that's what that is, Eddie Fulham died on his back."

Prye looked incredulous. "You saying the victim was already dead when he was run down?"

"You tell me, Lieutenant. You *are* a cop. Give it some thought while you're taking that leak."

6

Mig placed a call to Bernie D'Antino, his boss in Phoenix, who told him that Carl, who, with Mig, also operated forklifts at the clothing merchandise warehouse, had gotten over the flu sooner than expected and would be back on the job tomorrow. By this time of year bulk orders for jackets and coats had been down for a few months, but cartons of summer wear were stacking up. However, with the help onboard they could probably handle things just fine, so Mig could take some more time off.

" Let's say I take, I don't know, Bernie…a week. That'd be alright?"

"A whol'a week, uh?" Mig's boss said in his near musical accent.

"Just guessing. Maybe less, maybe…Hell, I can't really say."

Bernie's tone became serious. "Hey, you okay, Mig? I'm askin' you."

"Yeah, I'm…Yeah, Bernie, I'm okay."

"So…You musta got'a lucky, uh? Take'a all'a time you like— up to a week, week and a half. You be wore out by then, anyway, even at'a your age."

Bernie thought Mig wanted time for some woman.

"Shipments are coming in, I know. Will I still have a job if I—"

"Sure, sure…You a good worker, Mig. We get'a by, okay. Don't'a worry."

"Thanks, Bernie. I'll bust my butt when I get back."

He heard his boss chuckle on the other end of the line. "Your butt already busted up 'nough by them fuckin' Nazis. Listen, Mig…You take'a the girl to heaven, uh?"

"It's not like that. There's no—"

"Let her see stars…" Bernie chucked again. "…with her eyes shut'a tight, know what I mean?"

"Bernie, that's not wha—Yeah, whatever you say."

"Good. That's'a good." Then Bernie lowered his voice, turning serious. "I'm askin' again, Mig. Really, you doin' okay? In your head, I mean."

Mig reassured his boss, thanked him again before hanging up.

That was the easy phone call.

The next one was to Carmen. This time he regretted that she could take his call at the clinic. Before Mig could say never mind, he'd phone back another time, the woman at the reception desk rushed off to get his mother.

When Carmen got on the line, Mig asked her how she was doing and how was Jack. She said fine on both counts, asked him the purpose of his calling. She knew there was a reason beyond pleasantry, always saw through him. When Mig told her he'd been delayed, would be taking some extra days where he was, his mother was less than pleased that he might miss some of his finals.

"Can you make them up?" she wanted to know. "Will your teachers let you?"

"Uh—sure…Probably."

"Which is it, *hijo*?"

"Mama, look, I just can't leave right now."

"Something came up, you said. What 'came up' that's more

important than your college education?"

He wasn't about to comment on his view of himself and classroom learning. After a moment he said, "It's too hard to explain."

"Angel Miguel, you're dancing with me."

"I'm not! Really."

He regretted how he responded. Made him feel like a kid. "Don't even know enough yet to explain," he said. "About college, Mama, I promise you—"

"Oh, not me, *hijo*. Make promises only to yourself. You are a young man now. It is your life."

Mig heard the weariness in her voice, hated causing it. "Just need to be here right now, that's all," he said.

"Of course, being a young man…" Carmen's voice took on a lighter tone. "…I realize you naturally have…urges. There are plenty of girls—young women—here in Phoenix, you know. Some very attractive ones."

If Bernie and his mother both thought Mig was just having some wild fling, he'd go along with their assumption in common for now. Better that than him saying, "I need to look into what I think could be a murder." They'd both roll their eyes at that.

He asked Carmen to wire him a hundred dollars by Western Union. Then upped it to a hundred and fifty. He could barely hear her sigh on the other end of the phone before reluctantly saying that she'd send him the money, following it up with, "I only hope you're not being foolish, *hijo*." That stung, because he had made some bad choices growing up for which he still couldn't shake some guilt.

He gave Carmen the same time frame that he had to Bernie. Saying he needed a week wasn't based on a damn thing, just to put some cap on whatever he was getting himself into. Mig had no idea how much time he'd have to take, not even how he was going to use the time with any effect.

But he was drawn toward something he couldn't turn away from. Mig was being pulled, or pulling himself, toward a compelling need. He realized, in a strange way, Eddie Fulham was once more picking him up from hopelessness. Rescuing him one last time, now from a dying spirit. By needing to find out what had happened to Eddie, there was a stirring of purpose like Mig hadn't felt since he'd come home from the war.

Eddie's death was bringing him back closer among the living.

He drove a few miles south to the small community of Montalvo, to Korb's Trading Post that he'd seen on the way into town to buy a change of clothes and some skivvies and socks. Then Mig went back to the Ventura Police Station on South Garden.

As he walked from his car toward the entrance, there was a human howling sound from just inside. A mournful sound. The doors burst open and a slender, shock-stricken woman in her early thirties came out, struggling it seemed to get emotional bearing. She was followed through the door by Lieutenant Prye. He reached out to her, but she flailed behind her with one hand, pushing back at him.

For a brief moment her eyes locked with Mig's. The woman's posture was stiffened, as if bracing herself.

Prye called after her, "Please, miss. Let us take you home."

She made the rejecting motion again, then lowered her arms stiffly and clenched her fists as she continued across the parking area toward the sidewalk.

The lieutenant looked over to see Mig approaching him.

"Irina Temiarov, Dimitri's sister," Prye said.

"Guess I'm all you got now for translating."

"No need anymore. Her brother hanged himself in his cell."

Mig reflected sadly, said under his breath, "No more terror…"

"What's that?"

Mig shook his head. "Nothing," he said.

The place that Eddie Fulham had rented a couple of blocks off the Ventura beach was in a row of one-bedroom cottages built in the 1920s, all roughly finished stucco, painted in variations of off-white. One-car garages were set down unpaved driveways alongside the little houses. Patches of wind-blown sand drifted low extended out from the edges of the street fronting the row. Strips of tar crossing at right angles had been poured into stress cracks in the concrete roadway. Mig saw the street ahead appearing as a long, complex hopscotch pattern for gigantic girls.

He matched the metal numbers tacked next to the front door with the address Mrs. Fulham had written for him on a page of notepaper, turned into the driveway and parked. He found the front door key under a potted succulant plant where Eddie had told his mother he kept it hidden.

Once inside, Mig closed the door behind him, stood there in the tiny living room and looked around. He wanted an overview of Eddie's home space, of how he'd lived. Oak flooring without any carpets. A card table was set up, two folding chairs at opposite sides of the table.

Mig glanced through an archway to what looked to be a dining area. No furniture in it. Eddie must've eaten at the card table. Who would be in the other chair? Or was it set up just in case he had a visitor? An armchair faced out from one corner of the living room, its cover had a small tear on one side near the bottom. A scratched end table, a crudely made ceramic-stemmed lamp on it, was next to the chair. Mig saw a tag tied by a string on a leg of the table. He moved closer to see that the tag read, SOCIETY OF ST. VINCENT DE PAUL. He looked at the back of the armchair to see a similarly marked tag safety-pinned on it.

Maybe Eddie hadn't cared that much for home comforts. Or, he hadn't planned on being here in Ventura that long.

This second possibility intrigued Mig. If it was the case, why would Eddie have come here and set up a place to live, even this sparsely, only to know he'd be leaving soon? What might've been his reason? And did it have to do with his being killed? Mig didn't want to invest too much in groundless thought, but filed it away in his mind.

The bedroom didn't reveal anything. A used single bed, made up neatly; dresser; reading lamp, all tagged. One delivery of a St. Vincent de Paul truck had probably taken care of Eddie's more than modest settling in needs. Mig looked in the closet to find one suit, some white shirts, two sport coats, two pairs of slacks, wingtip shoes and penny loafers on the floor next to a half-filled laundry bag. Then he looked in the dresser drawers. A tie clip, skivvies, T-shirts. No magazines or paperbacks here or in the living room. No radio, either. Did Eddie only eat and sleep here?

Mig noticed the edge of something underneath a tucked together pair of socks. He moved the socks aside to find a small square box embossed with STELLER'S JEWELRY STORE. He picked it up and opened it. Beneath a square of cotton was a delicate silver chain attached to a heart-shaped locket. The initials *M.M.R.* were engraved in a flourish of script on the front of it. He opened the locket to find no picture inside. He noticed engraving also on the back. One word set diagonally to fit on the heart in the same script: *Remember.* Mig thought of the other folding chair by the card table. Maybe Eddie had had a girlfriend. He never got to insert his picture in the locket, much less give it to her.

He put the chain and locket back in the box, and was about to set it back where he'd found it, then thought better of it. He set the box up on the closet shelf, in the back in a corner by the wall. He was going to put the laundry bag up there for even more concealment, but figured that would only signal the police as something to look behind when they came here.

He didn't know why he was taking this precaution with the locket, wondered if he was trying to "play cop," as Lieutenant Prye would say. Mig also thought, with their attitude about Eddie's death, the police might not bother checking the back of an apparently empty shelf. But, besides clothes, the locket was the only personal item Mig found and he wanted it for safekeeping, not having any idea why.

He had missed lunch, and was hungry. He left the house, without locking up. This modest neighborhood was likely populated, Mig thought, by those who'd have little to fear from burglars. He got in his car, backed out of the driveway, and turned in the direction from which he'd arrived, remembering there was a café and bar a few blocks back down the street.

SAL'S AT THE BEACH was on a short commercial block that dead-ended at a hill of sand obscuring a view of the ocean. Paint, white and nautical blue, was peeling off the wood and plaster fronting all the buildings, punished over years by wind, sun, and sea air. There was a sports clothing shop, small enough that it could have fit into most home dens; a one-pump Standard station; a used book, record, and card store.

Mig parked in front of a bait and tackle shop. When he got out of his car he heard from the café's jukebox a bouncy, clarinet-dominant tune. Artie Shaw and the Gramercy Five playing "Summit Ridge Drive." He walked in.

Sal's was as worn inside as out, but looked clean and kept

up. It was still early, only a couple of tables were occupied. Three weatherbeaten beachcombers chomped on burgers and fish and chips. Toward the back where the light fell off, an older fellow was slowly cutting into a chicken fried steak with near ceremonious deliberation. The only other customers sat at the bar, four men and a hefty woman, blond hair some years younger than the rest of her. They were all regulars, Mig could tell from the collective indifference to their surroundings. Those at the bar were nursing beers, the blond woman and man to her left had whiskey backs.

Mig sensed them all looking suspiciously at him.

He took a seat at the end of the bar, as far as he could away from the others, hoping their indifference in this place would soon extend to him. He didn't want to have to endure any stares that his imagination would use to mess with him.

He guessed it was Sal himself who bounded up to him from behind the bar to take his order. Hair slicked back, trim Clark Gable mustache, crisply pressed shirt that showed pride of ownership. Sal reached under the bar and produced a one-sheet typed menu covered in a plastic sheath. Sal introduced himself and he and Mig shook hands. The man had the welcoming attitude of a caring host. Mig liked that.

"What can I get you to drink, Mig—Mig, right?"

Mig nodded. "Whatever you got on tap, Sal."

"An Acme comin' right up."

As Mig perused the menu, Sal set his glass of draft beer in front of him on a cocktail napkin.

"You're in luck. Early Bird Special before six. Fifty cents off."

Mig glanced behind Sal at a clock on the wall next to a mimeographed flyer. "It's a few minutes after six," he said.

"Well, yeah," Sal said. "But you're a new customer—and an honest one."

A bedraggled looking man in loose-fittting jeans and soiled sweatshirt, entered and sidled up to the table of beachcombers. "Hey, d'ja see all them big ol' blues lyin' dead on the sand yesterday?"

The three men nodded, more interested in eating than talking, at least to him.

"Wad'nt it the damnedest thing?"

More disinterested nods.

"Must'a been fifty of 'em at least."

One of the men let his eyes droop shut, shook his head. "More like fif*teen*. Maybe not even," the man corrected.

"Well, there was sure a buncha' sharks. What'cha s'pose it was caused it?"

"Red tide," one of the other men said after he swallowed.

The interloper scrunched up his face in disbelief. "Red tide, my fuckin' ass!"

Sal turned to face the man who'd just come in. "None of that kind of talk, Amos." He indicated the woman down the bar. "Not while Noreen's in here."

"Sorry," Amos said low, chastised. "Sorry, Noreen," he called out.

The woman smiled graciously at him. Raised her shot glass in a hail, then downed the contents in one gulp.

"Red tide killin' blue sharks…" Amos muttered to himself as he shook his head. "Act a' God, clear as anything. Must'a had it in for them sharks."

"That must be it," one of the men at the table said. He flashed a look at his two tablemates. They all smiled secretively enough that Amos didn't notice.

"Weird thing is," Amos went on, "God made them sharks, Hisself." He panned a look of confusion to each of the three men.

"Wouldn't'cha think He'd just change 'em instead to the way He wanted? Not just kill 'em off like that, mean as the fu—" He glanced at Noreen. "Mean as they are."

"Like they say," one of the men offered, "God gets pissed in mysterious ways."

Mig had ordered a sirloin, fries, and a side of broccoli. But eating it was delayed when a stubble-faced man in his cups, ordered another beer, moved from down the bar, sat next to him. He pegged Mig as an ex-GI, insisted on gripping his hand. He kept shaking it as he explained that he was too young for the first war, too damn old to have been in the recent one.

"My hat's off to you young fellas. Saved us, you did. Saved the whole damn world, s'matter a' fact."

Mig sensed himself starting to feel anxious, enduring the man's beer breath as he went on with his intended tribute.

"D-Day—that must'a been somethin'—Hey, come to think of it, third anniversary's day after tomorrow."

Mig didn't say that he was in the 82nd Airborne Division's contingent of support for the pathfinders who'd parachuted in soon after midnight on D-Day. Didn't want to feed the man with what he'd think was glory, but to Mig was only a near botched, deadly mission—with so much killing. It was all he could do to stay in control, his breathing becoming shallow and quick, as the man kept on.

Sal finally came to the rescue. "Let the fellow just eat his dinner, Mort. Come on, leave him be."

"Just expressin' my gratitude, s'all."

"I'm sure he'd be grateful if you'd let him eat in peace." Sal looked at Mig. "Isn't that right, soldier?"

"Not…not a soldier…anymore," Mig said through labored breathing.

"But you sure 'nough was," Mort said. "An' we can all be gla—"

Sal picked up Mort's glass and poured it out into the sink under the bar.

"Hey! Whad'ja do that for?"

"You've had enough. Now go on home to Sadie."

Displaying an offended look, Mort muttered weak protest under his breath, slid off his stool, and turned toward the door. He looked back and sloppy-saluted before exiting. Sal leaned over the bar to Mig.

"Sorry Mort zeroed in on you. He can be a pain after he's put down a few."

"It's okay...okay" Mig said, starting to regain composure.

Mig had his dinner in peace. When Sal picked up his plate, he asked him if he wanted coffee.

"No, have enough trouble sleeping as it is." He tapped his empty beer glass on the bartop. Take a fill up on this, though."

While Sal was refilling Mig's glass, Mig looked up at a mimeograph taped on the wall behind the bar next to the clock. Under a grainy photo of a grinning, broad-shouldered man in his mid forties was "SID BELEDAYNE FOR CITY COUNCIL—HELPING VENTURA GROW AND PROSPER."

"That the man whose daughter is missing?" he asked, indicating the mimeo.

Sal set Mig's refilled glass down on the bar with a fresh napkin. "The very same, yeah," he said. "Sid's brother-in-law, Lucius Jefford, drove his silly-looking ice cream truck with the big painted clown's head—red nose stuck on it—all over town, handing out these posters, getting store owners to put 'em up. It seemed real important to Luc…. Some folks think it's kinda coincidental, though."

"What is?"

"Little Peggy going missing again right when her dad's making a bid for city council. Like it's made up for sympathy, you know? Some think she'll 'be found' in a day or so. Headline in the *Star Free Press,* pictures of the family hugging and grinning. And tears, if Sid can work 'em up. But I don't know…"

"Sounds like you're not so sure about all that," Mig said.

"Just a little far-fetched, it seems to me."

"The man's daughter is missing. How can people be so. . ?"

"Doubtful? Probably 'cause Sid Beledayne rubs a lot of folks the wrong way."

Mig smiled ruefully. "Know first-hand about that," he said to himself. "What'd he do, Beledayne?"

"Being new in town doesn't help. Only moved here, oh, not even two years ago. Hardly had a chance to unpack, really, before he courted and married a widow in town. Adopted her two kids and had a ready-made family—to look good, some people figure. He opened a used car lot. Now he's running for city council. Probably thinks that'll help him with what he *really* wants."

"And what's that?"

"Talks up big plans for a housing tract development. Works overtime to pump up interest with potential investors hereabouts. And he...tries too hard to be your sudden best friend, if you know what I mean. Ventura's a place they like to look you over some before inviting you in."

"Small towns are like that," Mig said, remembering Phoenix. He looked up at the mimeographed flyer. "He looks confident in that picture he'll have enough supporters to get him elected."

"If he's luckier than I think he'll be. Sid Beledayne has opposition from most of the influential ranchers around here— especially old Hector Kierney."

"Why the ranchers and this Hector Kierney?"

"Oh, they're established and hidebound. Don't care for newcomers. They live outside the town limits, so they're ineligible to vote. But they have more to show for their ranching than dusty overalls, and do hold their sway."

Mig quaffed down the rest of his beer, set his glass down, and put cash on the bar to cover his tab and a tip. Sal picked up the money, thanked Mig, said with a smile to come on back, then took a towel and started to wipe down the bar.

"By the way, did a fellow name of Eddie Fulham ever come in here?" Mig asked. "He lived in the neighborhood."

Sal nodded, looked regretful. "Yeah…awful what happened. You knew Eddie?"

Mig nodded. "Did once."

"He used to sit here at the bar, too." Sal shook his head. "Just a damn shame…"

"You knew him fairly well?"

"Hard to say. Eddie was friendly as they come, but seemed kinda private, like there was stuff he didn't want to bother anyone with. We'd talk some."

"Anybody you know of have a problem with him?"

"Well, not a problem, really. Just the way he was looked on by some of my more soured-on-life customers. His positive way of seeing things. They used to call him Eddie full of it….This world could use more guys like Eddie Fulham."

"What I meant were enemies."

"Eddie? Can't imagine who….He had the nicest way about him. Face set friendly, sort of, in a natural way. Like he could make things around him better."

"Know what you mean, Sal."

"The look in his eyes was, I don't know…"

"Sweet. Had a sweet look," Mig said.

"Hmm, yeah. Good way to put it."

Mig asked Sal if he had any empty boxes, that he was going to pack up Eddie's things to take to his folks down in L.A. Sal unloaded a carton of soda water, saying he regretted that was the only box he could give him since trash pickup had been that day.

7

Even with the cover of seasonal overcast, it was still light out when Mig parked back in Eddie's driveway. As he started toward the cottage with the empty carton Sal had given him, through a window facing the driveway he noticed a hint of movement in the living room. There was someone inside.

Mig hesitated a moment, then ducked low and crossed the brick path to the front door. He turned the handle slowly and threw the door open. It slammed inside against the living room wall. He saw a young woman standing there, wide-eyed in shock.

"Who are you?" he demanded.

She caught her breath before answering. "Louise Kierney... and I might ask you the same question."

Mig told her his name as he scrutinized her. She was attractive in an offbeat way. Wide set eyes and small pouty lips triangulated her face. "Kierney…Heard that name just a few minutes ago. Hector Kierney. Any relation?"

"He's—We're related," she said.

"I have business being here. What's your story?"

"Eddie Fulham was a friend."

"Doesn't tell me why you're in his place."

She indicated the crudely made ceramic table lamp. "To get that back. I loaned it to Eddie."

Mig had noticed that the lamp was not tagged as was the end table it was on and the armchair next to it. He set the empty box on the floor.

"The folding table and chairs, too," she added.

"Okay," he said, easing his guard.

Louise bent down and unplugged the lamp, rolling the cord up.

"Never seen a lamp like that."

"I made it…when I was sixteen," she said, seeming to reflect. "My clay period."

" 'Clay period'?"

"I've always done crafts. One kind or another."

He studied her a moment. "How good a friend of Eddie's were you?"

"Why are you asking?"

"You feel free to just walk into his place...Could seem like that he might've been sweet on you."

Louise stared off with a pained smile. "That wouldn't be Eddie."

"And giving him the lamp and table and chairs..."

She looked at him with directness. "Loaning him them, as I told you. I think you're testing me for some reason, and I don't like it."

He walked to the card table, pulled out one of the folding chairs and sat down. "Have a seat, Louise. On one of your own chairs."

She looked at him, warily.

"I won't bite," he said. "Just need to ask you about Eddie."

She relented, sitting across the table from Mig.

"Why was he here? What brought him to Ventura?"

She shrugged, answered if by rote as she set her hands on the table, picking nervously at her fingernails, "…Well, I guess…just to settle in a nice little seaside town, you know…"

Mig shook his head. "No, I don't know. All I do know is his place is barely furnished, mostly by St. Vincent de Paul, some by you. Could indicate he didn't plan on being here that long."

She lowered her eyes, gazed at the tabletop, stopped with the fingernails. "Well, that's what came to pass, wasn't it?" A whispered regret.

"Not by his choice."

"An accident, they—"

"I'm not buying 'accident'. And, Louise, do *you*, really? Eddie out on that road by himself at night?"

He saw no reason to mention the possible circumstances that Lieutenant Prye had brought up, since he didn't believe them.

After a moment she shook her head, her eyes looking sad. "Eddie came here to…" She took in a deep breath, let it out. "…to get away from a bad situation."

"Where? Down in Los Angeles?"

Louise nodded. Mig noticed her jaw muscles tensing, and that she started in again picking at her fingernails.

"So, seems like sixty miles wasn't far enough away. What do you know about it, this bad situation?"

She sighed before continuing. "At first, Eddie wouldn't say anything. But I just knew something was on his mind. It weighed heavily on him. I asked him a few times to tell me what was bothering him, but at first he wouldn't. He didn't want to put me in any danger, he said."

"At first, he wouldn't tell you. But eventually he did."

"Not give any names. He said he'd never do that. But I think he had to get it off his chest, even to me."

"Go on."

"After the war ended in Europe, medical supplies the Army

had were packaged up and sent to the Pacific, for the troops still fighting the Japanese those last few months. Eddie was a medic assigned to get the supplies ready for shipping. It was all rushed, he said. No real inventory taken. But Eddie took his own rough accounting of what there was—or should've been. He found something short by what seemed to be quite a bit."

"Morphine," Mig said.

"How did you know?"

"Some guys used to talk about that. Used to say they could set themselves up real good back stateside if they could only get into a medical supply tent."

"Eddie was so forgiving—except when it came to this. In the war, he told me, he only cared about easing pain, saving lives."

Mig nodded, remembering.

"What was needed for our wounded servicemen on the other side of the world…stealing that bothered Eddie a lot," she said. "He reported it. But after V-E Day, no one was concerned, it seemed. Even the officers. They were just relieved their part of the war was over. Just wanted to get home."

"What then?"

"So Eddie followed up on his own. Somehow, he traced the morphine, not to New York or Boston, ports of debarkation from Europe, but across the country to Los Angeles. He thought they figured bringing it all the way to the West Coast would be easier to cover up."

"But he never said who 'they' were."

"No, he wouldn't tell me." Louise paused, as if in recall. She interlaceded her fingers tightly on the table. "He almost slipped one time, though."

"Yeah…"

Mig saw her squeeze her intertwined fingers. "He started to

say a name, then stopped himself. All he got out was Bobby."

"No last name?"

Louise shook her head. "This Bobby…his father was a lawyer for one of the movie studios."

"Movie studio. Which one?"

"I don't remember."

"Try," Mig said.

"Could've been…Metro-Goldwyn-Mayer…Warner Brothers…Twentieth Cent—that was it, I think. Twentieth Century Fox."

"Okay. What else?"

"That's all I know," she said. "That's all Eddie ever told me."

After Louise Kierney left, Mig went to the bedroom. When he'd first seen her through the window she was coming into the living room from the rear of the house. Maybe she had had to use the bathroom. Maybe she was looking in Eddie's bedroom, reminiscing about him. Mig wondered if she didn't only come here to get what she'd said. If she had been looking for something else and he'd interrupted her search.

He opened each of the dresser drawers and found all clothing items as he best remembered them being placed. If Louise Kierney had taken anything from any of the drawers he didn't know what it would be. He looked in the closet. Clothes were as he'd remembered them. She could have taken something from one of Eddie's pockets, but Mig would have no way of knowing.

The jewelry box was still up on the shelf, locket still inside. He thought about the initials engraved on the locket. No connection he'd be able to know between Louise Kierney and *M.M.R.* Maybe Louise really was just a friend. And *M.M.R.* the woman in Eddie's life. But since he wasn't sure about Louise's true feelings, he'd chosen not to ask her about the locket and the intials on it.

Mig hunkered down and looked at Eddie's shoes. They were lined up as he thought they'd been. But he couldn't be sure. Something could have been moved and put back within an inch of where he had seen it.

He was about to stand back up when he noticed that the laundry bag on the closet floor had been looked through. The drawstring top had flopped to one side when Mig first saw it. Now it draped the other way. He emptied the bag, and then felt foolish having done it. If there was something in Eddie's laundry that Louise wanted, she would've taken it.

He put the dirty clothes back into the laundry bag, brought the empty carton he'd gotten from Sal into the bedroom, and stuffed the bag into it. He loaded what would fit from the dresser. There'd be more to pack up, but he'd bring the carton to Eddie's parents when he drove back down to L.A. That would be in the morning to look up this Bobby whose father was some big shot lawyer in the movie business. It was all he had to go on so far to find connection to the stolen morphine.

Mig was tired, so tired he just took off his shoes and shirt and lay down on the bedspread. His head sank into the pillow. He didn't need covers. It was early enough that night hadn't yet chilled the air, and he soon fell asleep.

Then came another of his dreams

Shouting crowds in a city parade, crazed spectators. Bands playing blaringly loud and out of key. A procession, seemingly endless, of wild-eyed civilians and blank-faced soldiers, some in the crowd bleeding profusely from head wounds, and amputated stumps of arms and legs. Black confetti floating down so thick in the sky that the city is almost blotted out. The buildings are tall, stretching to blurs up toward a roiling dark gray sky. Some of the buildings are twisted, as if wrenched by God's hands. The strange ritual keeps moving down the street—joyless…inexorable.

A soldier appears from around one of the buildings, his uniform unfamiliar. He leaves the concealment of the building and comes closer, lowering his rifle, as everything turns silent. The soldier is Jurgen Gutfreund. He smiles and waves to Mig, who doesn't wave back. A scream, then more shouting as before. Mig aims, fires his rifle. Jurgen Gutfreund falls and is still. Mig, as if paralyzed, can't go to him. Then another soldier appears from around a building. Then another from the other side of the street. Then another, and another. All the strangely uniformed soldiers shoot into the crowd. Mig can do nothing. There's screaming between the loud cracks of the rifles. And shouting like cheers and laughter, hysterical laughter, even as people are falling out of cars and trucks. Bodies dropping where they'd stood. The band keeps playing, even louder now, rifle reports blending as rapid percussion. The parade continues, mirthless revelers unaware of the growing carnage around them.

Mig sat up, taking in deep breaths. The cool night air enveloped him, brought him back. On an impulse, he got up and locked the front door, checked the back one and locked it, too. He lowered himself to the floor, did pushups until his arms gave out, and then went back to bed. He wrapped himself in the bedspread and dozed on and off until shortly before dawn, the way it was with him most nights.

Once again, the light of day brought relief.

8

In the morning, as soon as Western Union opened, Mig picked up the money that Carmen had wired to him. Then he gassed up and got on the road. On the drive back down to Los Angeles, the aching of his wounds became increasingly bothersome. He read a sequence of little signs posted every several yards along the highway. Single lines of corny poetry were displayed from one sign to the next.

> CAR IN DITCH
> DRIVER IN TREE
> MOON WAS FULL
> AND SO
> WAS HE
> BURMA-SHAVE

Even with its humor, the implicit warning and reference to the moon made him think of Eddie and his fear. Mig pulled over to the side of the road, got out, and started to pace out his aches. He looked across a field to a dilapidated old barn. An advertisement from a prior generation had been stenciled in large letters across its roof, faded white paint that looked to have been peeling off for years: CHEW MAIL POUCH TOBACCO.

He thought about the old man from the drive up to Ventura the day before. His spitting tobacco juice, their go-around about signs to the lion farm not being put back up yet, his comment about opportunity becoming greed. "Sunshine'll fade to shadow," the old fellow had said. Mark his words.

After a few more minutes working out his pain, Mig got back in his car and continued south. As he drove, he imagined something that chilled him. It was like one of his dreams, but not weirdly unreal like them. It was clear as glass. Vivid. Mig imagined that *he* was the one trudging through the snow patches that night two years ago. Ploddingly slow, he came upon Eddie lying on the ground, staring up at the moon that could no longer hold him in dread. Mig had been too late to save him. It didn't matter that he never knew Eddie was in danger. He was too late.

Now that he had brought himself out here, Nate Prye felt like a goddam fool. He chewed his toothpick into soggy splinters before taking it out of his mouth and dropping it in the dirt. He couldn't help but feel foolish standing out here by the side of the road. Like an idiot. All because some half-Hebe, half-wetback youngblood he'd never met before had some harebrained idea about a simple hit-and-run being murder. Probably got it from reading too many crime paperbacks. Some cops read them, too, but not to take seriously. They knew real crime cases made more sense than the dumb idea this kid with names that didn't fit together came up with.

Prye had had bacon and a waffle that morning at the Hob Nob Cafe as he did every Thursday. Sometimes one other day of the week, depending on how tired he was of his usual bowl of Wheaties. When he had breakfast out on workdays he would leave the Hob Nob, head north for a few blocks on Thompson Boulevard, which conveniently turned right, becoming South Garden Street, and into the police station to park.

This was his routine for the sixteen years he'd been in Ventura. Prye went out for breakfast at the one coffee shop, never anyplace else. His wife Harriet used to bemusedly call him an uncurable creature of habit. He agreed with her, while remaining satisfied with who he was. She had always been the more imaginative of the two, Prye the solid, this-is-the-way-it-is rock. Their balance of natures had served them well. On cool winter days Harriet used to sometimes make the family oatmeal with half and half and Log Cabin syrup poured on top. Prye missed that. He didn't make oatmeal for himself now.

This morning, after breakfast at the Hob Nob, he took his usual route back to the station. He checked the desk duty officer reports to see what had gone on the night before, which of their usual "guests" were still sleeping it off in the cells in back. He waited until patrolman Hank Elias came on duty at nine, continuing his review of last month's phone log. He always liked to have that done by the end of the next month's first week. Prye was up to the twenty-first of May by the time Hank came in.

" 'Mornin', sir. Ready to head on out?"

"Yeah, Hank, yeah. Be right with you."

Prye finished scanning the last of the entries for the twenty-first and closed the log book. He snatched his hat off the rack, joined Hank, and they left the station.

The evening before, Prye had asked him about the hit-and-run scene, since Hank had taken the call that night. Wanted to know if there was anything Hank might think of to add to the report he had written, that Prye had just read again and still found sketchy. But, no, the patrolman couldn't think of anything.

Prye had also taken another look at the photos. That ex-G.I. did have a point that he resented admitting: there wouldn't be a shadow on the back of the victim's neck that the camera flash hadn't eliminated. That didn't mean the youngblood was right about the ridiculous idea he'd come up with, only that the darkened area wouldn't be a shadow.

Yesterday Prye had told Hank Elias that he was going out to check the crime scene the next morning. Hank had volunteered to drive out with him to see if anything might jog his memory. Besides, Prye figured, Hank would probably be glad to go back and examine a crime scene with the lieutenant, something uniforms saw as a minor privilege. Prye liked it when a young cop picked up out in the field what he had to teach. He liked being able to groom them for rank on their sleeves.

There was the long shot chance Hank might've overlooked something from last Thursday night that would come back to him, Prye floated as a thought. But experience didn't allow him to really expect it. Due diligence in police work all too often wound up as evidentiary dead ends. Could even make you feel foolish, like it did today.

The ride out on One Twenty-Six started in silence. The two men had never had a real conversation with each other before, and now Prye didn't know what to talk about. Finally, to end the awkwardness, he asked Hank how his cousin was doing now that he was out on parole. Buddy Joe Lamont was a career loser, a small-time burglar with more wrong instincts than sense. His major achievement so far was in making it to the big house, to San Quentin for a two-year burglary sentence, reduced for good behavior.

"Hell, Lieutenant, that lunkhead...The family just doesn't know what to make of him. Royal foul-up..."

Prye was sorry he'd broached the subject. It seemed embarrassing to Hank. "Sure hope he learned his lesson up at Q," the lieutenant said, meaning to bring the discussion to a close.

"Me too. With Buddy Joe…" Hank shook his head. "…what was a big deal to him up there, what he goes on about, was the mess hall."

"Food was that good, uh?"

"Yeah, sure it was swell. No, sitting at the table in the mess hall with who he claims are the smartest cons in there. 'Specially some guy named Chessman. To hear Buddy Joe talk about it you'd think Jimmy Cagney invited him to dinner."

"Well, he's out now. Needs to get a job," Prye said.

"He did, Lieutenant, if he can keep it. At Strohmeyer's Heating. Gonna bend my ear about it at a barbeque at my place Sunday. Can hardly wait…"

They drove on in silence, until Hank asked the lieutenant if he'd heard how Sergeant Ballinger's wife was doing with her pregnancy.

"She's on bed rest. Nearly two weeks overdue now."

"Two weeks, wow…"

"Doctor's keeping a close watch on her. I'm sure she'll be okay," Prye said, though he had his concerns.

"What about the baby?"

"No problems reported. I doubt the wait's bothering it."

Hank smiled. "If it's a boy and it takes much longer, right after they slap its butt, it's gonna need a shave."

Prye smiled, too. "Could be," he said.

Nearing some planted acreage Prye began to slow down.

"Up here is what you wrote in the report, Hank. This look like it?"

"Yup. Little ways back from that field—celery, I think."

Rows of irrigated vegetables bordered the south side of the highway. On the north side there was no cultivation. A lone, broad-branched oak tree stood as if on sentry duty in the tall weeds several yards away from the road.

Prye parked on the shoulder. Upon actually arriving here, he felt even more strongly that he was on a fool's errand, had no sensible idea why he had brought them the few miles out of town to where some guy had been run down the week before. They'd give it a look around with the benefit of daylight, then head on back to the station.

After they'd gotten out of the car and Prye, feeling stupid as mud, dropped his well-chewed toothpick, he looked down the road, back toward the approach they had made from town.

"Vehicle came from this direction, right?"

"Heading east, yeah, Lieutenant. Just like in the report."

Prye then peered way down at the road ahead. He started his side-to-side amble in that direction, Hank keeping up.

"Think back where we were was closer to it, best I can remember."

Prye walked several more yards, stopped and squatted down, looking at a few feet of paired skidmarks. Hank came up and also looked at the marks.

"Could be wrong, though, sir. It was dark out."

"Tried to stop, looks like," Prye said. "See anything you might say is a little off here?" He would test the young guys on the force who'd occasionally ride to a crime scene with him.

"Off? How you mean?"

"Only one set of skids," Prye said. "Which vehicle made 'em?"

"Which vehicle, Lieutenant?"

Prye stood up. "The one that hit the victim, or the one that came on the scene right afterwards?"

"Oh, you mean the not quite witnesses that called in."

"As I remember, your report said they didn't see the body

until they were nearly up to it, wasn't that right?"

"That's what I remember putting down, yeah. Looking at the skids now, just assumed they were from…"

"So, the other vehicle could've been the one skidded to a stop," Prye said.

"Yeah. Coulda been, I guess…Still, you'd think the one that impacted…unless the driver somehow just didn't see—"

"You'd think so. Think there'd be two sets of skids, wouldn't you?"

"I…guess I would, yeah."

"You got a close look at the body, right?"

Hank shifted his stance a little. Seemed ill at ease. "Oh, well, naw, not really. Just pointed the camera where I needed to."

Prye regarded him with a critical look. "Just pointed the camera, Hank?"

The patrolman looked sheepish, glanced away, then turned back to Prye."Truth is, I'm really not much for stuff like this." Hank shrugged, shook his head. "Funny thing for a cop to say, I know, but…that's the way it is, Lieutenant. I mean if the guy was still alive, I'd do whatever I had to, but…"

"But you just pointed the camera. Looked away while you took the flash."

Hank nodded, gazed off, set his hands on his hips in a posture meant to seem grounded, Prye thought. He also figured that Hank wished he'd been less forthcoming.

"Reason I brought it up, the victim was hit hard, face messed up bad," Prye said.

He walked down the road several feet east from where they had stood. He stopped, signaled with his arm for Hank to come look. The uniformed cop trotted up.

"Bloodstains. Still see 'em. What do they indicate, Hank?"

"The guy…he slid quite a ways."

"Uh-huh, sure did."

Prye paced the length of the smeared trail of bloodstains, turned back to Hank.

"I'd say about sixteen, seventeen feet."

There was the sound of a vehicle approaching, so they walked to the shoulder of the road as a pickup truck came from the direction of town, driving fast. It slowed down when nearing them and drove past comfortably close to the speed limit.

"Got a tape in my glove box, Hank. Get exact on that stain before we leave."

Hank lowered his head, shaking it slowly. "Lieutenant…shit. Stain details, that's not in my report."

" 'Preciate your honesty, Hank. But not your carelessness… What does this length of stain tell you?"

"Victim was hit hard, Lieutenant. Like you said."

"Indicating what?"

"Uh, like the vehicle didn't, you know, brake much."

Prye nodded. "Or at all. Indicating the one set of skids was from the second car. Makes you wonder, doesn't it?"

"Wonder about what, sir?"

"Whether the driver of the impacting vehicle was too drunk to brake…"

Hank nodded with renewed confidence. "That'd be my guess. Same story we've heard before. Some beaners out joyriding with a case of brews. Accidentally plowed into the guy, jabberin' to each other to keep on goin', hightail their brown butts outta there. Don't get caught, sent back across the border."

Prye had looked away, less than patient for Hank to finish his imagined scenario.

"…too drunk to brake, or whether the victim was run down

intentionally." He wasn't that ready to accept what he had just heard himself saying, but Prye knew he couldn't rule out the possibility with this possible evidence.

"Check out the north side of the road, Hank. I'll take this side."

"Okay, Lieutenant. What are we lookin' for exactly?"

"Beats the hell outta me. Whatever you might find that maybe makes you wonder about what happened here that night."

Hank nodded even as he looked blank. Prye had started to doubt this patrolman's usefulness at investigation—now or maybe ever. He was convinced that he'd need to scope out anything Hank would miss.

Prye edged himself down a short, steep drop-off to the edge of the field by the road, digging his heels into the dirt to keep his heavy bulk from slipping. But he did slip when his foot gave way on some slick weeds, and his foot splashed into a shallow streambed. He dropped against the side of the slope, grunted loudly, and then swore even louder.

"YOU OKAY, SIR?" he heard Hank call from the other side of the road.

A car passed by, drowning out Prye's expletive response.

"LIEUTENANT, YOU OKAY?"

"I'M FINE, HANK. JUST CHECK THINGS OUT OVER THERE."

Prye was relieved that Hank hadn't seen his awkwardness. He got up and stepped just to the side of the streambed, on dry ground. Once his footing was stable, he looked around where he was standing, then a short distance in both directions along the V between the roadside slope and the slight rise to the irrigated land. There was a concrete culvert a few yards to the east of him, indicating water runoff was in that direction.

He started walking toward the culvert, glancing barely at eye level across the road to see Hank throw a round red object into the weed field on his side. Prye waited until another car passed before calling out across the road.

"I SAW THAT. WHAT ARE YOU DOIN', HANK?

"JUST SEEIN' IF MY ARM'S STILL GOOD, SIR.. PLAYED LEFT FIELD AT OXNARD HIGH, YOU MIGHT'A HEARD."

Prye, along with everybody else around the station had heard about Hank Elias just missing out making all-state. His failed grab for glory.

"WHAT WAS THAT YOU JUST THREW?"

"LITTLE KID'S BALL IS ALL, LIEUTENANT."

"QUIT FOOLIN' AROUND."

"I CAN GO GET IT IF YOU WANT, SIR—FOR EVIDENCE." He belted out a laugh. "'COURSE IT LOOKS IT'S BEEN LAYIN' AROUND OUT HERE FOR MONTHS."

Prye didn't care for Hank having his fun with him.

"JUST...CHECK THINGS OUT, HANK."

Continuing toward the culvert, Prye straddled either side of the streambed. He'd never been that well-coordinated, but with middle age and added pounds he was even less sure-footed than in his youth. When he reached the culvert, Prye saw small patches of grass growing between expansion joints in the concrete. The grass was flattened by water runoff, mostly from irrigation, he knew. There were two or three scraps of paper, nearly disintegrated from age and dampness. Half-buried in the flattened grass and partially obscured by mud collected on the culvert's drain was the end of a dull gray strip about two inches wide. The rest of it had washed into the culvert.

He reached down and pulled on the strip. Duct tape. Prye pulled out the rest of the tape out of the culvert, about a seven or eight foot length. It was knotted close to the end, with an apparent small loop that had been torn. Prye wiped away the mud to see that it wasn't a tear, had no residual threads. It was a clean cut, as if made with a knife or scissors. He rolled up the tape and stuffed it into his side coat pocket.

He looked for what else might have washed to the culvert, seeing nothing, but knowing that possible evidence could be well on its way to the ocean by this time. He climbed back up the slope and crossed the road.

When Hank saw the lieutenant coming, he suddenly looked diligent, bending over and scouring the roadside ground with a darting, intent gaze. Prye just shook his head.

"Well, anything over here?" He pretty much knew what the answer would be.

Hank waited a dramatic moment before breaking off his posed scrutiny and looking up at his boss. "Nothin', sir. Clean as a nun's reputation."

"Uh-huh," Prye said with some skepticism.

Prye walked back on this side of the road, corresponding to about where he'd gone down the slope on the other side. It was sloped on this side as well, but to a lesser degree. He found a section where the weeds had been scraped away, roughly, it seemed, in no particular pattern. Dirt was exposed in broad striations.

"Come over here."

Hank rushed up, dutifully. "What'cha find, Lieutenant?"

"Look at this."

"Uh, ground sorta messed up. Coulda been anyth—"

"Disturbed, looks like. We had rain last week," Prye said.

"Uh…yeah. A little sprinkle. Unusual for this time of year."

"On Wednesday, I remember. The twenty-eighth. Day before the hit-and-run."

"That's right, Lieutenant, I remember, too. Was just a little sprinkle."

"This is the north side of the road. Shaded slope coming down from the pavement here would dry off slower."

"Suppose so, a little slower, yeah." Hank nodded solemnly. " 'Specially since June gloom's set in. "

"Not till Sunday, Hank. On the first. Like clockwork this year. Folks were out in jackets before then."

"Well, it bein' Sunday I guess you'd…"

Hank's voice trailed off. They both knew why any Sunday would be memorable to Prye. Everyone at the station knew. But no one talked about it, not to him.

"So…what are you sayin', sir?"

"Ground on this side might still be damp some a warm day after even that little bit of rain Wednesday…Appears to be something—someone scrambling for purchase here, like they might have to if the weeds were still damp and slippery. Hard to get footing."

Hank shrugged. "Well, it's possible, yeah…"

"It's what might've caused this," Prye said, mostly to himself.

Hank set his hands on his hips, looking away from Prye. "Lieutenant, I don't know how to say this, but…"

"How to say what?"

Hank faced his boss. "You're, uh…You seem to be runnin' with something here, Lieutenant, with nothin' much really to go on."

"Think so? You could be right." He scanned his view across the field, then looked at Hank. "Could be right…"

"I'd keep it to yourself, you know. Guys around the station, they like to talk and kid around, 'specially about who's in charge. Just bein' truthful, sir."

Prye smiled. "Pretty much like we used to do when I was in uniform. Never thought it was any different in Ventura than it was up in Visalia."

"I wouldn't want you to…well, you know…"

"Be joked about? That what you're trying to say?"

Hank just nodded, seemingly ill at ease to have broached this.

"I appreciate your concern, Hank."

"Heck, sir, I feel funny even bringin' it up."

"Don't fret about it."

Prye was well aware that being in a position of command there'd always be talk behind his back. Came with the job and long ago ceased to bother him much. What occupied his attention now were the flattened weeds and dirt striations. He lowered himself to one knee and moved his hand lightly over the disturbed area of the slope, as if that could help him understand.

"Coulda been caused by…just about anything, Lieutenant."

Prye glanced up to the young patrolman and nodded. Then he looked back to the ground. "Like some sort of struggle," he said under his breath.

9

"Well, young fella, you *are* in Hollywood, sure enough. But this is Columbia Studios you've come to."

The old gate guard pointed up to a sign above the arched main entrance, painted a non-Hollywoodish dull brown. "Says right there, see?"

"I can read," Mig said. "Like I said, I'm trying to find Twentieth Century Fox."

The guard grinned. "And my counterpart over at Paramount was having some fun with you, sent you here…You know, all the studios aren't in Hollywood, no matter what people may think."

"I'll do a study on it someday."

"Fox is nowhere near here."

"That right?" Mig said. "The other guy only sent me a mile or so. How much *more* fun are you cooking up?"

"Naw, naw. I can see you're in no mood to be kidded. Fox is way over in the west part of L.A. On Pico Boulevard."

A new Packard convertible turned into the entrance, slowed down as the guard gave the boyish, pompadoured driver a wave, then continued into the studio.

"One of the new writers on contract. Hope that car's paid for before 'ol Harry C. cans him. Just chews 'em up and spits 'em out…"

"So, how do I get there?" Mig asked.

"Fox? I'll write down directions for you."

"Thanks. That'd be a big help."

The gate guard made a rough map for Mig, handed it to him, saying that even a nice looking young guy like him has a slim chance of breaking into the movies. Mig told him that wasn't what he wanted, but the guard didn't seem to hear.

"There's gonna be television," the guard said. "It'll come on real strong next few years. That's what they're saying. You might have a better shot there, lad."

Mig thanked him again for the map and was on his way.

Work was going on with streetcar tracks on some major routes, and the slowdown in traffic caused the drive to Twentieth Century Fox to take Mig nearly an hour.

By the turn off Pico to the entrance of the studio there was a billboard advertising the upcoming release that month of *The Ghost and Mrs. Muir.* Across the wide driveway another billboard showcased a movie already in theaters, *Miracle on 34th Street.* A young couple beamed at each other just above the title, and between them a joyful Santa Claus figure held a smiling little girl. Mig thought it peculiar that a Christmas-themed movie was already being advertised as summer was just beginning. Now that times were finally looking up maybe it had to do with priming the Holiday shopping spree even during the start of bathing suit season, Mig thought. Still, this movie coming out six months before Christmas seemed to him a little odd.

He drove inside by a huge windowless building, adjacent to which was a closet-sized wood shack with a guard inside. Mig hoped the guard would be as friendly as the one who'd given him directions here. Not so. Without a pass he would not be allowed to drive on the lot, farther, that is, than to turn around and head out the way he'd come in.

There was no available space on Pico Boulevard, so he parked on a side street bordering a fenced-in huge expanse of lawn. He paced by the fence for a few minutes to relieve the pain in his backside and try to figure some way to get into the studio. He looked at his watch. A few minutes before noon. Mig guessed that some people who worked there would be driving out the gate to lunch at nearby restaurants.

He stood off the curb half a block down from the studio by westbound traffic on Pico Boulevard, hailing cars that came out from the studio gate. The first four or five ignored him. The next one stopped, but the driver thought Mig was signaling that there was something wrong with his car, was irked at having been inconvenienced, and sped off. A few more employee cars drove past his attempts to wave them down.

Then a LaSalle coupe pulled over and stopped. Mig leaned down to look in the passenger side as the window was rolled down by a middle-aged woman leaning across the seat. She had a kindly expression. He could easily picture this woman kneading dough for her fruit pies.

"You having car trouble, young man?"

"No, ma'am. Trouble, yeah, but not with my car."

"You didn't look like you were hitchhiking. Your thumb wasn't out."

"That's right, ma'am." He smiled. "Not hitchhiking."

She smiled back. "You going to keep me guessing?"

"Look, I know I'm interrupting your lunch—I'll buy you lunch—but the guard at the shack wouldn't let me drive into there." He gestured back up the street. "Into the Twentieth Century Fox place."

"Not without a drive-on pass, he wouldn't, no."

"Drive-on pass. How do I get that?"

"By knowing the right people. I can tell you don't know anyone."

Mig looked away in frustration, and then back to her with all the sincerity he could muster. "Just you, ma'am. I mean, I don't know you, but…"

She studied him a moment, amused. "You'd like me to drive back in, with you hidden in the trunk."

Mig nodded. "Or down real low on the floor in back, yeah."

"How do I know you won't rob me, steal my car, or, heavens…" She took on a look of shock. "…even worse."

"You don't, ma'am. Simple fact is, you don't."

She sighed, feigning weariness. "Get in."

Mig opened the passenger door, started to move the seat back away.

"Sit in the front. I *do* know people, including Clifford, the gate guard."

As she drove down the next block to turn around, they introduced themselves to each other. Her name was Margie Kellings, and was the secretary for the assistant head of the Production Department. She asked Mig if he was looking to be cast or crew.

"Don't know what that is," he said.

"You want to be in front of the camera or behind it?"

"Neither one, ma'am. I'm just trying to find someone."

She asked him with a smile to quit calling her ma'am. Studio people preferred first name basis. The young ones did it as a matter of course. Others out of wishing their youth back. She admitted probably being in the latter category. They drove through the gate, Margie giving the guard a little wave, him waving back. Once inside, she looked over at Mig, again with amusement.

"You didn't have to do that, Mig. Slump down in your seat like that."

"Thought that guy Clifford would recognize me."

"So what? I could drive in here with Joe Stalin if I wanted. Well, maybe that's an exaggeration these days."

She parked near the commissary, said the food there was not bad, but she liked a change every so often. Lucky for him this was one of those days, Margie commented, even though, oddly enough, she was right back to her usual lunch haunt. They entered a vast room to a din of clattering plates and silverware, in competition with a hundred or more conversations. Margie told him that important deals were being made over lunch. Mig wondered how with all the racket going on.

Over in a section of cloth-covered tables, she pointed out Henry Fonda and his agent, asking Mig if he wasn't impressed. Sure he was, he said, but he could tell that Margie didn't believe him. She ordered a club sandwich, the "Tyrone Power" it was called, and a small salad. Mig had a "Don Ameche" cheeseburger. He followed her lead with ice tea. Margie picked at Mig's fries as well as his reason for being there.

"You have lawyers here, right?" he asked.

"Oh, yes," she said. "Enough to field a softball team with a full second string. More lawyers than—well, no. There's not more of anything than producers, a few of whom actually produce movies."

"You know a lawyer at this studio by the name of Robert..? Bob..?"

"By last name is a better way to inquire."

"Don't have a last name."

She regarded him curiously. "Mind if I ask why you're here at Fox, Mig, looking for one of the staff attorneys named Robert anything?"

"It's hard to explain," Mig said. "Even the Robert part's only a guess."

"You *do* mind, I can tell."

"Like I said, it's—"

" 'Hard to explain.' Translation: none of my business."

Mig shrugged, ill at ease. "Wouldn't put it that way, Margie. Sounds rude."

"A young man with manners. I like that. Your mother did a fine job rearing you."

"Did her best." He smiled ruefully. "I sure wasn't easy."

She advised him that the way to conduct his search was with the studio Personnel Department. He should ask for Betty Kay Dolan and give her Margie's name. They played bridge together. Betty Kay would be helpful. As much as she could, that is, with such lack of information. When the check came, Mig picked it up. Margie offered to pay since it was his first day "immersed in the glamour of movieland." But no, he insisted. He had said that he'd buy her lunch.

"Then let's go Dutch, at least."

"Deal's a deal," he said, as he put bills on the table. "Betty Kay in…which department was that?"

"Personnel. She has the list of everyone who works here."

He reached out and they shook hands. "Well…thanks a lot, Margie."

"You're welcome, Mig Czerniak. And thank *you* for a nice lunch and your most pleasant company." She pressed her hand to his cheek, looked at him warmly. "She did a fine job indeed."

Margie gave him directions to Personnel before getting in her car and driving back to her office. She had just rounded a turn by a sound stage when Mig felt the bottom drop out of somewhere deep inside him, and then the shakes came. He made his way to a bench in a small area of grass and sat down, wrapping his arms around himself. Two workmen wearing tool belts were walking by. One of them nudged the other, nodding toward Mig. The other man just shrugged.

"Rehearsin' for a part, prob'ly."

"He's sick, man. Can't you tell?" He walked over to Mig. "Hey, buddy…"

Mig managed to look up at him. "I'm…I'm—okay…Be…okay."

The man reached for Mig's arm. "You need to go to the infirmary. Come on…"

Still shaking, Mig jerked away. "Won't help…Nothing…"

The workman took Mig's arm, but he jerked away.

"Fuck off! Just…lemme be."

The man backed off, looking offended. "Okay, just tryin' to—jeez."

The other man shook his head, smiled. "Goofy damn actors…"

After a couple of minutes the shakes subsided. The workmen had gone, so Mig was relieved he couldn't apologize. He was so tired of having to do that.

After he introduced himself to Betty Kay Dolan in Personnel and told her how he came to be there, she said something complimentary about Margie Kellings as she gestured for him to come around the counter. She took him into her private office and brought out a thick loose-leaf binder, saying with a smile, that if he ever said anything about her letting him look through this, she'd do serious damage to his manhood. Mig could feel himself blush at her frankness. He was in a different world here.

"It's alphabetical by last name," she told him, adding, "not by what their jobs are, unfortunately for you…" She moved a notepad and pencil on the desk closer to him. "Position with the studio is right after each name, as you'll see. Then office number, followed by home number."

"Really appreciate this, Betty Kay."

"Yeah, yeah, right…"If you ever tell anyone I let you tour through this binder, I'll deny it right up till they fire me."

"Won't happen, believe me."

"I certainly hope I can. This is Tinseltown. All too often you can't even believe 'Good morning'."

He opened to the first page, all surnames beginning with A.

"Too bad you're not looking for an Ellsworth or Marmaduke. You'll find a pile of Roberts…grips, sound guys, editors, gofers…"

"Gophers?"

"Different kind than you're thinking. They're people, too, almost…Well, dig in, have fun."

On her way out, Betty Kay started to close the door behind her, stuck her head back in. "I'm closing the door. This is our little secret. Don't even cough or sneeze."

Over most of the next hour, Mig poured over the pages of lists, writing down the names of all the staff attorneys, just to be sure. Only two of them were Roberts: Garfinkel and Lanyon. He'd start with them first, hoping that a sense of personal pride would be evidenced in passing down a first name from one generation to the next. The junior factor of ego boost.

When he had finished his list of studio attorneys, Mig opened the door a crack to see that there was someone else in the main Personnel room with Betty Kay, a guy filling out an employment application. Mig closed the door quietly and waited until he heard the man thank her and ask when he should check back. He heard Betty Kay's response of "Oh, in about a year, maybe two." "Huh." "Just kidding. Check back every week. You never know when someone'll quit, retire, or just keel over." The man left, thanking her all the way out the door. Then Mig came back in.

"Well, monk's out of his cell," she said. "Got what you want?"

Mig nodded, thanked her, adding, "Would it be okay if I use your phone?"

"You don't mean to call the lawyers you've looked up."

"Uh-huh, yeah."

"Oh, no. My largess only goes so far. Margie's a friend, but you making calls to studio attorneys from this office where you got their home numbers, that's where I draw the line."

Mig felt stupid, realized he should've known the welcome mat was only out for the one request. "You've been nice enough already. I shouldn't have asked," he said.

"Forgive yourself, you're still a pup. But do me one favor."

"Sure, anything."

"Never say that, someone'll take you up on it. The favor is, make your calls from anywhere you want—just not from here on the studio lot."

10

Mig checked back into the King Charles Hotel downtown, where he'd stayed the night after Eddie's funeral. It was easier making calls from his room than feeding change into a payphone. He dialed the first number on his list.

"Hello, Garfeenkel reseedence…"

"Hello. Is Bobby there?"

"Um, lemme get the meesses."

After a few moments another woman came on the line. "This is Babs." Her voice had a huskiness, from years of cigarettes and/or whiskey.

"Mrs. Garfinkel..?"

"Yes, how can I help you?"

"Is Bobby there? I mean, does he live with you?"

A throaty chuckle on the other end. *"Bobby*, you say?" Another chuckle. "Neither one of us has filed papers. Not so far, at least."

"Pardon…"

"It's an odd question, if my husband lives with me. Who is this?"

"I'm—I was overseas with Bobby."

"Really? Old Army buddies, were you? You and, uh, Bobby?"

"Yes, ma'am. Just trying to look him up. Your son."

"Oh, you mean Bobby, son, not Bob, spouse."

This had turned into a weird exchange, made Mig feel uncomfortable, like he was being toyed with.

"Yeah. I should've been more clear, ma'am."

"It's a Bobby *Garfinkel* you're looking for."

"That's right," Mig said, maintaining certainty on the phone, even though now realizing he must be on the wrong track.

The woman told him that she and her husband would've been proud to have had a son who'd served his country during the war, but had been blessed instead relatively late in life with a daughter. She would soon turn sixteen and they were hocked up to their eyebrows with Chrissie's upcoming coming out party. There were a fair number of Garfinkels in L.A., she surmised, and wished this ex-G.I. luck in not having to call too many of them to find the Bobby he was looking for.

Mig's next call was to the Lanyon household. And he found out that he'd never needed to write down the numbers of all the Twentieth Century Fox lawyers. Bobby Lanyon had been in the Army in Europe, his mother said. He'd been in the Quartermasters, supplies. Mig thought maybe this might include medical supplies.

"May I say who called," she asked.

"Well…deal is, ma'am, Bobby and me, we'd kid each other a lot. Kinda set each other up for practical jokes."

"Oh, that sounds like Bobby, alright."

"Yeah, and I'd rather it was a surprise," Mig said.

"Of course. I'll just tell him that someone—"

"Actually, be better if you don't say anything. Even that anybody called."

"A total surprise, then," she said. "Sounds just like what Bobby would do, too."

"Yes, ma'am. Want to really fool the shi—fool him."

"I see. Well, then, I suppose you'd like his address."

"That'd be good," Mig said.

"You have a pen and paper, young man?"

Bobby Lanyon lived in a stucco, Spanish style quadraplex apartment house a block off San Vicente, in an upscale West L.A. neighborhood. Mig parked across the street and waited, listening to a ball game on his car radio. It was the bottom of the third, the Los Angeles Angels playing the Portland Beavers. It was still early in the season but the Angels were starting to shape up as a Pacific Coast League powerhouse.

After all the years away from Brooklyn, living in Phoenix, Mig still missed the Dodgers. The Negro fellow, Jackie Robinson, signed this season to play first base, was a big deal. Mig thought it was a step in the right direction. He remembered passing a convoy of black soldiers on a farm road in northern France, thinking at the time that if enough of them made the same sacrifices as white GIs, they weren't going to go along that easy with being second-class citizens anymore. Things would start to change.

Maybe this Jackie Robinson signing with the Dodgers was an early sign of that change. Mig hoped so, seemed right to him. Being half and half himself of two sub-groups not always looked upon with favor, he was sympathetic to outsiders. He was glad, though, that the new guy, Robinson, who'd once been a shortstop, didn't take that position away from Peewee Reese. That wouldn't be right.

The game ended with the Angels nearly shutting out Portland. Mig turned the dial to the next clear signal station, and heard a cheerful baritone voice. "Welcome to Johnny Valentine's Riddle Griddle Show, brought to you by Sparkle Bright Toothpaste!" This was followed by, "Hello, boys and girls! Greetings to all of you at home and to those of you in our studio audi—" That was enough of that.

Mig turned to a pop music station. Tex Beneke led his band in selections from Glenn Miller Masterpieces, Volume 2. Then the Mills Brothers harmonized on their latest hit, "Paper Doll." After that, Frankie Laine crooned his version of "On the Sunny Side of the Street." Mig didn't remember the name of a Les Baxter instrumental, only the title of the album, *Music out of the Moon*. Made him think of Eddie, of how a symbol of romance to so many was only of dread to him.

The sun had burned through the June gloom by late afternoon, and then had faded to a weak glow by the time a Lincoln Continental with the top down pulled to a stop in front of Bobby Lanyon's apartment house. A tall, broad-shouldered young man jauntily got out from behind the wheel, scooted around to the passenger door, and offered a hand to help out the pretty young thing with him. As they started up the paved walk to the apartment, Mig crossed the street toward them.

"Hey, Bobby…Bobby Lanyon…"

The young man turned to see Mig approach. "Do I, uh, know you?" he said, forcing a smile.

"Friend of a friend, you might say."

Mig glanced at the girl with him. She was wearing shorts, and about three quarters of her were tanned, well-shaped, dancer's legs, no stockings, a backlit trace of blond down above her knees.

"Who would that be, the friend in common?" Bobby asked.

Mig resisted looking at the stunning legs, said, "Eddie Fulham."

There was a flash of apprehension. Bobby tried to cover it with a broad smile. "Eddie…What a swell guy."

"Yeah, he sure was," Mig said.

"*Was?* What do you mean?"

Mig glanced again at the girl, those fantastic gams, then looked back at Bobby to see what he could read. "He died last week."

"Aw, no, that's too bad. Eddie…Christ, too baaad."

Bobby's distress seemed fake. He didn't even ask what had happened to Eddie, the way people do as if explanation could somehow undo awful truth.

"Listen, can you excuse yourself for a few minutes?" Mig asked.

"To talk about Eddie?"

"Yeah…and things."

"Now's not really a good time, buddy."

"Just a few minutes." Mig glanced at the girl. "She can wait."

"Yeah, but we're going to a final cut screening. Elia Kazan's new flick, *Gentleman's Agreement.* Kind of short on time, as it is. It's frowned upon to be late for a screening, you know."

"No, I wouldn't. But you have time to stop here first," Mig said.

Now Bobby looked over at the girl, back to Mig with a grin. "Gotta change clothes," followed by a wink.

"Uh-huh. How about tomorrow then?"

Mig could almost see the wheels turning."…Sure, I guess. We can get together sometime tomorrow."

A whine from the girl, "Bobbyyy…"

Bobby glanced back toward her. " 'Kay, Mandy. I'm coming."

"Bet you'll be," Mig said low to himself. "What about tomorrow morning?"

"Have to check my schedule. You from out of town?"

Mig nodded.

"Where you staying?" Bobby asked.

"Downtown. King Charles Hotel."

"Okay. Give you a call."

"In the morning, right?"

Bobby clapped him lightly on the shoulder. "You bet'chum, Red Ryder. First thing."

"You might want to know my name."

"Was just gonna ask."

Bobby took a gold fountain pen from his shirt pocket and pulled out a money clip from his trousers, ready to write on one of the bills.

"I'll be sure not to spend this one. Go ahead…"

Mig spelled out his name. Also he said which hotel he was staying at again, doubting to what degree this slick young guy had tuned in to their brief conversation. Bobby annoyingly clapped Mig on the shoulder again, promising that he'd call by nine, nine-thirty the latest tomorrow morning. Then he walked briskly up the walk toward his apartment, arm in arm with the girl. Mig gazed at her practiced stride, watched them enter, and close the door behind them. He sorely wished he could keep from thinking about what he knew they'd be doing in there.

He crossed back to his car, put the key into the ignition. A weak attempt of the engine to turn over, then nothing. The battery was dead from Mig listening to all that radio. He could just imagine Betty Kay Dolan making some smart aleck comment about it. Using a crescent wrench from his tool kit in his trunk, he got the battery out of its hold-down bracket and carried it several blocks to a gas station. Then he waited for it to be charged back up.

By the time he got back to his car with the battery, it was dark, the Continental no longer there. Bobby and the knockout girl had left for that movie screening. Or maybe they'd missed the screening and just gone out to wolf down a big dinner, having worked up a couple of hearty appetites.

Mig didn't have much of one, himself. He drove back to the

King Charles, flipped through a few pages of a *Saturday Evening Post* he found in the lobby, and then chatted for a few moments with the desk clerk, who asked him if he wanted a woman. He could get him one for only five bucks. Mig passed on that idea. If he couldn't have some gal on a par with the one on Bobby Lanyon's arm, he wasn't interested. He bid goodnight to the clerk and went up to his room.

As he looked out the window to neon signs flashing garishly in the darkness and heard traffic noise, Mig remembered it was June 5. He thought of three years before on this date, close to midnight. With other men he was loading up on a plane in England, about to fly across the Channel. From the time they parachuted into somewhere in northern France till nearly dawn the lights weren't neon, but flashes from machine guns. The sounds not traffic but mortar and grenade explosions. For him it was all about the killing he'd seen. And that he'd done.

It took a couple of hours before Mig fell into another restless night of sleep. He made it mostly through the night before the shakes came over him.

11

It was almost ten o'clock the next morning. Mig had grown tired of waiting for Bobby Lanyon to phone him. He walked downstairs to find a new desk clerk there, a younger one with a crew cut, probably working his way through college. Mig told him that he was going out for breakfast, if by chance anyone called, please get a number. The young man said he would, then nosed back into his zoology textbook.

Mig entered a greasy spoon on the corner of the same block as the King Charles and took a seat at the counter. He ordered coffee and picked up a menu from a chrome rack in front of him. There was a dissipated older man perusing a racing form on the stool just to his right. Mig ordered coffee and started to look at the menu as the waitress set a filled cup in front of him.

A burly guy in a dark topcoat came in carrying a folded section of the *L.A. Times* and whispered something to the man with the racing form. Within moments the track fan put money on the counter, got up and left. The big man took his stool. He picked up a menu out of the rack and glanced at it. He turned to Mig, tapping him on the arm with the menu. "What's good here, sport?"

Mig took a sip of coffee. "Couldn't say. Never been here before."

"Can't go wrong with hotcakes, sport, can you?"

Two comments from a stranger, both including the word "sport." Mig found the familiarity forced. He hadn't decided yet what he wanted to order, but didn't want to encourage conversation with this guy. He thought about Bobby Lanyon, as he took another drink of his coffee. Wondered if he was still tangling bedsheets with that girl.

"Bacon or sausages and eggs. That'd be a good choice, too," said a man on the other side of Mig. He was shorter, cadaver-thin, sunken cheeks. This one had arrived out of Mig's view, and also wore a dark topcoat. It was unsettling, these two bookending him. The waitress behind the counter appeared in front of Mig, pencil point set on tablet.

"Ready to order, sir?" she asked Mig.

"No better choice than sausage and eggs," the one with sunken cheeks said. "How you like your eggs, my good man?"

Mig shot him a look, turned toward the waitress. "Just oatmeal, please. And an order of toast."

"I didn't expect him to order that," the burly one said. "Surprised me." He looked past Mig to sunken cheeks. "He surprise you, too, Wally?"

The other man nodded, looked at Mig. "You sure looked to me like a pancakes and sausage ma—"

"Then why'd you ask how I like my eggs?" Mig snapped at him.

The one called Wally opened his hands in a puzzled gesture. "Hey, just tryin' to be friendly—friend."

"I'm not your damn friend," Mig said. Turning to the burly one, "Yours, either. You're both annoying the hell outta me."

"Get a load 'a this guy, Malcolm," Wally said across Mig to the big man. Then he leaned closer to Mig with a dead-eyed smile. "In this town…," turning solemn, "…good idea if you try to get along."

Malcolm opened his palms and shrugged. "Yeah, know what we mean, friend?"

"Either of you call me that one more time…"

Mig stared hard at Malcolm, who opened his topcoat and suit jacket, and put the section of the *Times* in front of a slick periodical with green lettering in his inside jacket pocket. Over the pocket Mig saw a leather shoulder holster with a blued automatic.

"We got off to an unfortunate start with this fella, didn't we, Mal?"

Malcolm shook his head for dramatic effect. "Real unfortunate, yeah."

The waitress popped over, set Mig's oatmeal in front of him. "Toast'll be right up." Indicating his half empty cup, "Top that off?"

"Sure, thanks," Mig said.

She filled his cup, looking from Malcolm to Wally. "You gentlemen ready to order yet?"

Malcolm said nothing, just waved her off.

Mig looked from Wally to Malcolm. "Think you two have me mixed up with somebody else."

"No mix-up. You just happened to be sitting here," Malcolm said.

"And we're just trying to spread good will," Wally offered.

"Not enough of that these days," Malcolm added. He patted his topcoat where he'd put the newspaper next to the pistol. "Like in the news, you know? Powers that be are leaning on legitimate businessmen. Hassling 'em. What they say about Mr. Cohen, for instance."

"Don't know any Mr. Cohen," Mig said.

"He's a fellow does a lot of good for this city," Wally said.

"And still they give him trouble."

"Can't blame him if he shoves back, can you?" Malcolm said.

"Couldn't say, I don't even—"

"And he's a man that can shove back real hard," Wally said, leaning in close enough for Mig to see he had dentures. "Anybody interferes with his business, starts askin' the wrong kinda questions, say, and Mr. Cohen rightfully takes offense."

"Yeah, bothersome questions that are nobody's business. That really heats him up," Malcolm added. "Good thing for any smart young fella to keep in mind."

He gave a quick nod to Wally and they both stood up to leave. Malcolm put a dollar bill on the counter.

"Breakfast's on us, sport."

When he finished eating, Mig took a walk in the downtown area to loosen up. The traffic noise reminded him somewhat of New York, buildings and sky as gray as his mood. There was no reason to head back to the hotel and check for any message from Bobby Lanyon. He'd just gotten it from these two thugs. After walking a few blocks, he saw a branch library and, on an impulse, went inside.

There were two librarians behind the reference desk, an older man who looked like he'd been there since McKinley's funeral and a plump young woman with no lipstick but rouge on her cheeks to cover slight acne. The older man was busily setting books on a wheeled oak cart, so Mig directed his attention to the young woman.

"Excuse me…looking for information about some important man here in Los Angeles, a Mr. Cohen."

"The card catalogue is right over there, sir, referencing all of our books."

"Well, I don't know the name of any book about him."

"There's listing by author as well."

" 'Fraid that won't help."

"Well, then I…" Looking slightly flustered, she turned toward the older librarian methodically placing returned books into the cart. "Mr. Falkenberg…"

The man looked up from his task. He had the bespeckled appearance of knowing every tome in the place. "Yes, Rebecca?"

"This gentleman, could you please see if you can help him?"

Mr. Falkenberg set his cart a few inches away from the narrow passage to the reference section, shuffled over to Mig, offered a pleasant smile. He indicated the young woman who'd traded places with him and was now sorting books on the cart. "Just started this week, Monday after Memorial Day," he whispered. "Takes it so to heart that she doesn't know everything yet, poor girl." Then, speaking up, "Now, what is it you're looking for that we might have?"

"Just some basic information," Mig said. "About someone here in Los Angeles. A big, uh…businessman, maybe. Name of Cohen."

"Cohen, hmm…That's not an uncommon surname here. Is he a philanthropist?"

"Pardon?"

"Does he donate money to charitable causes?"

"That could be, but he's probably considered more like, you know, shady."

Mr. Falkenberg smiled broadly and raised his eyebrows. "Oh *that* Cohen."

After the librarian filled him in some on one of the city's biggest mobsters, Mig expressed his appreciation and left. So the heist of Army morphine came all the way across the country to Los Angeles because Mickey Cohen had brought it here.

Mig thought back to when he was fifteen, soon after he and Carmen had moved from Brooklyn to Phoenix. He was hiking in the desert one day with a new friend when he saw some movement at the edge of a flat rock. Mig bent down to pick up the rock, but the friend grabbed him and pulled him away. The other boy upended the rock with his foot to reveal a nest of baby rattlesnakes. "Don't mess with 'em," his friend said. "Them little ones, they got the strongest poison."

Eddie Fulham had gotten into a nest of rattlesnakes.

Mig had no idea what his next move would be. Whatever he'd do, he was in way over his head. He walked back toward the hotel, on the other side of the street from where he'd walked before. The sun had started to challenge the day's dominant grayness. As he approached a sidewalk newsstand, he reached in his pocket for change. Might as well read about what was going on in Los Angeles. He didn't know any more about this city than his sharing a name with it.

He briefly scanned the newspaper selections, looking for the *Times*. The last one had been sold, the vendor told him, so Mig bought a copy of the *Herald Express,* one remaining from the previous afternoon's late edition. He glanced at the headlines. There were some L.A.-based stories, one about war vets camping out in MacArthur Park in protest over a housing shortage. Another headline announced the Marshall Plan for relief aid to Europe. At least they were being taken care of over there, Mig thought.

He folded the paper to carry with him and started to walk away. Then he paused after a few steps and came back to the newsstand, looked again at the racks of other periodicals. One seemed familiar, sort of a multi-page newsletter on slick paper, wide green lettering at the top. He reached over and took it out of the rack.

The ceiling-mounted task light flashed brilliantly off the top of assistant medical examiner Chet Ewing's bald head as if passing under it caused brainstorm. But not so this early afternoon in the Ventura County Morgue, just recount and complaint.

"Two cars last night, three bodies, Nate. Head-on, half mile or so out of Point Mugu. Pretty messed up. Haven't even gotten to the third one yet. Plastered sailors couldn't even've done me a favor and waited till the weekend…They don't pay enough for this work in this damn county. Should've applied up in San Luis Obispo when there was an opening couple years back."

Prye let the man finish his vent before questioning him.

"Last week, late night, the twenty-ninth. Hit-and-run out on Foothill Road, a few miles outside of town."

"Would've been next morning for me. What about it?"

"I'm looking for autopsy details," Prye said.

The examiner started for the file cabinet.

"Never mind, Chet. I already read that. Want to know what might *not've* been written down. Your impressions."

The examiner shrugged, looked blank. "Impressions?"

"Jesus H. Christ, Chet…Anything that comes to mind that maybe didn't seem significant at the time? That maybe you might not've put in the report?"

"You sure it was *my* signature on that report?"

"Guessing it was yours," Prye said. "Just a scrawl. Coulda been goddam Harry Truman's signature."

"What was the victim's name?"

"Fulham, Edward. Young guy, early to mid-twenties."

The examiner thought a moment, looked blank at Prye,

shrugged again.

"Goddam it, *think*, Chet."

"What day was it?"

"Twenty-ninth, I said."

"What day of the week?"

"Thursday night it happened. You woulda got the body on Friday."

"*Thursday* night. Sure about that?"

"Was only last week. 'Course I'm sure," Prye said.

"Only checking."

"So now that you have, Chet, beyond the shadow of any possible doubt..."

The examiner looked relieved, shook his head. " 'Fraid not. Traded to get that Friday off since it was Memorial Day. My uncle bought the farm in the first war. Wanted to put a wreath on his grave. After that, I watched the parade."

"Then who did the workup?" Prye looked wary. "Not Kretzler, I hope."

"Yup. Al's who I traded with."

"That old Jew couldn't find his keister with both hands."

"He just comes to the job more relaxed lately. Marking his days to retirement, kinda like you, Nate."

Prye jabbed his finger at the examiner. "Don't *ever* make that comparison. I don't 'mark goddam days'."

The examiner put his hands up defensively. "Okay, Nate. I was just saying…"

"Kretzler around today?"

"Uh-uh. It's Friday again. His day off."

"Then give me his home number," Prye said.

"Okay, but I doubt you'll get him. Most likely Al's with his grandson, in his rowboat up on Lake Casitas, trying to catch trout like he talks about more than he usually does."

"He in tomorrow?"

"Yup. Weekends are his, when most of the stiffs are brought in. But Al doesn't seem to mind."

"I'd think not, the sloppy job he does," Prye said.

"No offense to you, Nate, but like I said, he's close to retirement."

12

Mig had stopped by Eddie's parents' house near downtown to drop off the carton of Eddie's things that he'd packed up. But they weren't home. He didn't want to just leave the box on the porch, so decided to come back the next day.

It was just past ten that night before he saw Bobby Lanyon's Continental parked in front of his apartment. Mig had checked a few times throughout the afternoon and earlier in the evening before finally finding Bobby home.

Most of the lights in the other apartment units were off, the tenants probably having gone to bed. Mig looked up to a brightly lit room on the second story, north side of the building. From the room he heard male outbursts of disappointment and some loud boasting, guffaws of laughter. Mig got out of his car and crossed the street to the apartment house. As he got closer he smelled cigar smoke wafting down from the open upstairs window.

He opened the apartment house door of heavy oak, crossed the tile lobby, and just started up the stairs when he heard a voice of hushed irritation.

"Just a second, young man."

Mig turned to see a thin, ferret-like elderly woman, gathering her robe protectively around herself, peering around the door of a downstairs unit. Her hair was rolled in large curlers. Her eyes narrowed at him. "I've had just about enough of that commotion up there. And now you think you're going up to make even more of it." She stared at him bright-eyed. "Well, you have another think coming."

"I'm not—no, ma'am, not at all."

"Don't you be sarcastic with *me*. I know your kind, and I've a good mind to call the police."

Mig thought for a moment, then said, "Somebody already did, ma'am."

"What do you mean?"

"I'm a co—policeman. I got the call."

Her eyes narrowed again. "Where's your uniform?"

"I'm, uh…undercover, ma'am. The department thinks that, uh, without a uniform is better for situations like this."

"And your badge? I want to see it."

Mig hesitated barely a second before digging out his billfold. "Good that you asked, ma'am. The public should always be sure."

He flipped the billfold open to reveal the snapshot of Aaron Czerniak on one side and his own Social Security Card on the other. He held the billfold out in front of him, his hand covering the photo, Social Security Card prominent, hoping that she wouldn't leave the security of her doorway to have a closer look. She squinted at the card.

"That's just paper. It's no—"

"Undercover we don't carry a badge, ma'am, just ID."

She seemed to accept that, retreating into her apartment without further comment. Mig stuffed his billfold back in his pocket and quickly moved up the stairs.

When he got to where the boisterousness was coming from, he tried the knob to find the door unlocked. He opened it and stepped inside. All eyes looked over at him from a poker game.

Bobby Lanyon and three other young men.

"Hey, the guy from yesterday," Bobby said with forced good humor. "What was your name again?"

Mig strode up to Bobby, grabbed him by the back of his collar with both hands, jerked him out of his chair.

"What the hell you think—"

"Hope you had a lousy hand, Bobby…"

"What the fuck!"

"…'cause you just folded it."

Bobby squirmed violently to get loose, but Mig pulled him off balance and started hauling him toward the door.

"Help me, goddam it!"

Two of the others just sat there stupefied, but the third, a stocky guy who looked to be a lineman, jumped to his feet and rushed over, blocking the door.

"Just hold on, buster," he said, jabbing his finger two or three times in Mig's chest for emphasis. "You're way outta line here."

Mig looked at him hard. "Do that one more time, I'll feed you that finger."

"Oooo, big talk…"

The stocky guy lunged at Mig and wrapped his arm around his neck in a headlock. "Don't know what your beef is, buster, but it's—"

Mig stomped hard on his patent leather shoe and metatarsals snapped. The now broken-footed fellow loosened his grip and bent over in pain. Mig shoved him aside and hauled Bobby through the open doorway. His handsome face twisted in humiliation, Bobby made a last ditch effort to enlist aid.

"HELP ME, YOU ASSHOLES!"

Mig pressed one hand up against Bobby's throat, almost choking him as he dragged him down the hallway. "Shssh. Some people are trying to sleep, Bobby."

When they reached the top of the terracotta pavered stairs, Mig let go of Bobby's neck and grabbed the back of his head, forcing him to look down the tiled stairway. "Make one sound and I throw you down."

Bobby's voice came out in a low quake. "No, no, don't…"

Mig eased Bobby down the stairs, continuing to hold him firmly by the back of his collar. As they reached the bottom of the staircase, the old woman opened her door again, this time with a look of haughty disdain. Bobby looked at her imploringly.

"Mrs. Dellaway, *please!* Don't le—"

The old woman shut the door and deadbolted it.

Mig hauled Bobby out into the night. He forced him around to the side of the apartment house into a stand of yucca trees and slammed him up against the apartment house wall, grasping him by his shirtfront.

"Malcolm and Wally weren't invited to the poker game, I see."

"Wha—what do you mean?"

"Next time you send a pair of phony gangsters to scare somebody off, make sure when one of 'em shows off his gun some movietown trade paper isn't folded next to it. *Daily Variety* it was called."

"It was just a joke, that's all."

"Not funny, Bobby."

Bobby averted his look, gazing woefully down to a flowerbed by the trees. "I didn't mean any harm…"

Mig backhanded him across the face. "Don't like to be messed with."

Bobby rubbed the slapped side of his face. "What do you want from me?" he almost cried.

"Tell me about the morphine."

"What morph—"

Mig grabbed Bobby by the collar and lifted him up against the wall, fists pressing against his throat, until only the toes of Bobby's shoes touched the ground. His face turned red and his eyes bulged out. He sputtered drops of saliva, straining to breathe.

As if in a sudden spell, Mig was looking not at Bobby's face, but at that of Jurgen Gutfreund. He released his hold on Bobby, who started to squirm away. Regaining of purpose snapped Mig out of it. He reached out and caught Bobby by the arm and dragged him back among the yucca trees, bracing him against the wall.

"Now…tell me about the morphine shipment."

Bobby looked away, still struggling to get his breath back.

"The one here to L.A. after the war ended in Europe."

Bobby looked pathetically at Mig. Around the corner, by the front of the building, they heard muffled voices as the other young men came out. Within a few seconds, the sound of cars starting up and driving off. Bobby turned his head toward the sound, all hope gone.

"There go your true blue buddies…About the morphine, Bobby."

"I…don't know…anythi—"

Mig slapped him again.

"Think about how ugly you could wind up in the next few minutes, Bobby. So battered to shit that dollbabe on your arm yesterday would stride her gorgeous legs as far away from you as she could. It's all up to you how much damage I'll do."

"…I got taken out of the deal…soon after I got back stateside."

"Uh-huh. No doubt by Mickey Cohen's guys."

Bobby shook his head. "Never went anywhere near…that high up."

"You don't say. Who else was in on it?"

"Overseas it was…just me and another guy."

"His name."

"McPhee. Lester McPhee."

"Go on. What was the setup?"

"We were both in Quartermasters, Les and me. Right near the end, spring of forty-five. He got attached to medical supplies, field command-level."

"Two skunks in just the right place," Mig said. "Things so rushed after V-E, anything could go missing."

"Yeah, that was about it."

"Too easy an opportunity to pass up, wasn't it? You slime…"

Bobby cast his eyes down, trying on shame, not convincingly.

"Never gave a whole lotta thought about the wounded guys in the Pacific that morphine could've helped save, did you?"

Pitifully, Bobby looked at Mig. "I know, I know…It was wrong, I know," he said weakly.

"You pathetic fuck…Eddie Fulham knew this was going on, didn't he?"

"Eddie, he worked in the medical supply with Les, trying his best to keep track of everything that went out."

"He ever say anything to this Lester McPhee about what he suspected?"

"I guess, yeah."

"Your skunk partner, he threaten Eddie any time lately?"

Bobby looked perplexed. "Lately?"

"Yeah. Where is McPhee these days?"

"Les, he used the morphine himself back then, too. He shot up too much one night and died."

"That's more than perfect. So who else would've had it in for Eddie as recently as last week?"

Bobby looked at Mig in desperation. "Hey, you don't think

that I—"

"You wouldn't have the stomach for it, Bobby."

"I don't know who would've done Eddie in. I don't."

"Then trace it back, rich boy. How exactly did the morphine get to L.A.?"

"Film cans. I coordinated shipping movies my dad's studio sent overseas for GIs. We sent the morphine back to the States in the film cans by ship."

"And who received it here?"

"Les's contact at the dock in San Pedro before the cans were delivered back to the studio. I got a payoff, not that much."

"The contact. Who was it?"

"A voice over the phone. I don't know."

"A couple actors brought in to do their best Bogart…some mysterious voice over the phone…You're starting to make me mad, Bobby."

"The phone call is true! I don't know who it was. He told me that if I ever said anything he'd—"

Mig pulled him forward, then slammed him back hard against the wall. "One way or another, you're gonna give me more than you have so far."

"Come on, please…he'll find me and—"

"Don't worry about him, Bobby. Your problem's with me, right here and now."

Bobby started to break down, openly blubber.

The ache from Mig's wounds was kicking in from physical strain. It took him off purpose enough for him to think of the leggy girl from yesterday, to wish she could see Bobby now. But Mig dismissed that as petty schoolboy envy—on the heels of his schoolboy bully. Guilt took over. No matter how justifiable the reason he'd broken this privileged creampuff down, it didn't sit right with Mig. He couldn't help but feel like he was being a real shit.

He spoke in a calm voice. "Need a name, Bobby. Point me to someone I'd want to talk to."

13

It was almost midnight by the time Mig found the place. A few miles the other side of Compton, it seemed far removed from the city. Desolate. As desolate as he felt now after he'd leaned so hard on Bobby Lanyon. He wondered if he'd taken satisfaction from that. It seemed too easy to just blame it on the effect the war had on him. Was this who he had become, or was becoming? One who victimizes because he likes doing it? Boy, would Carmen be proud.

He scanned his gaze to see the only lights around were those illuminating oil pumpjacks. Like bulky-framed beasts scattered across the dark flatland, as if bowing their massive heads to an unseen ruler, they continuously circled down and came back up to bring black crude from deep in the earth. A strange location for a jazz club, Mig thought, way out here. Then again, way out here was inconveniently remote for police patrol. The draw of music could be cover for a lot of things.

The red neon sign above the club's doorway sputtered BIT A' HEAVEN. Even at this hour, things were hopping. Mig could hear the pulse of music even from back where there was room to park his car, see spots of red glow of a few lit cigarettes, bare outlines of figures in the dark. He grabbed his leather jacket from the back seat and got out of his car. The chemical smell of petroleum was in the air. Holding the jacket over his shoulder, he limped toward the entrance, feeling the price his backside was paying for having braced the one who'd given him directions here.

Once inside, Mig could tell the music was coming from a jukebox. The band was between sets. He encountered stares from where he stood just inside the door. The stares spread like a wave across the room. Elbows were jabbed and shoulders tapped for those too absorbed in conversation to notice, and they turned to also see him and became part of the wave. The stares were curious, uncomprehending, some hostile.

Mig felt on display, the only white person before a sea of Negroes.

He made his way through a parting crowd to the bar. The bartender's gaze lined up on him as the man stretched his arm out to set down a customer's fresh drink. He leaned halfway over the counter toward Mig with a broad smile.

" 'Evenin', officuh, what can I serve you?"

"Whatever you got on tap," Mig said. "And I'm not police."

The bartender leaned forward, face-to-face with Mig, shook his head, agreeably. "No, suh, this be county. Outta *po*-lice jurisdiction." Then he grinned. "Deputy sheriff'd be more like it."

"Not that, either. I'm not the law."

"Oh, you ain't got no badge then?"

Being checked out, Mig sensed that if he didn't pass muster he'd be in a room of total clam-up. He took out his billfold and set it on the bar.

"Have a look."

The bartender just stared at the billfold as if it were germ-infested.

"Here," Mig said, as he picked up his billfold and opened it, holding it up for the bartender's inspection of an old snapshot of another man and Mig's Social Security card. He nodded in contemplation, then that smile again.

"No badge in your pocket, I s'pose."

Mig almost smiled himself over the irony of the situation. Earlier the same night he'd easily convinced someone that he was the law, now he had to put in some effort to do just the opposite.

"Search me, if you want. I'm no kinda cop."

The bartender nodded, starting to believe him it seemed. "You sure this the place you want to be, suh?"

"I like jazz," Mig said.

"They got plenty jazz joints up in town."

"Been to some of 'em. Hear you got some good new stuff here. Bebop."

The bartender's eyebrows rose in surprise. "You be a bebop man, my man?"

"You bet. Dizzy Gillespie…Charlie Parker…"

In truth, the only thing Mig knew about emergent jazz was what he'd heard from Carmen's benefactor and boyfriend, Jack Tolafsen. Jack had played his collection of 78s for Mig, from early Coleman Hawkins up through the latest innovative musicians, only a couple names of whom Mig could remember. And he'd already dropped them, so didn't want to be trapped in a conversation about something it would soon be obvious he knew little about. He leaned closer to the bartender.

"You got a drummer here who's kinda hot, I hear. Mason Garrett."

The bartender's look took on a sadness. "You mean Sticks, yeah…Had his day, had his day…"

"He on tonight...Sticks?"

The bartender indicated the bandstand. "Every night 'cep Mondays. Keeps tryin' to find his ol' groove. Him and the boys'll be startin' back up any minute now." He pushed back from the edge of the bar to stand upright. "Lemme get you that on-tap."

There was an empty chair at a table occupied by two couples and a woman withoug escort, somewhat older than the others. The men were decked out in pinstripe suits, fake boutonnieres in their lapels. The women wore brightly colored, shiny cocktail dresses. One of the men slid the chair out for Mig's easy reach, then backed away in dubious respect or possibly in fear of catching whatever disease this young white buck had. Mig raised his beer glass to them and smiled to seem pleasant before sitting down.

Reacting to all the attention on him, Mig had not taken immediate notice of the men of the combo that had just come back onstage, including the drummer, who he'd come here to talk to. Three of the five in the group wore dark glasses in a room of subdued lighting. It lent an air of mystery to two of them, the one on sax and the bass player. Their shades gave an I-exist-for-my-artistry-that-transports-you image.

But Mason "Sticks" Garrett, was blind. Mig could tell when another instrument was on a riff, when Sticks wasn't playing. He reached over to each of his drums and hi-hat cymbals, touching their perimeters to make sure all his instruments were in an ordered spatial relationship with his seat. It reminded Mig of a story his mother had read to him when he was little about a blind woman gently touching each of her brood of children to make sure they all were accounted for. Sticks touched his drums and hi-hats with what seemed near parental love.

Into the first number, Mig knew the bartender had been right. Sticks's drumming was off. He missed beats more than once, blind also to a solid groove.

When the set was over Mig went up to the bandstand, introduced himself to Sticks and asked him if they could talk in private. Without hesitation, not even inquiring what this stranger's business was with him, Sticks bent over, picked up a white cane with red tip from the floor by his feet, and told Mig to come out back with him.

Outside, by the back door, the steps were lit by a bare bulb at the end of a curved metal conduit, mounted high. When they sat together on the steps Mig now could see why Sticks was blind. Outside the frames of his shades were gnarled beads of healed tissue, darker than the mahogany tone of his skin. Acid scars. Sticks dug in his coat's side pocket, took out a wooden kitchen match and a self-rolled cigarette that had been previously lit. He struck the match with his thumbnail, put the flame to the cigarette, took a deep drag. He held the smoke in for a moment, and then exhaled—not tobacco smoke. Sticks held out the self-rolled to Mig. "You do reefer?" he asked.

This was an opening for mutuality, maybe trust even, but Mig needed to keep his head straight, didn't know what the effects of marijuana might be.

"No, uh-uh. Thanks, anyway—Really like your drumming," Mig quickly followed up with.

"You do, uh?"

"Record guys, they ever come into the club?"

"From time to time," Sticks said.

"You might get a deal one of these days," Mig continuing the lie and hating it.

Sticks took another hit of the reefer, held it in before answering. "One 'a these days, ya think?"

"Never can tell," Mig said.

Sticks nodded, seemingly to himself. Then asked, "Folks ever call you Mick, 'stead a' Mig?"

"Often enough, yeah."

"That's 'cause they have a *pre*conception. What they're used to 'stead a' the what is. They don't pay no 'tention to that."

"Never thought much about it, Mr. Garrett."

Sticks took another drag, held it in as he pinched the lit end out, exhaled, and put the reefer back in his coat's side pocket.

"Now me, I don't *pre*conceive a whole lot. 'Stead, I tune in to the what is." His lips spread into a wide smile. " 'Course I got me an advantage, bein' able to hear better than most. Lord's way of makin' up some for my *dis*advantage…Now then, what you *see* yourself lookin' like, Mig Czerniak?"

"Me?"

"Nobody else out here I can sense."

"Well, I'm, uh, about five-ten, brown hair, blue—"

"All that don't mean nothin' to me," Sticks said, waving his hand dismissively. "I aksed what you see yourself lookin' like, not what you look like."

"You lost me there," Mig said.

Sticks chuckled. "Was messin' with ya. Just to illustrate a point, what I meant by preconception. See, you do it, too."

"I'll try to remember that, Mr. Garrett."

"One thing you could see yourself lookin' like—inside, that is, below skin deep— is real patient."

Now Mig laughed. "Patient? If Carmen could only hear that."

"This Carmen, she's…"

"My mother. She wouldn't say I was patient about anything."

"Well…could be you're just bein' that way with me, 'cause you think that's the way to be with ol' Sticks. Jus' warmin' me up some 'fore gettin' to why we're talkin' together. So, Mig Czerniak, tell me, why we talkin' together?"

"I got your name from Bobby Lanyon. Remember him?"

Sticks thought for a moment, "Movie lawyer's boy. Vaguely

'member. Vaguer yet be fine with me."

"We hold pretty much the same regard for him then."

"Fry up a dog turd, pour good country gravy on it, still got what'cha got."

"He said you might have a line on some morphine that came into the Central Avenue area a while back."

"Things shuffle fast around Central. How long ago you talkin'?"

"Around the end of the war," Mig said. "Late spring, early summer of '45."

"Oh, yeah, 'member that load a' stuff…Gone with the wind, my man. Gone-with-the-wind."

"That right?"

"Yesterday's high. That Miss Emma's used up long time now."

"What I want to know is, how did it get here?"

"Oh, you want history 'stead a' high."

"Seems you preconceived about me, Mr. Garrett."

Sticks laughed. "Got me there. Yeah…"

"Who brought that morphine into Los Angeles?"

"You know, Mig Czerniak, I talked outta turn one time years back. My big mouth cost me, it did."

Mig nodded, and then realized that wouldn't communicate with Sticks. "Thought something like that."

"Was a hard lesson, but it taught me to keep my mouth shut, be blind to jus' about everything. *Be* a tomb 'stead a' *in* one."

Mig knew he was being stonewalled.

"Look, Mr. Garrett, I need your help. Could deal with Bobby Lanyon in a way I know I can't with you. Someone I credit for my still being alive I think was murdered. And it had to do with what he knew about that morphine. I owe it to him to find out."

"You could be killed, too. S'pose, though, you thought about that."

"If I am, I am."

"You be crazy, boy?"

"Seems like it sometimes."

"And you 'spect me to feed that."

"Don't *expect* anything. Just hope you'll help me is all."

Sticks said nothing for a moment, just bobbed his head and rocked from side to side as if listening to jazz in his mind.

"Puttin' aside the bullshit you was tryin' to slide my way before, truth is, my timing's off. Didn't used to be, but is now."

"You mean your music," Mig said.

Sticks nodded. "My beat. Might's well say my life…Won't be gettin' it back, my beat. That's just the what is 'bout that."

Mig fumbled for encouragement. "Maybe if you, uh…"

"I'm dyin', Mig Czerniak. Got the cancer."

"Oh, didn't know."

"No one does, 'cep me and a doctor I go to. Don't want a lot a' fuss."

As Mig started to stand up, "I won't bother you any more, Mr. Garrett."

Sticks reached up, grabbed at air, before getting hold of Mig's wrist.

"Sit back down here, boy."

Mig did, feeling uncomfortable now.

"It's freein', in a way, facin' death."

"Been close to it myself," Mig said. "Know the feeling."

" 'Specially freein' to me. I be past fearin' threats. Can say whatever comes to mind. What they gonna do?"

"You got things you want to say, Mr, Garrett?"

"That big M you was talkin' about…word is, it came in through the used car business the Early brothers once had."

"The Early brothers? Tell me about them."

"Zeke and Zack Early…nothin' much to tell. Two a' them were just a front for the bin'ness. Black smilin' faces sellin' mostly black market cars to folks down here… thems who thought they could trust the brothers." He chuckled at that. "But the Earlys, like I say, they were just a front for someone."

"Front for who?"

"Some white man, we all thought—just not who he might be. Zeke and Zack, they were…" Sticks tapped the side of his head "…a little spare in the attic. Could never run a bin'ness, 'cep into the dirt. Naw, it was somebody else they was shuckin' for. Some pale cat, we all figured."

"Guy named Lester McPhee. Ever hear of him?"

"He white?"

"Guess so."

"Hmmm, McPhee…That was the name of a scrawny, shifty-eyed kid, I heard about, doin' cleanup at the car lot 'fore the war. A white workin' for coloreds wouldn't go down, not unless somebody else but the Earlys put him on the payroll. This McPhee boy, as I recall, got hisself into some scrape with John Law. Robbery… sum'um. Hear tell the draft got him outta trouble."

"Not in the long run," Mig said.

Sticks shook his head, made a tsk-tsk sound.

"All a' them young boys…Ya know, while I'm bein' so run-at-the-mouth, you ain't the first one aksed about this."

"Really? Who else, Mr. Garrett?"

"Was a while back. Some months ago now. Young cat name a' Eddie."

"Eddie Fulham?"

"That'd be him," Sticks said. "There was sum'um about him…a innocence, you might say. A sweetness…Not a funny fella kinda sweetness, just a good way about him."

"Yeah, I know," Mig said. "That was Eddie."

"Told him what I told you just now. Didn't even know I was sick yet, not then. This Eddie, though…" He cocked his head, remembering. "I thought the Lord'd frown on me if I just turned him away. Sorta hard to explain."

"It's not necessary. You said the morphine was used up."

"Oh, yeah. Dry as a granny's snatch."

"What about the money from it? Where'd the profit go?"

Sticks chuckled deep. "I'd tell ya if I had a hint even. Things be finally good now after so many years a' hard times. Plenty a' places for that money to go legit-i-mate, find its way to some smooth groove after the war. Plenty a' places."

Mig reached over, put his hand in Sticks' hand, gripped it.

"Thank you for your help, Mr. Garrett."

Sticks nodded. "Luck to ya, Mig Czerniak. And if you run into that Eddie fella, give him my best."

"Eddie, he's—Yes sir, I'll do that."

14

Saturday was usually Nate Prye's day off, but he'd come down to the morgue because Al Kretzler would be on duty. Kretzler was out of the room when Prye got there, so he cooled his heels for a minute, reading over the report again that this assistant medical examiner had made on Eddie Fulham. There wasn't much in there. It seemed to Prye to be slipshod work.

As he stewed over this, Kretzler, an aging morgue worker, bumped the door the rest of the way open with his hip and walked in holding two chipped enamel cups.

"Good morning, Lieutenant Prye. I heard you had come in. Hope you like yours black, otherwise I can—"

"That's okay," Prye said with irritation. "Thanks," he begrudgingly added. "But already had mine for the day." Then he got straight to the point. "Why is your report so goddam skimpy, Kretzler?"

"Which report is that?"

"One on Fulham, Edward. You did him a week ago Friday." Prye swiped the back of his fingers dismissively on the first page of the report. "Might as well be on a skinned goddam knee."

Kretzler set the cups down and turned his droopy basset hound eyes up to Prye. "I didn't have a chance, Lieutenant, to really do a full autopsy on that one. Didn't have a chance to cut and really do much of an examination."

" 'Didn't have a chance'? You that overworked, Kretzler? I mean, did I miss the PanAm crash around here last week?"

"They wanted the body back. The parents."

"Last I checked, you're paid by the city of San Buenaventura as well as the county—not anyone's goddam family!"

"It seemed respectful, is all. So I released the body to them. To their mortician."

"That's nice, your sense of respect for the grieving parents. But just maybe they'd like to know what happened to their son. And you've compromised any investigation."

"I was never told there was one, Lieutenant. In my experience, there usually isn't much of an examination with a hit-and-run. Not unless there's something suspect."

This point calmed Prye down somewhat. Kretzler was right. In the absence of corroborating evidence of criminal intent, H and Rs didn't normally rate much probing.

"Okay, I'm gonna ask you the same thing I asked Chet Ewell when I thought he was the one who did the autopsy. Was there anything you noticed about Edward Fulham's body that didn't make it to your report—didn't, but should have?"

Prye watched as Kretzler tried to concentrate, knowing this was futile. It was all this geezer could do to get himself to work each day, not be that much on top of his job. Still, he felt badly that he'd laced into the old Jew like he had.

"I...didn't mean to sound..." Prye started to say.

Kretzler put his finger up near his chest, waving it slightly in recall. "Some bruising on the wrists."

"Both of 'em?"

Kretzler nodded. "Could've been some ligament tearing. I don't know..."

Prye controlled himself from getting steamed again. Any examiner worth his salt *should* know. He thought of what that young ex-GI had come up with as a theory.

"What about the back of the neck?"

"Oh, yes…yes." Kretzler said, a memory returning.

" Yes, what?"

"Come to think of it, there was bruising there, too."

"Sure it was a bruise?" Prye asked.

"It wasn't dirt, Lieutenant, if that's what you mean."

"A stain from blood settling. Could it have been that?"

Kretzler shook his head with confidence. "You mean lividity. No. He was hit from behind, expired face down." He looked at Prye as if catching him being naive. "That was obvious."

Prye knew he was going on weak logic, uneasy with his next question. "Could he have been killed before?"

"You mean, that the hit-and-run was only—"

"A throw-off, yeah."

"Well, I would think…" Kretzler raised his eyebrows. "… being in actual police work, you'd not be very much inclined to read lurid crime magazines, Lieutenant Prye."

Prye pursed his lips, glanced away. That's all he needed to hear. He looked back at Kretzler. "So the back of the neck…You're sure that couldn't possibly be lividity." He didn't know why he was sounding so invested in the idea.

"Where you getting this notion, Lieutenant?"

"Police photos," Prye said.

"I see. It could look like that in a black and white photo maybe…" Kretzler gave another confident shake of his head "… but not in actual view. Lividity has a redness to it, being blood settled just below the epidermal surface. A bruise, after a short time, is black and blue, just like it's termed. The victim's neck was bruised."

"So that means the back of the neck was impacted."

"That's what's indicated."

For a moment, Prye imagined having the satisfaction of telling that youngblood ex-soldier he was way off-base.

"So, back of the neck…probably happened right then, when he was hit."

"That would be a fair assumption, yes. If the nape was impacted much before that, the bruising would look different."

"And bruising would also be on his back, would it not?"

"There was, Lieutenant. Generalized on the back and buttocks…But now that I think of it, the bruise on the neck was separate. There was separation of bruising from the neck and back."

"Separate. And that would mean?"

"Well, there's, you know, soft tissue, hard bone tissue…"

"I'm not here for a goddam anatomy lesson," Prye said.

"There was no bruising just above the scapulae—shoulder blades. The rounding there would've avoided impact. But, thinking about it now, oddly enough, the nape was a bit further in and still bruised anyway."

"And that would mean?"

"Can't say for certain."

"Go out on a limb, Kretzler. Make a guess."

Prye let him take his time to consider.

"…Maybe impact was to the back of the neck first, followed a split second later by the more generalized impact."

"Like there was something that projected out neck-high from the vehicle?"

Kretzler shrugged. "I can't imagine what that would be, but... yes."

•   •   •

It was almost noon before Mig got up. It was late by the time he'd gotten to bed and his sleep was fitful. No dreams of the war. But questions about the trail of morphine money had kept him awake for most of what was left of the night and well into the morning. Had Eddie found out anything more than the blind old drummer knew? And what had brought Eddie to a town sixty miles up the coast from here?

He took a shower, got dressed, and then walked down to the corner cafe. The same waitress took his order across the counter, smiling as she scribbled on her pad.

"My, my, you're really hungry. Must've scored last night."

Mig was surprised by her frankness.

"Then she'd still be with me. I'd be buying her breakfast."

"A gentleman, no less…Where's your two friends, the 'tough guys'?"

"They were just actors," Mig said.

With mock surprise, "No…really?"

"You knew?"

"Sweetie, when you've been in this town long as I have… Could tell they were rehearsing their parts. Trying out on you before some casting agent." She looked at Mig with amusement. "You'll know, too, when you've been here a while."

Mig shook his head. "I won't be, that's for sure."

Even though he'd found out more than she assumed she knew about Malcolm and Wally, Mig still felt stupid at having been had. L.A. must be full of Hollywood phonies. Not his kind of place. He was glad to be leaving. He loaded up on ham, over-easy eggs, pancakes drowned in Aunt Jemima, and three refills of coffee. After he'd stuffed himself with food instead of the answers he'd driven down here for, he paid his bill and walked back to the King Charles to check out.

Mig pulled up in front of the Fulham's house. This time a DeSoto sedan was parked in the driveway. He took the carton full of Eddie's clothes and laundry and started to carry it up the walk toward the front door when he stopped, hearing a sound he recognized from years before, impacts of leather against wood. From the back yard of the adjoining property, the sound continued in short repetitions, staccato-like briefly, then slowing, uneven, losing momentum.

He crossed over to the next driveway, walked up its length, past the house, to see three boys of about twelve years old or so. Two of them watched as the third took wild right fist swings at a punching bag hanging from a platform cantilevered off from the side of a garage. With his next roundhouse the boy missed the bag, staggering to keep from falling down. The other two laughed at his awkwardness.

"Jeez, Chipper…you really got…a heck of a right," one of the boys managed to squawk between guffaws.

"Yeah. Joe Louis woulda been out for the count," the other boy added, smirking, as he stepped up for his turn.

Then, they noticed Mig watching them, and seemed a little ill at ease. They looked wary to Mig, as if they didn't know what to make of him. Recalling himself as a boy, hardly welcoming adult interference, Mig ventured anyway with, "You guys want a few pointers with that bag?"

"You a prizefighter, mister?" the one called Chipper wanted to know.

Mig set down what he was carrying. "No. But I learned a little about boxing when I was about your age."

He thought about Paddy Burkette, who'd befriended him and his mother back in their Brooklyn days, when they'd moved to the walk-up where he lived. Paddy had boxed enough years for his brain to go a little soft. And binge drinking didn't help. But even bordering on punchy, he still had enough of his wits left to teach the thirteen-year-old Mig some basic moves down in his basement apartment.

He remembered the clutter down there: second-hand furniture scrounged from here and there; a hotplate stained with spillovers; copies of *Ring Magazine* scattered about; a forgotten, partially-filled drinking cup, gray mold forming in it; posters of the young Paddy as a once promising bantamweight, reminders of his old fighting days. Paddy Burkette didn't cross Mig's thoughts that much anymore, not since the war. And he was more than glad about that.

He walked up to the bag. It was set too low for him, so he stood crouched a bit.

"Speedbag like this isn't for working on a knockout punch. It's more for timing, coordination."

He took an easy right to the bag, followed by a return with the side of the same fist. He repeated the motion with his left fist. Then turning to the boys. "Like that…with your right *and* left."

He took the same light punches with his right, then duplicated with his left. He repeated a few times, punching easy and slow, increasing speed only slightly. Less than sure, out of practice.

"I seen it in a newsreel where Manuel Ortiz did it real fast," one of the boys said. "Can you do it fast like that?"

"Not anywhere near like Ortiz, Graziano, those guys," Mig said. "They're pros. Best there is."

"Can you do it *kinda* fast?"

Mig nodded dubiously at the challenge. "Don't expect that

much, fellas. I'm ten years out of practice."

Mig worked the punching bag as before. Then he speeded up some, still with good timing, he leveled off speed, kept at a steady pace. Same steady pace. After a time his confidence started to build.

While Mig worked the bag, cranking up his speed, a memory flooded back to one day when he was thirteen.

There had been a pickup softball game that afternoon after school. The score was tied for the last three of eleven innings, until the other team finally got a winning run, so Mig was coming home later than usual. He hoped his mother wouldn't be upset with him.

Walking up the stairs past the second floor, he heard her. She was pleading.

"Paddy, don't…You're not like this…*don't …*

Mig rushed up to the landing, grabbed the newel post for a faster turn, and ran down the hall toward their flat.

"No, paddy! Stop it!"

Mig threw open the door.

Paddy Burkette had Carmen pinned on the floor next to the couch. She was struggling fiercely under him. Buttons on her blouse were torn off, her bra exposed.

Mig grabbed Paddy and pulled him off his mother, punching him hard in the gut, knocking the wind out of him. When Paddy went down Mig threw him on his back and straddled him, pounding his face with both fists. Carmen tugged at Mig's collar, trying to pull him away.

"Angel Miguel, *that's enough!"*

Blood poured from Paddy's nose, and Mig kept hitting him. The old boxer was barely conscious and still Mig hit him, until he was stopped when Carmen wrapped both arms around him and pulled him off the ex-pug.

"I said that's enough."

He wrenched from her grasp and lurched to hit Paddy again, but she clutched his arm with both her hands.

"He was drinking again, *hijo*. He was not himself."

She looked down at the bloody pulp of Paddy Burkette's face. "We'll have to call a doctor."

"But, Mama, he was—"

"He was drunk. And you know his brain isn't right, anyway."

Ignoring her, Mig started for Paddy again. Carmen grabbed him, wrapping both her arms tightly around him as he struggled to get to the beaten old boxer.

"Hey, mister…*mister!*"

Mig found himself swinging at the bag maniacally, as if it were Paddy Burkette's head. He was breathing hard, sweating. He stopped working the bag.

"You were missin' a lot after a while," one of the boys said.

Mig saw the three them staring at him wide-eyed, apprehensive, then glancing furtively at each other.

"Lost it there, I guess….Anyway. like I started out's the way." Mig attempted to smile to cover his embarrassment. "And don't lose control like I just did. Keep a cool head, keep in control… You guys got any questions?"

Each of the boys shook his head, saying nothing. Mig hated himself for having made them afraid of him, of how he'd become. They were only kids. Why did they have to see him like that?

"Well, remember…This kinda bag's for timing. Practice easy on it, just to build up speed."

Mig couldn't think of anything else to say, neither it seemed could any of the boys. He smiled awkwardly at them, as if to undo what had happened. Then he picked up the carton he'd brought and walked down the driveway, crossing to the next one and up the walkway to Eddie's parents' house.

When he knocked on the door, Mrs. Fulham answered, putting her finger up to her lips, signaling him to be quiet.

"Warren's asleep," she whispered. Looking at the box, she said, "You can set that down here, Mig. Just inside the door here."

Mig put the box down where she indicated. Mrs. Fulham ushered him back out on the front porch, closing the door quietly behind them.

"Thank you for bringing this." She looked puzzled. "Was that all Eddie had?"

"There's more, Mrs. Fulham. I had to come down to Los Angeles in kind of a rush to find ou—there's more. I'm heading back up to Ventura. I'll pack up the rest of his pants and shirts and stuff."

She looked reflective. "You know that expression, 'give the shirt off your back'?"

Mig, nodded. "Sure."

"Well, Eddie did just that one time. When he was…seven. Seven, I think, yes, He and a friend had climbed over a fence. A shortcut to the malt shop, Eddie said. The other boy's shirt caught on a nail or something on the fence and tore. It was a new shirt, one he really liked. He started crying, so Eddie gave him the shirt he was wearing. Told him he could keep it…Eddie was such a dear. An angel."

Mig thought of his own first name. "Not an avenging angel," he heard himself saying.

"Oh, no. Eddie was too gentle for anything like that…You know, Warren would've rather seen our son be a 'real soldier,' as he used to say. 'Carrying a rifle, not—as he used to put it—'a damn first aid kit'."

"Think your husband got over that point of view, Mrs.

Fulham."

"Oh, he did, yes. Eddie was awarded a medal, you know."

"I know, ma'am."

"He sleeps a lot now, Warren. He can be looking at the paper, listening to the radio. Falls asleep in his wheelchair every afternoon. Never used to before Eddie died. He just doesn't take much interest in anything now."

"He needs more time, Mrs. Fulham. You both must. It's only been just over a week now."

"He feels badly, I think, for how stern he used to be with Eddie. Never understood our son's gentle nature. Warren could be so hard on him." She looked off, wistful. "I did the best I could to try to soften his father's harshness…Looking back, it seems that I was always the protectful parent."

Little did she realize, Mig thought, that her protection of Eddie would implant the irrational fear he'd had, the secret dread that Mig knew about, and which impelled him to track down Eddie's killer.

Then what came to mind was the locket he'd found at the beach cottage.

"Mrs. Fulham, was there a woman Eddie was seeing?"

"A woman? Do you mean up in Ventura?"

Mig hadn't considered that *M.M.R.* could've been someone in Eddie's life from when he'd still lived in Los Angeles. But, he had a hunch that she wasn't. "He probably would've met her up there, yeah."

"No…I mean, no woman he ever mentioned to us."

Now, talking to Mrs. Fulham, Mig wondered about the reason for Eddie's decision to go to Ventura that he might've told his parents. Would it only be misleading, or could it shed some light?

"Mrs. Fulham, Do you remember *why* Eddie told you he was

moving up to Ventura?"

"It was a job he applied for. As a bookkeeper. Eddie studied bookkeeping day and night when he found out that job would be available."

"Bookkeeping. He could've done that here in Los Angeles."

"Oh, I well know. We used to tell him that, but it made no difference. His mind was set on that particular job, the one up there."

Eddie's having been employed in Ventura hadn't occurred to Mig—and now finding out that job was so important to Eddie. It must have had everything to do with why he was up there. Mig realized that up to now he'd overlooked something vital.

"Who was it that he worked for, ma'am? Do you know?"

"Oh, some car dealer. Sold prewar cars."

"His name?"

"It was, umm…Billy, something, I think…Billy Dale…Billy Dane…"

Mig remembered his conversation with Sal at his beach café in Ventura a couple of nights before.

"Was it maybe just a last name?"

"Possibly, I suppose."

"Beledayne, Mrs. Fulham. Was it Beledayne?"

15

Mig started the drive north from L.A. a short while later with a clear focus of suspicion. He'd asked Mrs. Fulham to let him read the last few letters Eddie had sent them, allowing her to believe it was just because of his and Eddie's friendship. Most of the notes were only brief assurances that things were good with him and expressions of concern for his parents. Eddie's writing as a dutiful son didn't give much in the way of clues. That is, until Mig read the last letter that Eddie had sent.

In it he had written, "Pretty soon I'll be leaving here to find my own place in Los Angeles. It's high time, don't your think? I have to take care of someone up here first, and then I'll be moving back down." Mig was fairly sure who it was that Eddie had "to take care of." That is, as soon as he could find the evidence in Sid Beledayne's books of unexplained amounts of cash. And from what he'd written in that last note, Eddie must've been getting close—too close it turned out.

He felt badly turning down Mrs. Fulham's invitation to stay for dinner and to spend the night before heading back up to Ventura the next morning. Being with the Fulhams was difficult for him. Mig couldn't just make polite conversation with him now being sure who was responsible for their son's murder.

He knew he couldn't share with the Fulhams what he was

convinced about Eddie's death. Mrs. Fulham was managing to hold up as well as possible in her grief, while it sounded as if Eddie's father was mired in his. If Mig could uncover the chain of events that led to what had happened to Eddie, maybe it would give them some relief. Or learning the truth might weigh them down even more. He hoped not.

He arrived back in Ventura just after four that afternoon. Mig drove for several blocks on Main before turning left onto Seaward, heading toward the beach community and the cottage that Eddie had rented. Mig planned to grab a bite at Sal's, see if he could get more information on Sid Beledayne. Sal seemed to know what was going on in town.

His instinct was to go straight to Beledayne's used car lot now that he knew that Eddie had gotten a job as bookkeeper there to dig into Sid Beledayne's accounts to find the hidden cash flow from the sale of morphine to the Negroes down on Central Avenue. But for Mig to just barge in and confront Beledayne wouldn't be the smartest way to go. Like heading straight toward a machine gun nest rather than around and behind it.

Mig hadn't figured yet what his plan of attack would be. He doubted he'd have that police lieutenant Nathaniel Prye on his side. The guy'd been doing his job for so long, he was stuck in routine. Besides, Prye seemed to have a sour attitude toward Mig. The Polish/Jewish half of him, the Mexican half of him, the youth of him. The big old cop could take his pick whatever it was about him he didn't like.

After a few blocks, he saw a group of Mexicans, about a dozen or so, mostly men and a few women, on the sidewalk down the street a little ways from the Sunkist lemon packinghouse. Hands were waving, fists in the air. Mig slowed down as he got near, heard shouting in Spanish.

"Communista puta!" "Vuelva a Russia!" "Salte de America, puta!"

Moving away, trying to distance herself from the crowd that was hounding her, was the sister of the poor Russian vagrant who'd hanged himself in the Ventura jail. The woman, clutching a small grocery bag, looked scared.

Mig pulled to a stop by the curb and got out of his car. He hurried to the sidewalk as much as his limp would allow and put his hands up in a gesture to hold back the Russian woman's accusers, demanding to know why they were harrassinging her.

"Calmense! Que maldad ha hecho esta mujer a ustedes?" he shouted at the mob, slowing its advance for the moment. He glanced back at the woman, and then faced the Mexicans, asking again what this woman had done to them.

"Que maldad?"

Most of them quieted down, except for a barrel-chested man in a short-sleeved plaid sport shirt, who tried to keep up the angry momentum. Focusing on this man, who appeared to be the ringleader, Mig asked what they thought they were going to do to the Russian woman, going for potential guilt to defuse the group's rage.

"Y que prerser hacer ella!?"

Mig remembered an attractive girl in her late teens or early twenties in a French town, Mayenne. She had been a waitress in one of the taverns he had been to before the awful winter in the Ardennes. She had been flirtatious, with a dimpled smile, giving forth with lusty laughter as she would toss back her dark, wavy hair and joke with the GIs she served, those who'd liberated her village.

The last time he saw her the girl was terror-stricken, surrounded on a street, being accused by the townsfolk of sleeping with the local Nazi commandant, even if it might've been only to secure food for her family. Mig and other soldiers just watched, as if helpless, when the people of the town threw the girl down on the cobblestones and cut off her hair, jabbing her scalp with scissors. Blood had coursed down her face and neck as they ripped most of her dress off.

Now he couldn't just watch this.

He stood between the Russian woman and the crowd of Mexicans. He asked the men in the mob why they were doing this, directing his question mostly to the enraged plaid-shirted man, demanding to know what the woman had done to be so tormented by all of them.

"Que hizo, companeros!?"

And then Mig glared from one woman to another, to force explanation from each of them.

"Hermanas..? Porque la tormenta?"

The man in the plaid shirt stepped forward, accusing the woman's brother of having killed the little girl, Peggy Beledayne, the one who'd been missing. Mig spoke in the Russian woman's defense, about the loss of her brother.

"Su hermano ya esta muerto. La tormentan en su luto!?"

"El mato la chica, Peggy!" the man in the plaid shirt accused.

Mig answered back, questioning their knowledge of events. He asked what did they really know about anything that might've happened to the girl?

"Lo sabes que es cierto..? Como sabes por seguro que el hermano mato Peggy Beledayne?"

He stared directly at various faces, exacting knowledge of the truth from each one about the Russian woman's brother's unproven guilt.

"Lo sabes..?" "Y usted, senor..? "Senora, lo sabes por segura..?" "A su hermano lo ayaron culpable en tribunal de

justicia..? Pues...si era..?"

There were brief spurts of objection, but the mob's anger was waning. Conviction started to give way to uncertainty; some doubt had wedged in. Even the man in the plaid shirt had lost some steam. With the lessening of their passion, Mig appealed to these people's better natures, imploring them to go home to their children.

"Vuelvan sus familias. Vuelvan en casas con sus hijos."

There was a shuffling of feet. Some in the crowd looked from one to the other for reenforcement about what they should do. Mig urged all of them to go home.

"No se averquezen aqui. Vuelven a casa...Vuelven a casa," he said.

One by one, the people started to disperse, the plaid-shirted man being among the last. When they were all walking away, conversing quietly among themselves, Mig turned to the woman, whose name he remembered was Irina Temiarov, and spoke to her in her language.

"Vu vmeste?"

She regarded him curiously, asking what he had said. *"Shto tu skazal?"*

"Vu vmeste," he repeated.

Her countenance softened into a slight smile. "I am not in pieces, as you asked. Only shouted at," she corrected him in English.

"I meant, are you alright. My Russian's not that good."

Her smile faded. "I've suffered insults in my life before."

"But that shouldn't happen here."

"In America, you mean?"

Mig nodded. "Yeah. That kinda thing shouldn't happen here."

"So naïve, you Americans. You think you are above cruelty...

You, you seem different, though."

"You mean you don't think I'm cruel?"

"You might be capable of that. But what I mean is you speak other languages," she said. "Even if one of them not so well. But I am grateful your Spanish was effective. Where did you learn it?"

"My mother. She's not from here."

"Then you are close to being foreign."

"In a way, I guess…My condolences about your brother."

Irina folded her arms more tightly around her grocery bag, looking down sadly.

"My poor, little Dima," she said. Shaking her head in regret, "He was such a delicate spirit."

"There was a town in Germany," Mig said, "Ludwigslust, near one of the camps. When my unit occupied the town, we made the people that lived there see what had been going on just a short ways away. Walked the townsfolk in line right up close to force them to look at what had been done to other human beings so close by."

"And what they would have known about—*if* they ever searched their conscience."

"Right, yeah," Mig said. "Many in that camp starved to death, others were shot or gassed. Being in one of those places..." He shook his head, remembering. "Your brother, he, uh, took it the rest of the way from what the Nazis…I'm really sorry."

"I was always more of a survivor than Dima. That may be a curse," she said.

"It's all about surviving."

"Some Americans would know about that. The ones who were there." Irina regarded him for a moment. "Do you drink coffee?" she asked.

"Yeah…"

"I make it strong."

A couple of blocks from there, Irina Temiarov had a one-bedroom apartment with a Murphy bed mounted on the living room wall. That's where her younger brother had slept before he became mentally destabilized and left to forage in the hills, she told Mig. There was a suitcase on the couch. She'd be packing to leave on a bus down to Anaheim the next morning. She knew a Russian family there that had taken Dimitri's casket from a train to a mortuary. They would bury him on Monday, and Irina would stay on with the family for a few more days.

As she went though the swinging door into her kitchen to heat water for coffee, Mig looked around the living room, seeing sparse, mismatched furniture. An overstuffed armchair; a couch upholstered in what he thought was Hawaiian cloth with big flowers and leaves; a scratched-up, dark-stained dining room table with four cane-seated chairs. There was a print of a stormy seascape in an ornate frame next to a delicate painting of a woman in a long dress from another era lighting a candle on a mantle over a warming fire. Nothing fit together. Everything seemed to have been scavenged by the landlord from different rummage sales.

There were a few worn snapshots taped in a cluster on one wall. He moved closer to look at them, seeing whom he thought were Irina and her brother at various ages of childhood. In some photos they were posed with people of different generations.

"These pictures on the wall…your family?" he said loud enough for her to hear.

"The photographs, yes. Family mostly," she said from the kitchen. "All gone, probably. I expect never to know."

Mig regretted that he'd asked. He looked some more at the pictures, some of them creased and tattered, precious possessions hurriedly gathered for escape, he assumed. The children were smiling in the photos taken in their early ages, but there was austerity in the adult poses, reflections of hard living. In pictures taken in later years Dimitri still seemed youthfully carefree, while the expression in Irina's eyes was serious, of one who already bore adult burden.

Mig took out his billfold and opened it to look at the snapshot of Aaron Czerniak that Carmen had given him. He didn't know why he had done that. It seemed to be an unconscious action. Aaron had a similar Slavic look to Irina's family. He put the photo back in his billfold.

In a few minutes Irina set a porcelain service for two on the table, on a doily yellowed with age. The cups were tiny, like the ones Mig had seen in Europe. Then she brought in coffee in a cylindrical brass container. "Turkish," she called it as she poured, apologizing for having no cookies or cakes. He wasn't much for sweets, anyway, he said.

After they sat down, he told her his name when she asked, realizing they hadn't actually introduced themselves to each other. She wanted to know if Mig was a common name in America, and for some reason he gave her his full name. He could tell Irina sensed his reluctance about it.

"I am not one to tease you about having wings," she said.

"Appreciate that," Mig said, recalling a day a long time ago on his new schoolyard playground right after he and Carmen had moved to Brooklyn from the West Side. He was taunted about his first name. A group of boys had started running around him in a circle, flapping their arms and sing-songing, "I'm an angel…I'm an angel…" Mig had grabbed the biggest boy in the circle and given him a bloody nose. From then on it was clear to all the boys that he was Miguel, soon shortened to Mig.

"Czerniak…You are also Polish," Irina said.

"On my father's side, yeah."

"That's how you speak some Russian. The languages, they are not that different."

"Didn't ever know my father. Or none of his family."

Irena reached in the pocket of her dress, took out a pack of Chesterfields, offered Mig a cigarette.

"No thanks," he said. "Never took it up."

She struck a kitchen match on the side of its box, lit a cigarette for herself and took a deep drag, expelling the smoke to the side, away from him. "He is no longer alive, your father?"

Mig shook his head, sipped some coffee. "Before I was born, he was murdered by a robber on the street one night. So I was told."

Irena nodded, taking in what he'd said. She took a short inhale and set her cigarette down in an ashtray as she looked at him guardedly, it seemed. "Violence, then…it was part of your life—your fate—even before the war. Even before you came into the world, no?"

Mig considered that, felt uneasy. "Suppose you could say that."

She took a sip of coffee, set her cup back in the saucer. "Have you made of it a friend?" she asked.

It seemed to him an odd question, unsettling. He drank some more coffee and set down his cup. "Don't know what you mean."

"Back there on the street, you were ready to fight those people, the men, all of them."

"Didn't think it would come to that."

"But you would have," Irina said.

He shrugged, smiled. "Lady in distress and all. Not much choice."

She didn't return his smile. "Have you made violence your friend? This is what I am asking."

"What do you—what are you getting at, anyway?"

"Would you turn it on me?"

Mig looked away, shaking his head in disbelief, then glared at her."What the hell you think!?"

A flash of fear at Mig's reaction, then she met his look with calmness. "I need to know who it is I have brought into my home."

"So why *did* you if you just thought I'd hurt you?" He looked away again, fuming, helpless. "Shit…"

Irena's expression relaxed. "I want to believe that I can trust you."

"Yeah, well maybe you can't. Maybe I should just go."

He pushed back his chair to get up.

She quickly stubbed out her cigarette. "No. Stay, please."

Mig hesitated at her pleading look.

"Please…"

She reached out to him. "I did not mean to insult you." She took him by the hand. "We each could know the other more, I think."

She stood, still holding his hand. She looked into his eyes as if willing herself to trust him. "Come," she said.

He stood up, too, and Irina led him into her bedroom.

She turned to him and embraced him hard, held him as if in capture. When they kissed what he felt from her was a disturbing hunger. Mig almost wanted to withdraw. There was something other than passion in her, more a desperation. It was like with a woman in Belgium he'd been with in a moment out of war. The attempt to shut out a nightmare existence by grasping, clutching another body to a final shuddering of physical release—it all being somehow impersonal. Apart from any real emotion, just a man and woman mechanically, uncaringly using each other to blot out the hell around them.

After their sex was over, Mig was left with unease. He had been taken back to a time and place he wanted to forget. Irina had rested her head on his shoulder and he'd put his arm around her, out of reflex. He felt her cooling tears on his skin before she fell asleep. As he lay there, Mig came to resent being with this woman, a refugee of the war that wouldn't stop plaguing him. Another victim of it. He slid his arm from under her and turned away, staring at the pattern on the wallpaper. Little flowers.

They reminded him of the desert wildflowers he'd seen out the train window when he and his mother were traveling west, nearing their new home eight years before. His anger about the whole idea of moving from Brooklyn had subsided enough to let him appreciate the beauty of the white and purple spring wildflowers that blanketed this flat desert landscape, the haze of a ridge of hills far in the background.

But as welcoming as the bloom was that he saw from the train, Mig knew he'd never fit in this place of no streets or buildings. And from what he could see from the train window, no other people. But eventually he would come to change his mind about this strange, empty-seeming land. He let his thoughts take him to Arizona, and their first summer there.

16

Carmen had gotten a position as nurse in a government-funded clinic just east of Scottsdale. Most of the patients were Pima Indians. Some of the men of the tribe were digging a network of irrigation canals nearby in a Civilian Conservation Corps program.

Mig was fifteen, too young to be employed in the CCC, but, when school let out for the summer, he did shovel work on the canals as a volunteer. He liked the men he labored with, even though he was as much an outsider with them as he'd been with the Puerto Ricans when they lived on the West Side, before Brooklyn. But here he was more accepted, not derided because of his lighter complexion, blue eyes, or different sounding last name.

Several of his dark-skinned fellow pick and shovelers worked with their shirts off in the hot summer sun. Mig did the same on his first day on the job. By mid-afternoon, he suddenly felt weak and passed out. When he woke up, he was being carried into the clinic where his mother was employed. He was set down on a cot in a treatment room and Carmen put a cool towel on his forehead. She told him to rest and he went back to sleep.

Then he recalled his arm being shaken. He opened his eyes to see an Indian girl a few years older than he was. She smiled down at him. There was a slight gap between her two front teeth.

"Turn over," she said. "So I can get to your back, *niño*." Only his mother had ever called him that when he was little, so it sounded out of place. "Come on, turn over," the girl said, and he did, although he didn't like being ordered by her. It added to his embarrassment at having passed out and been carried into the clinic like a child.

With a damp washcloth she gently cleaned the patina of dust from his back and shoulders, asking him if it hurt.

"No," he snapped. "Hell, no."

"Looks like it might hurt some."

"Well, it doesn't," Mig said.

"It serves you right, *niño*, for tempting the sun god."

He turned and looked up at her with disbelief.

Then she smiled. "Just kidding. I don't really believe in that stuff."

She took a little jar from the pocket of her smock, twisted off the cap, and scooped some white cream from the jar into her hand. She smoothed the cream on his shoulders and down his back. It felt cool and good on his sunburn. The girl chuckled and he asked what was so damn funny.

"You trying to be like one of us. But you're no redskin—just pink-backed."

Her name was Ruby Hinojosa, helping out part-time at the clinic for the summer before going back to college, where she was studying to be a nurse. The only thing Mig liked about her was that she spoke well of Carmen. "Your mom's really neat," Ruby said. "You better be a good son to deserve her," she told him, raising one of her eyebrows in mock reproach.

"You must spit real good with that gap in your teeth," Mig said. He objected to being reminded that one of the reasons they'd moved out here was because he'd lapsed in being such a good son.

Ruby regarded him with amusement for a moment, then tapped her front teeth. "Can spit farther than you, I bet." She snatched up his shirt from the back of a chair and tossed it to him. "Take it easy the rest of the day. And tomorrow…" she shook her finger at him, "…keep your darn shirt on. I gotta get back to work."

Mig watched Ruby step out of the room, saw her hand grab the doorjamb and tap it a few times with her fingers. She swung back in to face him. "Hey, Mig—That's your name, isn't it?"

"So what?" he said.

"You like the movies?"

"They're okay."

"There's a western down at the Rialto called *Stagecoach*. They made it not that far away from here. Monument Valley, up by Four Corners." She cocked her head invitingly. "Wanna go tonight?"

"Uh…with you?"

"No, with Eleanor Roosevelt. Sure with me."

Mig had fixed dinner from canned food by the time Carmen got home, surprising her. He'd never done that. He told her that he was going to the movies with Ruby from the clinic so they had to eat early. "A date, huh?" his mother said teasingly. He insisted that she had it all wrong. "Mama, she's in college, for crying out loud."

Ruby had picked him up in her dad's battered old truck. Its gears would grind every time she shifted. "Clutch wearing out," she explained, as she jammed from second to third. "Daddy said he'd get it fixed, but it'll probably be up to me. A lotta things wind up in my lap."

During the movie he noticed out of the corner of his eye that she'd look over at him from time to time, and it made him feel awkward. He didn't know how he should look back at this girl. Smiling? Serious? Mig didn't want to seem like a jerky high school kid so he kept his attention on the screen and just endured being observed by her.

Later, when he treated her to a root beer float at the soda fountain down the block, she asked about his sunburn. She'd noticed that he'd not leaned all the way back in his theater seat, and he was canted forward now. "It's kinda sore," he said. "Not that much, though." Ruby told him that she'd put some stuff on it, a special kind of stuff. When he said that he'd come by the clinic after work tomorrow she shook her head. "I'll put it on tonight. You'll sleep better."

They drove across town to her cousin Maria's. She had cactus growing in her yard, Ruby told him. The juice from it would help. He didn't understand, but didn't ask because he thought too much questioning would make him sound young. The house was dark; Maria wasn't at home. Ruby cut off an ear of cactus in the front yard with a pocketknife and they went inside.

She told him to take his shirt off and lie down on the couch on his belly. He did so and she applied cactus juice to his shoulders and back, caressing his skin, more lingeringly than she had before at the clinic. Then Ruby told him to wait there, she'd be right back. After a couple of minutes he heard the toilet flush. Moments later, the ceiling light in the living room was shut off.

He turned his head and looked up to see Ruby standing next to the couch. There was enough light spilling in from the hallway for him to see that she didn't have on a stitch. He realized he must've just gaped at her because she set her hands on her hips and said, "Golly, you never saw a girl in her birthday suit before?"

She knelt down next to the couch and reached under him to his belt buckle.

"Roll over a little," she whispered. "Help me out a little."

His heart was pounding as she undid his belt and unbuttoned

his Levis. He couldn't get erect right away, as nervous as he was, and feeling that he must look silly, his pants and shorts having been bunched down below his knees. But she patiently aroused him. Mig thought that heaven itself couldn't top this. "Should we go into the bedroom?" he whispered, a huskiness in his voice, trying to sound sexy. "Nope. It's Maria's bed." She told him to move over on his side to let her get next to him on the couch. "Better that way for your back," she said.

When Ruby dropped him off at home, Mig entered the apartment to find his mother reading a book and having a cup of tea. She looked up at him and said, "How was the movie? It must have been a long one."

We, uh, had a couple root beer floats after." Mig leaned down and kissed the top of her head. "Goodnight, Mama."

She looked up, regarding him with an odd smile. "You appear…fulfilled," she said. He knew that she knew and he was embarrassed. Carmen had a last sip of tea, marked her place in the book, got up and started for her room. "Sleep well, *hijo*. You must be tired."

The next afternoon there was a small paper bag on the side table by his bed. A note was next to it: YOU ARE OLD ENOUGH TO BE A FATHER, BUT I AM ENTIRELY TOO YOUNG TO BE A GRANDMOTHER. Mig opened the bag to find a pack of rubbers.

That magical summer put aside all Mig's doubts about living in this new place, this now excitingly wonderful place. It didn't bother him that Ruby must've been with other boys before. That summer she was his only, each of their hormones at full charge. They had sex at Maria's on nights when she wasn't home, coupled hurriedly in the cab of her dad's truck on dark side streets in town, got it on in an arroyo under the sun on an itchy wool blanket that smelled a little musty. Ruby taught him about sensual bliss such as Mig had never even imagined.

She also tried to teach him to ride horseback, but he bounced up and down clumsily when his mount trotted and said he was fine just watching rodeo contestants do all the riding; he was too much of a dyed-in-the-wool city boy for horses himself.

Ruby encouraged Mig to become a stronger swimmer. This came to save him on that night leading into D-Day, when other paratroopers drowned in fields flooded by the Germans. He and Ruby would race each other in a public pool, and Mig eventually was acknowledged as the faster of the two.

As they were drying in the sun after a swim one Saturday, Ruby asked him if he knew why she'd chosen him to be with. He made a glib remark alluding to his sexual prowess, which he regretted when he realized it only made him sound younger than her. He was always trying to obscure that.

Ruby told him that her "mission" was to make him smile more, to draw back from the anger she could see that he had from the first time they'd met. "You should be an eagle," she said, and he was puzzled.

"An eagle feasts on what it kills," Ruby explained, "while the buzzard pecks on whatever carrion it finds—decaying flesh. In the beginning of time, according to legend, they looked alike. But their good nature had turned eagles beautiful, majestic, while buzzards in their bitterness only became ugly." She looked at him, a drop of pool water spilling from her eyelash. "Be an eagle, Mig. Don't keep feeding off bad memories."

Though continuing to fall short of her advice, from then on, Mig struggled to take to heart what she had said, knowing her wish for him came from wisdom and caring. Ruby was very much his teacher that golden summer. Then she went back to college in

Texas, where she had a scholarship. Their time together was over.

The same month that she left, Hitler invaded Poland and the world changed.

Mig saw Ruby once again about a year after the war. It was in a Piggly Wiggly self-service market in Phoenix. She was Ruby Jordan now, introducing Mig to her husband, a former Army Air Corps supply pilot gone back to ranching. They had known each other slightly in high school and, by what seemed an unlikely destiny, their paths had crossed in Burma when Ruby was serving with the Red Cross.

She was pregnant now, just beginning to show, so planned to take some time off from her job. Mig told her he knew she was going to be a great mom. Ruby spread her lips, tapped the gap between her front teeth, saying, "I'll teach him to spit real good."

"Or her," Mig said.

"No, he'll be a boy. I just know."

The three of them talked for a few minutes. When they parted, Mig shook Todd Jordan's hand and told him that he was a very lucky man. It sounded so obligatory and trite to Mig when he'd said that, but he'd never been more sincere.

It was after dark before Mig stirred awake. He saw Irina, naked, standing almost silhouetted by a streetlight, looking out a window, having a cigarette. The smoke wafted by her and was drawn outside. Her body was almost skinny, boy-like with slim hips. Her legs were slender with a muscular fullness in her calves. Irina's straight brown hair fell to just below her shoulders, a few strands caught by a breeze.

"I have regret, Angel Miguel Czerniak, for the way I was," she said, continuing to gaze out the window.

"How did you know I was awake?"

"I have learned to sense what those who feel safe do not."

She put out her cigarette in the ashtray she was holding and turned to him. "Is it not still so with you? You were a soldier."

Mig nodded. "Yeah…Why the apology?"

She walked back across the room, put the ashtray on the bedside table, and sat next to him. "I used you. That was not right of me."

"Irina, both of us, we —"

She put her finger to his lips to silence him. "No, it was me."

She touched his cheek, tentatively, and then took her hand away. "Can we try to make love?" she said. "I want to know again what that is."

Mig pulled back the sheet and Irina lay next to him. They stroked each other for a while, not at first for arousal but only to become familiar through touch. This time each of them was with the other, entwined in the beginning almost chastely, then with a shared intensifying passion. This time there was no regret afterward.

The shakes came to Mig later that night. Irina held him. She held him tightly until he became still and his breathing relaxed.

Shortly after dawn she looked over to him, noticing the line of short surgical scars on his lower back. She pushed the covers down to see the rest of the scarring on his buttock and thigh. Irina circled some of the healed wounds softly with her fingers, and Mig awakened. Neither of them said anything, neither finding reason to. He squirmed a little when her touch tickled him.

After both of them drifted back to sleep until sunlight brightened the room, they made love again. And for a while they rested in each other's arms.

Then Irina removed herself from their embrace and reached

over to the bedside table for her pack of Chesterfields, shaking a cigarette out. She struck a kitchen match on the box and lit it. She sat up in bed, resting her elbow in her hand and smoked as she stared out the window. A blue jay alighted on the sill.

"Look," Mig whispered, so as not to disturb the bird.

"Very cute," she whispered back, glancing at Mig with what seemed to him discomfort.

The little bird cocked its head in jerky motions, staring at various places in the room. Then it flew away.

"So free…" Irina said

She stubbed the cigarette out in the ashtray. "I need for you to understand something," she said. "It is important to me."

"Okay."

"Dima did not take her, that child."

"Peggy Beledayne."

Saying the name gave Mig a strange feeling. Was the loss of Sid Beledayne's little girl fate's way of getting to the man in a way that Eddie could not, or that Mig might not be able to?

"He would not have done that. Dima would not."

"I know, Irina. I was at the police station when they brought him in. I knew then he didn't do it."

"My being with you so soon after what happened to my brother…Do you find that heartless of me?"

"Come on." Mig shook his head. "Heartless? That's just bullshit."

"Such a simple dismissal you have, Mig."

"Truth's that way. Simple."

She gazed up toward the ceiling, took a drag of her cigarette, blew out the smoke.

"In the camp where we were, one of the guards had his way with Dima. As a man rapes a woman. The commandant, a devoutly religious Nazi—how ironic—found out and had the guard transferred to another camp. And for his unwilling part in 'sinning against God' my little brother was castrated…So you see, what they accuse him of doing to this little girl, Peggy, Dima would have had no—"

"Irina, you don't have to convince me."

"Let me finish, please…The operation they performed on him took away more than…It damaged his mind, took away his essence. I had to care for him then. And after we were liberated—I got us both liberated—I brought him with me to America, and to this town. I tried to shelter him as well as I could from the cruel laughter of children and people's looks…One evening there was a loud noise outside. Something with a car that sounded like a gun. I don't know how you call it."

"A backfire," Mig said.

"Dima ran out and did not come back that night to our apartment. I searched for him. I found him eventually just outside the town, huddled in a ravine, eating what he had taken from garbage. I brought him back with me. But the next night he left again. The police brought him in a couple of more times and I was called to get him. But he would keep leaving to live in the hills, to be in some sort of refuge. Insane refuge…This is what I need to say to you, Mig." She stubbed out her cigarette in the ashtray. "Over the past few days I have found relief that Dima is no longer alive."

She turned to look at him.

"Who he really was died a few years ago, so now I am relieved. I have had my tears, but I am glad it is over, the burden of him. Some would think that terrible, no?"

""Some people," Mig said.

"I needed to make that admission."

"Don't know why, and why to me."

"I needed to admit it to myself," she said. "Aloud to myself. You were merely witness to that."

"Aw, you used me again," he said, smiling.

"It is not a joke, Mig."

He looked away, feeling badly at having tried humor where it didn't fit, but not badly enough to apologize. He turned back to her. "You're right, Irina. It's just sad. Sad as you want or need it to be."

She looked pensive for a moment. "I don't want to do that now with you." She leaned over and kissed him, and then lay back contentedly, her hands up behind her head on the pillow. "And I am glad to be here with you, Mig. With you in my bed."

Mig touched the line of numbers tattooed from her wrist to her forearm. He stroked his fingers down past the inside of her elbow through the patch of soft brown armpit hair to cup the low mound of her breast.

"Your touch makes my nipple hard," she murmured.

"Feels nice. But so much for *me* getting hard for a while."

She laughed. "The young stallion is spent?"

" 'Fraid so, for the time being."

"And hungry, too, I would think."

"*Starving*. How 'bout you?"

They drove to the Hob Nob Cafe on Thompson. It was crowded on a Sunday morning, but a booth became available almost as soon as they walked in. Mig ordered a big breakfast as he had the morning before in Los Angeles, the last meal he'd had. Irina asked for an order of rye toast and a hard-boiled egg, waving her hand in rejection at the waitress asking if she would also like to drink what the gentleman was having.

"Your American coffee, it isn't really coffee," she said.

The waitress looked offended. She added a pot of tea to Irina's order, then walked away, muttering to herself.

"She doesn't care much for your opinion," Mig said.

"With my accent, she probably thinks I am a Communist."

"Are you? We haven't gotten into politics."

She leaned back in the booth. "I once belonged to the Party. Are you shocked?"

"Why would I be?"

"With feelings here being what they are now. And you being an American."

"But a different kind of one, you said yourself."

"This is true."

"My mom was a so-called fellow traveler for a while, years ago. Communist sympathizer." Mig said. "She still sort of leans in that direction."

"She must find it difficult for her during this time, no?"

Mig shook his head. "She depends to an extent on government funding for her clinic, so she keeps some thoughts to herself."

As they were waiting for their food, Mig looked down the line of stools at the counter and saw Lieutenant Prye get up and take his hat from a rack. Mig's gaze followed Prye's metronome-like walk as he passed by, not taking notice of them, on his way out of the diner. Prye seemed preoccupied, not with anything having to do with the death of Eddie Fulham, Mig was fairly sure. He watched through the window as Prye shambled from side to side to his car.

"Mig…" he heard Irina say, and turned back to her.

She reached across the table and put her hand on his hand, bringing his attention back to her. "The large man who just left, do you know him?"

"Met him. Wouldn't say I know him. Not really."

"He looks like police," she said.

"Good guess, Irina."

"In my country, oppression existed much before the war. I was more certain than guessing."

He nodded. "He's a cop. Maybe not a bad one, but I don't know."

Mig wondered how Prye would be with his suspicion of Sid Beledayne, who was running for Ventura's city council. Would he have Lieutenant Prye's vote?

17

Nate Prye was making the same drive he did every Sunday. He used to make it midweek as well, but over time he allowed his workload to keep him from that. It was easier on him keeping it to the one day a week. So far nothing had changed, but he clung to the belief that there would one day be a breakthrough. Hope was unfamiliar to Prye. Something he'd never learned to place much trust in. But instead of his work and the investigative ability he'd learned to rely on over the years, hope was all he had with this.

Prye parked his car outside of the administration building, as he always did, and went inside to sign the visitor's register. Then he sat down on one of the oak benches and waited for his escort. He looked out the window to an expanse of mowed lawn, on the far side of which he gazed at a weeping willow tree. How fitting, he thought.

" 'Mornin', Lieutenant Prye."

Prye turned to see a rangy mulatto man approaching him.

"Hello, Wingate."

He didn't know whether this was the man's first name or his last. He'd introduced himself only as Wingate when they'd met many Sundays ago.

Prye stood up and shook Wingate's hand.

"Been to church already, sir?"

"First thing, yeah."

When Wingate would greet him, he'd always ask the same question. Prye didn't have the heart to tell him he wasn't a churchgoer. He didn't want to disappoint this kindly, religious man.

"That's good. Folks showin' up early sets Sunday up jus' right for the Lord."

Prye nodded in perfunctory agreement.

"Well sir, reckon she's lookin' forward to seein' you today," Wingate said as they started down the hall.

What he'd just been told, what Wingate always said, was also an evasion of hard truth, Prye knew only too well.

They climbed a flight of stairs and turned down another hallway. Prye heard a moan of distress from behind a closed door, followed by a profane shout in objection to something behind another door. Then a defensive response. Following Wingate, Prye ignored it all, kept walking down the polished linoleum hallway.

The two of them turned a corner. It was quieter here. Wingate stopped at a door and knocked on it, smiling as he did. "You got a visitor, ma'am." There was no answer from inside. Wingate opened the door, gesturing for Prye to enter. "Ya'all have a real nice visit, now."

Prye nodded to him and he entered, closing the door behind him. Inside a woman was sitting in a chair by a small table, doing needlepoint. She looked to be about Prye's age, and was trim, her graying auburn hair in a shoulder-length perm. The freckles across her nose and cheeks were faded under light makeup. At first, she didn't acknowledge Prye as he sat on the bed next to her.

"How you doin' today, honey?"

"I got a letter from Greg," she said, almost more to herself than him.

Prye looked off sadly.

"Want to read it?"

"Sure," he said.

She set her needlepoint in her lap, reached over to the table and picked up a sheet of paper, handing it to him. "He seems to be doing just fine over there."

Prye looked at the paper, a mimeographed announcement that bingo would be on Tuesdays as well as Fridays starting the second week in June.

"Doesn't it seem he's doing just fine, Nate?"

"Yeah…yeah. Doing fine."

"But that Andy…" She made a scolding utterance. "He hasn't written for almost *two weeks*. That boy is so inconsiderate."

"He's never been much for letters, you know that, honey."

He couldn't be sure what she knew, could only wish and hope.

"There's a war on, for goodness sakes. Doesn't he realize a mother worries?"

"He's probably just…" Prye rubbed his hand comfortingly on hers. "…just busy, Harriet. He's just busy, that's all."

"That's no excuse. I worry about him."

"I'm sure he's okay."

He didn't know what, if any, effect perpetuating the lie had. Was it considerate? Did it just fortify her illusions? Or did it make any difference at all? All Prye knew was that he loved his wife as much as ever, and would be patient for as long as it took for her to come back to reality.

Their son Andy had joined the Marines the day after Pearl Harbor was bombed. Their other boy Greg finished his last college semester, and then enlisted in the Navy on the assurance that he'd get into flight school. He'd kid Andy about the Marine Corps sucking hind tit of the Navy, getting his twin brother's goat every time with his teasing. Andy was sent to the Pacific right after boot camp. Greg was transferred there as soon as he'd earned his wings.

Prye was a rock for Harriet when Greg's Corsair was shot down near Corregidor, and she bore up as well as could be expected. She was inconsolable, though, when Andy was killed by a sniper in Okinawa. It happened when the major combat was all but over, less than two months before the Japanese unconditionally surrendered.

At first, Prye thought they both just needed time to mourn the loss of their sons. He could bring himself to do that. But Harriet couldn't, not after Andy's death. She took to her bed and was silent for days. When she finally did speak, she was delusional, in her own made-up world. On the advice of a psychiatrist, Prye had her admitted to Camarillo State Mental Hospital, a few miles from town.

For a time, he visited his wife every day, expecting her soon to come back to herself. She would, once in a while, in recounting memories accurately. And Prye would get his hopes up talking with her. But after a few conversational exchanges Harriet drifted back to the comfort of the fantasy she'd made up for herself. Now, almost two years later, his visits were down to Sundays only. Once a week was all he could take.

Harriet's psychiatrist had said that without a prior history of mental illness and her condition not seeming to be neurological, with therapy her prognosis was good. But, still, every time Prye witnessed the way she'd become it widened the crack in his heart.

He managed to hold his emotions in check when he was with Harriet, and then pause once back outside the hospital to take deep breaths to keep from openly weeping. When he left Camarillo, he'd go to the station, find out what had transpired on Saturday night, and busy himself with paperwork that could easily wait until Monday.

Hours after seeing Harriet he couldn't bear to go back to the home they had shared. Prye would spend Sunday nights in fellow Rotarian Norm Whelan's cabin up near Matilija Hot Springs, not far from from Ojai. Norm and his family, if they had been there for the weekend, were always packed up and gone by late Sunday afternoon. After he would arrive at the cabin, Prye would sit on the porch rocker and gaze out through the trees with the company of a half pint of Johnny Walker Black Label.

18

A few minutes after Prye had left the Hob Nob, Mig and Irina were served their breakfasts. When they finished eating they were engaged in conversation over a second pot of tea for her and a couple of coffee refills for him. She glanced up at the clock on the wall and said, "I missed my bus."

Mig looked at his watch, as if knowing the time would make any difference.

"Damn—I'll take you where you have to go."

"You can reserve your gallantry," She said with a smile. "There is another bus to Anaheim late this afternoon. It leaves at 5:30."

At her suggestion, they took a long walk on the beach, barefoot, hearing the occasional squawking of seagulls, seeing a small sailboat in the distance bobbing on the chop. They put their socks and shoes back on and climbed the worn staircase to Ventura's pier. Mig asked some boys with a bucket of bait what they were fishing for. "Perch. Wall-eyes and number elevens," he was told. "Taste okay, but there's a lotta little bones." He and Irina continued to the end of the pier. They leaned on the railing and gazed out at the Pacific.

"Even it has an end, the ocean," she said.

He looked at her strangely. "What made you say that?"

"My people are fatalists."

"Don't know that word."

"Americans have little reason to."

"I meant, I don't know—"

"I understand what you meant. You are honest, Mig. And unlike many of your countrymen, you seem to be a fatalist."

He looked away. "Whatever that means."

"You do not expect, how do you say, a bowl of roses."

He smiled and shrugged, deciding not to correct her confusion of expressions.

"With me, being this way is in my blood. I expect it will pass, though, with you, Mig. You have some family, no?"

"Only my mother."

"Tell me about her."

He explained that Carmen's high class parents in Mexico had rejected her for having become pregnant with him out of wedlock, even worse, by a non-Catholic, a Jew. The situation didn't sit any better with his father's Orthodox Jewish family. The Czerniaks were leaders in their New York City's religious congregation, Aaron's father was the synagogue cantor. He sang prayers. They had even blamed Carmen's influence on the circumstances of their son's death, before her illegitimate child was born. Carmen was all the family he ever had. And she was more than what he believed most people had.

"Your grandparents…They are still alive, any of them?"

"Wouldn't know," Mig said. "Really don't care, either. With my mom I got all the family I need."

Irina hugged him and said, "I admire her, she who gave birth to you."

"Yeah, so do I…Irina, this morning you said that *you* got you and your brother out of the camp. You got you both 'liberated' is the way you put it."

"Yes. I managed to do that."

"How?"

" 'How,' you ask…It is something I have never talked about."

"That's okay if you—"

"Perhaps I should." She thought for a moment. "Perhaps it is something else that I need to speak about."

She pulled back the sleeve of her blouse enough to expose some of the tattooed numbers. She looked down at them.

"These numbers, they assured our imprisonment. The few who attempted escape tried to hide their numbers. And it didn't work. The Germans would look first for what was attempted to be hidden. So I did not try to conceal the ink on Dima's and my skin. It was better, I found, to…to hide boldly."

" 'Hide boldly.' How do you mean?"

"After what happened to Dima, his…operation…as added punishment for the 'sin,' the commandant assigned me as housekeeper for the camp doctor."

"You mean the one that..?"

She nodded. "yes."

"Jesus…"

"I came into his quarters every day and cleaned. The first few times he was not there. Then one day he came in after a 'tiring surgery,' he said. He looked me up and down like I was meat on display. Then he closed his eyes in rest and ordered me to give him a back rub."

"Your chance to kill him," Mig said.

"Oh, I knew that. But I had to keep from doing it. I needed escape for Dima and me more than revenge…I gave the doctor his back rub—a wonderful back rub. When we each put our clothes back on he told me what time to return the next day. And so I thought of a plan. He liked to drink, this doctor. Cognac, especially. When a case of it arrived in the camp, he took two bottles back to his quarters."

"To share with you?"

"Oh, no. No fine cognac for the concentration camp bitch. Only for himself. To drink before he roughly took me, and then to drink more when he ordered me to dance for him. I had trained in ballet as a child. Dancing came naturally to me."

She smiled wistfully, closing her eyes and swaying her shoulders slightly in reverie. "When I was a girl…on warm summer days I would go deep into the woods, to a meadow, my secret place. I would take off all my clothes and dance and dance. Dance until I was exhausted…I was always happiest then."

Then she held firmly to the pier railing, her eyes narrowed.

"I took what had once been innocent joy and 'entertained' this beast as I watched him get drunk. The erotic way I danced before him, he gulped down one drink of cognac after another…Then his glass dropped to the floor. He had become unconscious. Slouched like an ugly old cherub in his big wing chair, white-skinned and flabby, a stupid grin on his face."

"*Then* you killed him. Escaped from the camp somehow."

She wagged a finger in the air. "Oh, no. There was Dima to consider, remember…*Then* I got the doctor's camera. "

"Oh…" Mig smiled. "Blackmailed the bastard. Swell."

"The commandant, he was religious, I told you."

"Yeah…"

"He had given his officers crucifixes for Christmas. They probably appreciated the torture imagery. The doctor had the one he was given hanging on his salon wall. I took it down and placed it on his genitals—and took pictures."

"That's great, Irina. Had him right over a barrel."

"Yes, but what to do with that. The advantage I had over this pig could have caused his disgrace—and my execution…Power, Mig, rests in how it is used."

"Okay, yeah. I understand. Then what did you do?"

"Being the doctor there, he would sometimes have prisoners transferred to a medical facility for…experiments. And to get his roll of film back, he was most willing to schedule such a transfer, with my instructions."

"Out the gate in broad daylight. Hiding boldly, like you said."

She nodded. "Besides Dima and me, I had him order a few more prisoners to be on the list for transfer. To make it look normal. There was always a small group."

"And you could pick who was in it."

She shook her head. "Select who was to be spared? I could not. One of those he put on the manifest was a woman I did not like. But so be it. I would not have wanted the fate of that place for her more than anyone else."

Mig nodded.

"There was a guard with us in the truck. I sat next to him in the back. And when we were some distance away, maybe a kilometer or so, as he was lighting himself a cigarette, I stabbed him in the neck with a spoon I had sharpened. Then pushed him out of the truck."

"What about the driver?"

"I started shouting, urging the others to do so as well. The driver stopped the truck and came running around to the back, yelling in German. The moment he looked in at us, I shoved my weapon deep into his throat…Dima became hysterical." Her expression was pained. "He was so upset, so terribly upset…"

"Hope the film found its way to the commandant alright,"

Mig said.

"I threw it into the forest. There would have been reprisals after we left had I carried through with my threat. Others would have had to pay. With two of their dead soldiers on the road, that may have already been the case. But I hope not."

"They can't understand what we have to do, most people."

Irina looked at him as she had in her apartment the day before when she'd questioned him about being violent. "Are you still having to do it, Mig?"

"Don't know what you mean."

"You said what we *have* to do, not had to…Is killing not over for you?"

He looked off, toward the ocean. "We'd better go back, get your luggage."

They went back down the pier. At the bottom of the stairs to the beach Mig waited as Irina took off her socks and shoes. Then he did, too. As they walked through the sand, she paused once to enjoy a breeze on her upturned face. On their way to the car they held hands. Neither of them said anything.

They went to Irina's apartment and made love, lingering in bed for as long as they could. Then she packed her suitcase and Mig drove her to the Greyhound Station. They walked out to the bus and he handed Irina her suitcase. When she started up to board, he stopped her and she turned back to him, leaning down from the step to kiss him.

"Goodbye, my gallant young American."

"I'll miss you, Irina."

"You will not be here when I get back," she said.

Mig looked away, then back up to her and shrugged. "Not really sure. Hope so, though. I hope so."

"Wishing has rarely been kind to me, Mig."

"I might be still here."

She touched his cheek and smiled slightly with regret. "It is easier for me to believe that you will not."

Nate Prye stopped rocking in the chair on his friend Norm Whelan's cedar-planked porch. He finished half of his glass and poured the rest back into the bottle of Scotch. Wind whipping through the pine trees was especially strong this late Sunday afternoon up at Matilija. Not forceful enough, though, to intrude upon his disturbing memories of being with his beloved Harriet earlier in the day.

But that wasn't all that was on his mind. What else bothered him had caused him to go light on the Johnny Walker. After leaving Camarillo State Hospital that Sunday, he had gone to his office at the station, as usual, and finally finished reviewing the previous month's duty log. And he'd found something that didn't make sense about a week ago Thursday, the night of May twenty-ninth. Prye got up from the chair.

From what he'd been told, something didn't figure at all.

19

After driving down from Matilija, Prye parked his car on a quiet street a few blocks off Ventura Avenue. Townsfolk referred to the neighborhood, the street itself and the ones branching from it as "the Avenue." It was a modest neighborhood where many of the residents spoke Spanish, either because they came from Latin America or those of their families' previous generation had. The majority of the lawns were neatly mowed, houses painted every few years. Most who lived here were a credit to the community. Still, the Avenue was not considered the best part of town as some measure of criminal activity could be traced to it.

Once when Harriet told her husband that the tamales they were having for dinner she had bought at a street corner *mercado* down there, Prye became a little cross with her. "How do you think it looks for a police lieutenant's wife to be shopping down at the damn Avenue?" Harriet didn't respond at first, just gave him a forbearing look. "My tamale tastes delicious. Yours doesn't, dear?" He'd looked away from her, feeling judged once again for his ingrained cultural bias.

Deep down he knew that any blustering of self-righteousness would never go over with Harriet. Sometimes he seethed inside, resentful that this woman he loved more than life itself was trying to gently persuade him again. But over years, as his confusion and anger would subside, he knew that she was only trying to influence him to be more openminded. Even so, he had a hard time allowing adjustment to the man he'd always defined himself to be.

Because the cars of Hank Elias's barbeque guests lined both sides of the street in front of Hank's place, Prye had to park nearly a block away. As he walked closer he heard conversation and bursts of joviality coming from just outside Hank's house. There was a group of three young men having a smoke on the front porch, probably out here to share jokes unfit for mixed company and brag about their alleged sexual conquests, he thought. As Prye stepped up to the porch he looked at one of the men and nodded.

"Buddy Joe Lamont…Hello, Buddy Joe."

The man nodded back, furtively, seemed a little taken aback. "Lieutenant Prye…Didn't know you was comin'."

"That all right?" Prye asked with a note of sarcasm.

"Sure, yeah, sure. It's Hank's place—Here to see him?"

"Finding things better on the outside?" Prye asked.

Buddy Joe tossed back his head to get the hair out of his eyes and smiled. "Oh, yeah, you bet—lot better."

"Good. Glad to hear that."

"I got a job, ya know, Lieutenant."

"I heard, yeah," Prye said, affecting being mildly impressed.

"At Strohmeyer's Heating Supply."

"I heard. You hold onto that job, Buddy Joe. Keep straight now."

"Oh, yeah. Learned my lesson up at Q. You can count on that."

Prye smiled. "Good. Nice to hear. I suppose that's the reason they call it Corrections."

He glanced at the other two men, a shifty looking pair who quickly looked away from Prye. "Overton and Cathcart here…," Then he looked back at Buddy Joe. "…they helping you keep straight?"

Buddy Joe seemed to become uncomfortable under Prye's gaze. "Uh, Hank's inside somewhere, Lieutenant. Or in the back," shaking his head, "Somewhere."

Prye stood on the porch for a moment, regarding the three men, one by one, as they glanced with unease at each other, averting his look. Then he walked by them and through the open front door.

Inside, some of Hank Elias's older relatives and neighbors were chatting on the couch and facing chairs, balancing paper plates on their laps, heaped with spareribs and macaroni salad. Women in flower print dresses and their jowled husbands, muscle gone to fat, former workmen in sport shirts, some buttoned at the throat. They chatted quietly among themselves, having been invited but looking to Prye as if they felt isolated here.

The rest of the guests in the room, animated and loud men and women, vying for conversational dominance, were a generation younger. In thirty years, they'd be just like the others, Prye thought. Trying to talk themselves into retirement age contentment, but mostly just plain worn out. He scanned the room but didn't see Hank.

Standing just inside the back door, Prye looked out toward the yard. Young adults drank beer and Cokes, recounting recent events of their lives with each other. As little kids played tag, older ones stood around sullenly, in a teenage state of otherness, their own source of isolation. A few men and women, munching potato chips, picked charred meat off the grill of a brick barbeque. They packed their hamburger and hot dog buns, slathered on mustard and pickle relish. It was the beginning of summer. Gatherings like this would occur from now to Labor Day.

Prye thought back, before their sons were born, and in later years with them, when he and Harriet would've been having fun at weekend parties like this. To him now, besides his Sundays out at Camarillo, weekends mainly meant the department having to deal with booze-fueled antics in town on Saturday nights. Toward the end of each week Prye found himself wishing that things wouldn't get too out of hand.

He turned back inside and made his way through the guests to look in the rooms off the hallway. Prye saw a door open and Hank come out, startled to see him.

"Hey, Lieutenant, wow. I couldn't remember if I invited you or not."

"You didn't, Hank."

"Well, that was sure not very—I shoulda. Let's get you a beer, somethin' to eat."

With a seemingly forced smile, Hank started to move past Prye, who stopped him, putting his big mitt on his chest. "I want to talk to you."

Hank looked nervous. "…Okay…"

Prye nodded back toward where Hank had just exited. "In here'll do."

"That's the *bath*room."

"Good. We'll have privacy."

After closing the bathroom door behind them, Prye turned and stood against it, folding his arms across his chest. Hank stared down at the pattern of little octagonal white tiles on the floor.

"What's this all about? I do anything wrong?"

"Well, I don't know about 'wrong,' Hank. There's just something sort of odd, seems to me. A little strange."

He took a step forward. Setting one foot on the edge of the tub, he leaned toward Hank and rested his arm on his knee. "I want to check it out with you, that's all." Prye could almost feel Hank squirming inside.

"Whatever you want to know, sir."

"The night before Memorial Day, a week ago Thursday. That H and R out on One Twenty-Six..?"

"The one you and me went out to, right."

"You told me you just pointed the camera at the body. Didn't really look at what you were photographing."

Hank looked down, shook his head. "Yeah, I coulda' missed somethin'. Fine patrolman *I* am…Lieutenant, I know it's not the way to investigate but I just…"

"You just don't like messy scenes, isn't that it? Blood and all?"

Hank nodded quickly, repeatedly. "You prob'ly want to tell me I shoulda' picked another line of work."

"Oh, I'm not here to *tell* you anything, Hank…Just to ask you."

"Ask me what?"

"You were on the desk that night. If you don't like messy scenes, why'd you replace yourself—have Lefevre replace you—so you could take the call?"

Hank avoided his look, not saying anything.

"I'm sure there's a good explanation, Hank."

"Well, sir, I wish you hadn't found that out."

"That's why there's a monthly log," Prye said. "So I can fill myself in on what goes on. Find stuff out."

"I, uh…" Hank cleared his throat. "That night…the call that came in…"

"You trying to figure out how to say something, Hank? Or *what* to say?"

There was a knock on the door, followed by a man's voice from out in the hall. "Hey, 'bout done in there?"

Hank called out. "Yeah, pretty quick."

"I need to go—bad."

A chuckle from out in the hall, followed by another male voice. "Beer's wantin' outa me, too."

"Hold on. Be just be a minute," Hank said through the door.

"Those guys…" Hank shook his head. He looked to see Prye staring at him, waiting for an answer. Hank let out a breath. "It was a woman, sir."

"You went to see a woman."

Nodding quickly, Hank said, "On duty. On duty, I know."

"That could be cause for suspension. You're aware of that."

Hank nodded quickly again. "I wouldn't hold it against you, Lieutenant. Not one damn bit."

"So…you're saying the call that came in about the H and R, the timing was convenient. That it?"

"Yeah." Hank nodded vigorously. "It was a quiet night, no calls since around nine, nine-thirty. I was just waitin' for one to come in closer to midnight. Late like that wouldn't, you know…"

"Be so obvious."

Hank nodded.

"This woman, she call you at the station before that night?"

"Naw, not at the station. Never any time before."

"That same night, I mean," Prye said. "Was there any particular reason she might've called before on that night?"

Hank looked unsure, as if not knowing how he should answer.

"Hank, I don't come down real hard on my men. That is, if they got a half good reason for doing something that, you know, skirts on the edge."

"Earlier she called, yeah. Right after I got on shift."

"Uh-huh. I just want to understand your situation is all."

"She had this problem she said I could help her out with, and…Well, you know how it is with women, sir. They get all nervous and scared about things. Need a man to lean on, get 'em calmed down."

Prye nodded, understanding. "Yeah, I know how it is…Who is she, Hank? Someone in town?"

"Well, sir, she's a…sort of a private person."

"You mean she's married? Husband away on business? That kinda' deal?"

"Well, no, not that. I wouldn't…She's just sorta', you know…private."

Now there was harder knocking on the door.

"Hey, there's a line formin' out here…"

"Okay, damn it," Hank said, his voice strained. "Hold your horses."

Prye took his foot off the edge of the tub and stood up. "Thanks for being honest with me, Hank. Like I said, just wanted to check it out."

"And about bein' suspended, sir? I wouldn't blame—"

"Don't report in tomorrow. If we were staffed up better, you'd be on two week's suspension instead of just one."

Hank just lowered his head and nodded with resignation.

Prye turned toward the bathroom door and opened it as the first of the men in the hall pushed by him, starting to unzip his fly.

Buddy Joe Lamont and the two others were still on the front porch when Prye walked out the door. They moved aside for him to pass.

"Nice seein' you, Lieutenant," Buddy Joe said.

"I'm sure," Prye muttered drolly, as he walked down the steps.

"Hey, Lieutenant…," Buddy Joe called out.

Prye stopped, turned back. "What is it?"

"Up at Q, I used to eat at the same table in the mess as this guy, Caryl Chessman. He's a damn genius."

"Hoped it'd rub off on you?"

Buddy Joe snorted in amusement, shook his head, brushed his blond hair back out of his eyes. "What I'm sayin' is, I got out lookin' back at Chessman still inside. Just goes to show, maybe genius ain't as good as plain ol' smart."

Prye didn't respond to Buddy Joe's sorry attempt to impress him. As he walked away, he wondered why, though. Had he gotten away with something and was gloating about it?

Prye had run in Buddy Joe once or twice, as well as the two others on Hank's porch, Max Overton and Ronnie Cathcart. They were all career losers. For them, wearing out wouldn't come with years of hard work but a fate almost everyone else could see coming but them. They'd break society's rules once too often and either die on the street or get locked away until their teeth fell out. These three staked all belief in luck being a fountain that would never run dry. And each of them would end, one way or another, choking on dust.

As he drove out of the Avenue, Prye figured he'd dealt with Hank as he needed to. Maybe it was true about him getting together with a woman when he was on duty the night of the Edward Fulham hit-and-run. A woman who was too private to be named. That could be all there was to it. But Hank had stalled as long as he could to come up with that lame sounding excuse.

Prye had thought about letting him off, not disciplining him. But that might cause Hank to wonder why. He had given him a suspension not only because he had it coming. It was also to make Hank think that what Prye had asked him about was adequately explained, the matter now over and done with. The patrolman might be focused enough on having been meted out punishment to be off-guard. To make some slip if he was covering anything up.

Of course, he wasn't sure if Hank was bright enough to come

up with this degree of logical thinking. Likely not.

This was all conjecture, Prye realized. What he didn't know was how much all this conjecture had to do with him occupying his mind, not wanting to think about earlier that day and feeling the sadness of this weekly visit with Harriet.

But nothing could take that away.

20

As Irina's bus turned the corner and was out of Mig's sight, he instantly felt lonely. His brief time with this woman was an unsettling mix of experience. Even though Irina Temiarov was a connection to disturbing memories of the war, he already missed not still being with her.

Mig felt restless. He was reluctant to go back to the beach cottage. He hadn't been there in the last few days, and didn't want to spend any more time where Eddie had lived than merely to get some sleep, such as sleep usually was for him. He drove down Main Street just to keep moving, keep the plaguing questions of Beledayne and Eddie's murder at bay until he had some way of getting at the truth.

He drove past Ventura High School, then a section of small shops on either side of the street. Jue's Market was on the right. Mig figured the word spelled that way was a Chinese name. Down a ways, on the other side of the street was a Safeway. He drove past a cemetery that didn't look that well kept up. Not even grass planted. After that, on a slight downhill stretch there were a few houses with high windows and shingling detail of various shapes that looked to have been built in the first part of the century, maybe even in the late 1800s.

Then Mig was in the downtown area. What struck him most

was the Bank of America building of cement molded to look like huge stone blocks. It was so traditional, so solid, a place where you'd trust having your money. A few blocks down from that he saw the American Theater. An odd name for it, he thought, since the marquee posters only advertised movies in Spanish. On the other side of the street, there was a hot dog stand on a corner of the next block and Mig was getting hungry, so he parallel parked between a panel truck and a gray-primered jalopy a short ways past the stand.

After wolfing down two hot dogs, fries squirted with ketchup, and a Dr Pepper, Mig headed back toward his car. There was a pool hall a few doors down, which an amber neon sign above the door identified as HEINE'S. He considered going inside to have a beer and find a game of eight ball. But he looked to his left and hesitated.

Farther down the street he saw a tall evergreen tree, and through its broad branches there was a church that had a familiar look to it, topped by a bell tower. Beer and a game of pool could wait. He walked toward the church.

It was still light out and Mig was curious about this place of worship. He looked up above its carved wooden doors to see 1782 inscribed and painted dark on the plaster. It was one of the California missions, he realized. He'd read about them in school when he was a boy. As lacking has he had been as a student, history always had held some interest for him. He thought it was strange that a historical building like this was in such a run-down area of town. Maybe someday they'd fix it up. He went up the steps of the mission and opened one of the heavy oak doors.

Inside, the church looked bigger to him than it did from the outside. The ceiling beams were of dark wood, the uncomfortable looking pews of polished oak. Paintings of Jesus in various situations hung along each sidewall of the church. The altar area was painted in sunlit tones and set within columns. Tall gold candlesticks adorned the altar. "Gold and fancy vestments," was how he'd heard Carmen sum up her feelings about the ceremonial adornment of the religion in which she'd been raised. Her God would prefer what was spent on showy display be used to feed, clothe, and medicate the poor.

He went out a side door to a garden area. Four paved pathways between areas of grass led to the center of the garden and a fountain. From there, one of the paths led to a small building on the other side of the garden. Through a window he could see that it was a gift shop, closed now, with mission-themed cards, rosaries, and little statuary icons of saints for sale.

In the fading light, he sat on a concrete bench near the fountain and took in his surroundings. The look of the garden and mission brought to mind again his mother from Mexico and what he'd briefly related to Irina about her.

Carmen Quinteros was the youngest of four children. Her father, who proudly traced his heritage to Spanish aristocracy, had once been a highly successful investor in Mexican land holdings. But the upper class had lost favor during the revolution that began in 1910 with the overthrow of Porfirio Diaz's repressive regime. Carmen's father lost most of his properties. However, he had banked enough through the years for the family to live in comfort on a ranch outside Hermosillo. The parents, their oldest daughter, and two sons were bitter about the social changes for their class in Mexico.

To Carmen what was transpiring in the country promised fairness where before there had been oppression, as she'd heard and read about. She tried expressing this to her father and was severely scolded for her views, with her mother's and older siblings' concurrence. Carmen was never to say anything of the sort around those in their social circle. When she had matured a little, she'd give up all this Bolshevik-inspired foolishness. That's what they believed. But she held to her views, and freely expressed them no matter how much her family members objected. In time, Carmen was to become an embarrassment to them.

Carmen's father, who otherwise believed that higher education was not for girls, consented to allow her to attend college in the United States. Her parents' and siblings' desire for Carmen to be gone, she'd told Mig, coincided with her wish to remove herself from them. For once, all in the Quinteros family were in agreement.

She enrolled at the Columbia University School of Nursing in New York City. When she was having lunch one day in the school cafeteria while studying for a physiology exam, Carmen heard a male voice addressing her. She looked up from her book to see a young man with light blue eyes, holding a plate of food, asking if he could sit at her table. She had just taken a bite of her sandwich and nodded yes.

The young man thanked her as he sat down, introducing himself as Aaron Czerniak. He knew her textbook, having read it in his pre-med studies. Carmen had had little social contact since she'd arrived in New York, though she was teaching herself English while excelling in her academics. She liked the look of the young man sitting across from her having his lunch, too. She didn't say much, only gave the briefest responses to his questions, hoping she'd put the correct English words together.

Mig remembered his mother smiling wistfully when she recalled that day. Aaron spoke to her in faltering Spanish. He knew about as much of her language as she knew of his. He explained in a combination of both languages that he worked part-time at a medical clinic in Spanish Harlem. After they'd finished their lunches and were still struggling though a vocabulary-limited bilingual conversation, he asked if Carmen would like to attend a social with him at his parents' synagogue.

"Synagogue?"

"It's a place of worship," he'd said. "To talk with God."

Carmen had frowned. "This talk is with prayers, or money?"

Aaron smiled and took a moment to answer. "Some of both, I suppose."

She liked his honesty. Something she wasn't that used to.

"I'm Jewish," he'd said, cocking his head a little as he looked at her for any sign of objection. "Is that okay with you?"

Carmen had told Mig what her father had always expressed about Jews and what she knew he would have her say.

"It is fine," she did say and smiled. "I can learn to speak Jewish."

Aaron had chuckled. "Well, that'd be Yiddish, or even Hebrew. You've got your hands full as it is, linguistically."

"Ling…ling…What is this?"

He'd shaken his head, a seemingly private gesture. "It's me being a fool using such a word with you."

Aaron took her to the temple social, much to the disapproval of his parents, the rabbi, and the congregation in general, Carmen could tell. There were wary glances from seemingly everyone. She felt uncomfortable at first, but later realized that she almost took satisfaction in the heavy air of rejection. It was familiar in the strangeness of a new culture, making it not so strange. Maybe, she had thought at the time, the forces that opposed who she was would somehow direct her to know herself better.

And, she'd told Mig, the young man "with the pale blue eyes like you have," who'd brought her here, would turn out to be a guide in her growing from rebellion to purpose. She'd looked at her teenage son after she said that, as if willing him to understand some meaning of it. Mig remembered that, at the time, it had made him feel uncomfortable, without really knowing why.

Within a month Carmen and Aaron were lovers. Soon they started living together in a tenement on the Lower East Side. They rented one of three rooms from a young Lithuanian family that couldn't afford the whole apartment. The air was permeated with the smell of coal burning in the tenement's furnace, and when Carmen and Aaron made love they could feel fine soot on each other's skin. On some weekends they would take a train a short ways upstate and bathe in the pond of a farmer they had befriended.

Aaron introduced Carmen to the kind of political action that she was ready for even before they met. He took her to meetings and rallies of the CPUSA, the home-grown Communist Party founded a few years before. They listened to impassioned speeches and handed out pamphlets deriding the exploitation of labor by big business.

Her political fervor, however, soon made way for another involvement when Carmen became pregnant.

She knew better than to go to her family bearing the news of an out of wedlock conception, especially partnered as she was with a Jew, a "Christ killer."

Aaron told his mother and father, hoping for their approval of his and Carmen's marriage. But his parents wanted nothing to do with their son, their only child, until he severed relationships with this *schikse*, and told her to go back to her own kind with the "product of their shameful cohabitation." Until he did so, tuition for Aaron's medical school would be discontinued.

So he left school and started working full-time at an agency for the indigent, intent on becoming a social worker.

If he couldn't go to medical school to learn to heal people physically, he'd help them in other ways. Aaron devoted himself to the betterment of the disenfranchised: newly immigrant Puerto Ricans, Negroes, Irish, and Italians. He aided the forgotten and the shunned, was a witness in court for the accused who had resorted to crime in desperation merely for enough to eat.

He and Carmen decided to be married by a justice of the peace. They got their blood tests and marriage license. The event was to happen on a Friday, after which they would take the train up to their farmer friend's. He had a spare bedroom where they would honeymoon for the weekend.

Late Thursday night, after Aaron had completed his shift at the social service agency, he was walking back to his and Carmen's tenement when a robber confronted him. Aaron emptied his pocket of the little money he had on him and handed it to his assailant. In return he had a switchblade stabbed high into his gut, the blade shoved up to penetrate just under his ribs into his heart.

In grief, Carmen almost lost the baby, who was born eight weeks premature. Mig barely weighed four pounds at birth, scrawny and jaundiced. Carmen couldn't even hold her baby, only look at him in an incubator. And the doctors seemed to discourage even visual contact. She knew why. They didn't want her becoming attached to an infant that they thought would not survive. Nurses in the maternity ward rushed to Carmen's bedside when they heard her raging with sacrilege toward the ceiling. It took three of them to put her in restraints and tape her mouth.

Within the next few days Mig started to gain a little weight. His yellowish skin began to become pink, and Carmen was given her son to hold in her arms and nurse. Mig soon took on the glow of good health with Carmen's love, her milk, and, she believed, her demand to the heavens that her and Aaron's child be allowed to live.

When talking to him about his father, Carmen once said to Mig, "I was to have him, and then you. Having both of you together was more than God would allow."

In the mission courtyard, Mig took out his billfold and opened it to look at the snapshot of Aaron Czerniak, for the second time since yesterday. But it was too dark now to clearly see it.

He went back though the mission and down the front steps to the sidewalk. He headed back toward his car, and paused in front of Heine's, considering whether to go in for a beer and game of pool when he heard a man's voice.

"Hey, guy, can you help me out?"

21

Mig looked over and saw a figure in an overcoat, hunched in the shadow of a storefront alcove next door to the pool hall.

"Anything to spare for a fellow G.I.?"

Mig walked closer to the man and saw that he was about his age, maybe a few years older, and had a of couple days growth of beard, needed a haircut. His overcoat was torn at the lower side of the pocket into which his right sleeve was stuffed. When he pushed away from the alcove into more light and shuffled nearer to Mig, he saw that the sleeve in the pocket was mostly empty.

"You were overseas, too, weren't you?" the man said.

"Yeah, Europe."

The man nodded knowingly. "Figured. Limp an' all."

The man lifted the part of his left arm he still had and the lower part of the sleeve bent toward the ground.

"With Patton's Third. Tank fire…How'd you get it?"

Mig shook his head. "Don't like to talk about it."

"You got any spare change?"

Mig reached in his pants pocket, dug out a dollar and handed to the man. "Get yourself something to eat."

"I need cigarettes more. Thanks."

"That's okay." Mig looked toward Heine's, then decided against going in. He crossed to the driver's side of his car and reached to open the door.

"Hey, can I get a ride?"

Mig felt uncomfortable in the man's presence, but nodded anyway. "I guess, sure. Hop in."

"Soon's I get butts. Can you wait?"

Mig nodded, though he was reluctant.

The man went inside the pool hall while Mig got in his car. Soon the man came out, stopping on the sidewalk to place his newly bought pack of Lucky Strikes between the remainder of his left arm and chest so he could tear off the top paper of the pack. Mig watched as the man walked toward him, pausing to shake out a smoke, putting the pack into his overcoat pocket, taking out a Zippo and lighting up.

When he got in the car, Mig asked him to open his window. The man cranked down the passenger side window, and then looked over at Mig and smiled. One of his upper teeth was missing. He leaned back and reached forward to smooth his one hand across the dashboard.

"Nice wheels," he said, the cigarette between his lips.

"Thirty-six Chevy's all…Where you want to go?"

"Over on the other side of the fairgrounds. I camp out there."

"Need directions," Mig said.

The man nodded, took a quick drag, removed the cigarette from his mouth, and exhaled. "You're not from around here."

"Nope."

"I could tell from your plates. Just pull out the way you're headed. I'll show you."

He had Mig turn left a half a block west on Figueroa. Soon they were past any stores or houses. They drove by a sign designating the County Fairgrounds and the man indicated a narrow dirt road ahead that curved down through a stand of trees.

The man had Mig turn left at the bottom of the low slope. Mig's headlight beams revealed there was no road anymore, just a wide area strewn with rounded rocks partly buried in sand.

"Ventura River bed. Dry unless there's a good rain. Keep to the side where you won't get stuck."

"You hike your way out of here every day?" Mig asked.

"Some days." The man chuckled. "Shoulda' been infantry, not armor, uh?"

Up through the trees ahead on the same side of the riverbed, Mig could see a light flickering at ground level.

"That's it over there. Been campin' out with some other guys…Turn off right up ahead on that path there."

Mig steered up the narrow clearing, brush scraping his running boards, and they approached a campfire near a train trestle thirty feet or more over the riverbed. The light of the flames played on the trestle's lower beams and crossbars. Above that everything was black. There were a half a dozen scruffy looking men of various ages sitting around the fire. They looked up in surprise at the approaching car. A couple of them got up and turned away, heading into the trees.

"Were they in the war, too?" Mig asked.

"Naw, just hoboes. Ride the rails between San Diego and up north. Got some stories, lemme tell you."

"Suppose they would," Mig said.

He pulled to a stop several yards short of the campfire. Mig looked over at his unkempt passenger. "Good luck, buddy."

"Thanks for the—Say can I buy you a cup of coffee?"

"That's okay. Another time."

The man looked down sadly. "There won't be any other time." As if summoning whatever pride he had left, he looked at Mig. "We both know that, soldier."

Mig took a moment to consider. "Okay, then. Coffee's on you."

Mig grabbed his leather jacket from the back seat, and they both got out of the car and walked toward the campfire. There was a cold sea breeze coming through the trestle.

"How long you been with these guys?" Mig asked as he put on his jacket.

"Hard to say, *these* guys. Who's here keeps changin'. Train comes through, one or two leave, couple new fellas drop in."

"Interesting way to get through...to live," Mig said, mostly to himself.

As they got to the campfire, the four men around it looked at Mig suspiciously. He nodded to them, tried on a smile, glancing off to see the other two peering at him from the treeline.

"No need to worry, fellas. This guy was just good enough to give me a ride. He's no railroad bull or nothin'."

Starting from the one to the left of them, Mig's passenger introduced the hoboes.

"This here's Frankie...Come on, Frankie, get up and shake the man's hand." With some hesitation, the one called Frankie did. Then the next man was introduced. "Woodrow—not Woody, likes to be called Woodrow, like in ol' Wilson, used to be president." That man got up. He and Mig shook hands. Mig's passenger guided him over to the third man. "Burt, the old-timer of the bunch." Mig looked into Burt's eyes as they shook hands. He could've been seventy, or a hard-lived forty-five. The next man, giant-sized, backed off shyly a few more feet from the campfire. Mig was ushered over to him. "And Rumbles. Can't talk—or just won't—so we don't know his real name. Just the sound he makes when he walks, heh-heh." Mig shook the man's huge, roughly dry hand.

Mig's passenger moved to the fire. After wrapping his hand in a rag he picked up from the ground, he gripped the handle of a dented coffee pot set on rocks in the fire. He filled up a tin military mess kit cup, and then turned to Mig with a grin, holding up the cup. "You came here for some coffee, right, fella?"

In a quarter second Mig knew something was off—the man's expression, the cup held a little too high. He ducked as the steaming coffee was tossed where his face had been. A few drops of it burned his cheek.

"JUMP HIM! TAKE HIM DOWN! TAKE HIM DOWN, YOU GUYS!"

Mig picked up a short length of tree branch from the edge of the campfire. The few flames on it went out when he brandished it at the other men.

"COME ON, YOU GUYS. HE'S GOT MONEY ON HIM!"

But the other four men just stared off blankly. Mig lowered his arm with the branch. There was no threat. The giant shuffled off toward the trees. The others sat back down around the fire, fixating on it, as if only wanting the moment to pass.

Mig's passenger waved his whole arm once, a gesture of defeat. He looked at Mig and just sadly shrugged.

"Times are hard, man. You know. You made it back, too."

"You didn't," Mig said low.

"Wha—Whad'ju say?"

"You as good as died over there."

He dropped the branch, looked with disgust at his passenger, and walked back to his car.

As he was driving by the County Fairgrounds sign, back toward town, Mig started to get the shakes. He pulled to a stop to wait it out and let it pass. After a few moments he willed himself to stillness. He thought about the pathetic ex-soldier he'd just been with. No matter what the war had done to Mig, he realized he was nowhere near that irretrievably lost.

He felt himself breathing deeply, beginning to feel at peace right now. He relaxed, leaned his head out the car door, and became aware of the sound of crickets in the early night. For some time Mig sat there in his car, breathing in the cool sea air and listening to a thousand crickets chatter away. He wondered what all they had to say to each other.

On his way back to the cottage, he stopped for a couple of beers at SAL'S AT THE BEACH. Sal wasn't behind the bar, didn't work Sundays, he was told. It was his day with his wife, beginning with early services at the Methodist Church. Mig could easily picture it. Sal had had family man written all over him. He'd have been a good dad.

Mig parked in what had been Eddie's driveway. He tried opening the front door but it was locked. He hadn't locked it, he was sure. Figured that the police must've after Lieutenant Prye finally had gotten around to checking out the place. Mig picked up the key from under the potted plant. He opened the door, turned on the overhead light in the living room. It looked emptier than before. Not just from the lack of the folding table and chairs that Louise Kierney had taken back. Those and the table lamp. The crudely hand-crafted one she had made.

In the bedroom, Mig reached far back on the closet shelf. The Steller's jewelry box was still there. If the police had come, they didn't find it. Or, if they did, didn't find it significant. Mig took the lid off the box and lifted out the heart-shaped locket by its delicate silver chain. He opened the heart, imagining Eddie's grinning face where there was supposed to be a picture. He closed the locket, looked at the engraving on the front of it. Who was M.M.R.? He turned the locket around to see Remember on the back. Just the one word. Remember what? He put the locket back in the box and placed it again up deep in the corner of the shelf.

It had been a long day and Mig was tired after being awake a good part of the previous night with Irina. He undressed to his skivvies, turned the bedspread down and got under it, but, as a few nights before, not under the blanket and sheets. That much comfort wouldn't do in the bed that Eddie Fulham had gotten up from a week ago Thursday, without knowing that his next resting place would be in a coffin.

Mig had a rough night of sleep, interrupted as usual by disturbing dreams of the war. What had happened distorted into the weird imaginings of his unconscious. Amid the stylized carnage appeared the face of another soldier, his fixed expression strangely lighthearted. That his features were unfamiliar didn't matter. Mig knew in the nightmare that the other soldier was Jurgen Gutfreund.

Gripping the pillow from its underside shortly before dawn, Mig pulled out a piece of cloth. He turned on a light to see that it was a handkerchief. Coming fully awake, now he thought he knew why Eddie's laundry bag had been gone through on the day he'd arrived at the cottage. Louise Kierney hadn't just come here to get the furnishings she had lent Eddie. The lamp from her "clay period," as she'd called it, was when she was sixteen, Mig remembered her saying. As a woman in her twenties, she practiced another craft, and he was now looking at an example of it.

Her feelings for Eddie must've been more than she'd admitted having.

22

Sid Beledayne's used car lot was on Thompson Boulevard, between a DeSoto-Plymouth dealership and a Goodyear tire shop. Colorful little flags strung on a rope over the front display of prewar cars flapped in a gentle morning breeze. On either end of the lot were signs that proclaimed PRICES SLASHED! THIS IS YOUR DAY TO BUY! WE'LL MAKE YOU THE BEST DEAL POSSIBLE!

The lot had just opened for Monday business when Mig drove up next to it and parked on the street. When he walked onto the lot a salesman with a lip-splitting grin hustled up as best as his paunch would allow.

"Wanna make a trade?" the man said, bubbly-voiced.

"Nope," Mig said. "Not today."

"We can make you a reee-al good deal."

Mig shook his head. "Satisfied with what I got."

He saw the salesman's mouth twitch in an effort for something persuasive to say, as Mig turned away from him and walked toward the office. He climbed the few steps and opened the door.

In the outer office, a young woman was turned away from him, setting up coffee. She'd heard the door open. "It'll ready in a few minutes, Sid. I got in a little later than—"

When she turned around, Mig was surprised. "Well, I'll be

damned. Louise Kierney. 'Morning, Louise. Remember me?"

She looked discomfited, maybe even troubled. "Yes, of course."

"The other evening when we were talking about Eddie, didn't think to ask you where you knew him from."

"Why are you here?"

"To meet your boss. And..." He pulled from his pocket the handkerchief that he'd found under Eddie's pillow, It was damp and wrung out. "...wanted to give you back this, after I looked you up sometime today. Needed to wash it first." He held the handkerchief up and read what was embroidered on it. " 'Every little sneeze makes me think of Louise.' And these little doodads around it, like you see on music sheets. I remember Eddie saying his allergies would act up this time of year." He examined the handkerchief. "Careful sewing work, Louise. Must've taken you awhile."

"It was just a gift. A friendly gesture is all."

Mig read the rest. " 'All my love.' Hmm."

She turned away, busying herself with the coffee setup.

"You were looking for this in Eddie's laundry bag the other night when I walked in, weren't you?"

Louise whirled back to glare at him. "It was something private, okay?"

Mig held the handkerchief out to her. "Anything else down at Eddie's place you might want to get back?"

She took the handkerchief, stuffed in it her dress pocket. She shook her head.

Thinking of the locket with someone else's initials, he asked her, "Eddie...was he in love with you?"

"Like I said the other night, we were friends. Only that."

The front door opened and Sid Beledayne walked in. "Good

morning," he said to Louise.

She gave him a sympathetic look. "Any news yet, Sid?"

"No. Just a matter of time before they locate that idiot cousin. Peggy's sure to be with her." Looking at Mig, "And this is..?"

"His name I forg—"

"Mig Czerniak, Mr. Beledayne." Mig and Beledayne shook hands. "I knew Eddie Fulham overseas. Around the end of the war in Europe," Mig said, studying the other man for a read.

"Oh, God. Poor Eddie. What happened, it was so tragic."

"Yeah, sure was. I'm staying down at his place at the beach for another night or so to pack up his things."

"I see," Beledayne said.

"Eddie's mom asked me to." Mig looked directly into Beledayne's eyes. "That's why I came up here to Ventura."

"Give my condolences to his parents, will you?"

Continuing to look intently at Beledayne, "Glad to. It'll mean a lot to 'em."

Beledayne seemed uneasy under Mig's stare. Then his attention was diverted when the door opened and Lucius Jefford came in. Mig remembered him from the first day he arrived in Ventura. The one with the ice cream truck.

"This is my brother-in-law, Luc Jefford. Once brother-in-law."

Jefford nodded a silent greeting at Mig.

"Mig Czerniak. Was there when you came into the police station last week."

"When they brought in that tramp, yeah," Jefford said. "One less commie…"

"That what he was?" Mig asked.

Jefford shot Mig a look, as if in objection to being questioned.

"I saw your dad at Mass, yesterday," Beledayne said to Louise.

She nodded quickly once, turned away, setting cups for the

percolating coffee.

"Hector expressed his concern, was almost friendly." Beledayne shook his head. "Too bad it takes a missing child to bring that out in him towards me."

"He—can be a difficult man," Louise said, still turned away.

"On the stubborn side, alright. Sure wish he'd..."Beledayne looked out the window. "A customer just drove in. Arnie's already tied up with another one, so..." He walked outside.

Mig looked out the window to see Beledayne stride toward the potential buyer. Two cars were parked near the office that weren't there when Mig arrived. A Cadillac, Mig assumed was Beledayne's, and a Plymouth coupe parked to the side of it.

Mig turned toward Jefford. "See you're not driving your ice cream truck today, 'Uncle Luc'."

"Kids are in school till this afternoon."

"Of course, yeah." Mig looked at Louise. "So Hector Kierney's your father."

"What of it?"

"The other evening you just said you 'were related.' Seems like sort of an odd way to put it."

There was a moment of silence among the three of them.

"Well, Mr. Czerniak, you've done what you've come here to do," Louise said.

"Pretty much."

"And that was what? What is it you came here to do?" Jefford asked.

"Private matter," Mig said. " 'Bye, Louise."

He started for the door, glanced back at Jefford. "I'll get a popsicle sometime."

As he left the office Mig watched Beledayne romancing his customer, taking the man by the arm as he gestured toward a

Pontiac two-door sedan in the second line of used cars. He was no doubt telling the guy how much his family would appreciate him making the wise choice.

Mig continued across the lot toward his car, realizing that he hadn't accomplished anything. He'd tried to put Beledayne on edge just by saying he'd known Eddie Fulham. So what? Other people did, too. And none of them knew that Eddie had been purposely killed—almost none.

He thought of Irina, what she'd said about what had allowed her and her brother's escape. "Hiding boldly' is how she'd put it. All Mig had done for the past few days was ask questions, which didn't get him anywhere. He needed to be more out in the open.

"Hey, there. I can see you're reconsidering, young fella."

The salesman from before had made a rushed sweep to head Mig off. He grinned at him as he bounced on his heels a couple of times, primed for a sale. He thrust out his hand, Mig didn't shake it. The man lowered his arm, apparently oblivious to rejection.

"Arnie Cruikshank. I'll get you behind the wheel of something slick as a whistle for a young fella like you." He eyed Mig for a moment. "Convertible'd be big with the ladies. And I'll bet you're quiiite the ladies man."

Mig looked past him to see Beledayne moving away from his customer, starting to head back toward the office.

"Got a '41 top-down Ford, fresh paint job, midnight blue. Right over here."

He attempted to usher Mig toward a line of cars, but he shook the salesman off and advanced toward Beledayne.

"It's a honey," the salesman said, calling after Mig. Then his voice trailed off with a hint of disappointment. "Rather deal with Sid. Okaaay…"

Mig hailed Beledayne as he was nearing his office. "Mr.

Beledayne…"

Beledayne stopped and turned to see Mig approaching.

"…forgot to mention, I knew somebody else in the Army during that time…" As Mig stopped near the other man, "…Lester McPhee. Said he used to work for you."

A flash of recognition on Beledayne's face.

"Down in Los Angeles before the war," Mig said.

Beledayne nodded slowly. "I remember him. Skinny fellow. Hands-in-the-till sort, I was informed."

"Don't know about that," Mig said. "Lester and me, we were drinking buddies. Him and Eddie Fulham and me." Mig smiled, shook his head as if remembering. "When ol' Les had tossed back a few…" Mig shook his head and smiled, as if remembering, "…well, you couldn't shut him up. He'd just run off at the mouth like crazy. Said something about you once—hinted at it only. You can trust me, though. I'm not one to spread that sorta loose talk around."

Beledayne frowned at that.

"Really, you can trust me."

"I have no idea what any of that could've been." Turning toward his office, Beledayne said, "I need to go inside now and get to work." He went up the steps and started to open the door.

"McPhee died, I heard," Mig said. "In the service."

Beledayne hesitated, his hand on the doorknob. "The war was a terrible thing," he said.

"From using morphine...that he got somehow."

Beledayne looked back at Mig with what seemed to be insincere regret. " Too bad he did that to himself. I didn't care much for him, but still..." He shrugged.

"And now Eddie's been killed. Makes you wonder, uh?"

Beledayne looked incredulous. "What are you talking about?

One death was stupidly self-induced, while the other was a hit-an—"

"Hit-and-run. Yeah, that's what they say....Well, see you, Mr. Beledayne."

As he walked across the lot toward his car, Mig wondered if Irina would call what he had said to Sid Beledayne hiding boldly, or just plain stupid.

He knew he'd just set himself up. It was the only way he could think of to shake Beledayne loose from feeling safe. Now Mig started to consider the good sense of maybe enlisting some help with what he'd put in motion.

23

As he dropped the receiver into its cradle, Nate Prye wished he could've just gotten his answer, straightforward and easy. Wished he wasn't going to have to talk to Wilhemina Sykes. But he was told that he would have to speak to the manager since she was the only one who would have what he wanted. And Wili was the manager of the local phone company office, recently promoted from senior operator. She had a dental appointment and wouldn't be in until about half past nine. Prye asked to leave her a message regarding the phone company record of a late night call to the police station a week ago Thursday. He figured it would go easier if she had some advance notice before they'd talk about the phone company's record for that night.

Prye and Wili had met nearly two years before when she had bailed out her husband, Marvin Sykes, from Ventura's drunk tank after he'd stirred up a rowdy public display on V-J Day. Sykes had accused the officer who tried to lock him up of being unpatriotic and started swinging. It took that officer and Prye, who happened to be passing by in the hallway, to put Sykes in his cell.

When Wili came to pick him up the next morning, the desk sergeant told her what a fuss her husband had put up. "Even gave the lieutenant a heck of a shiner," he'd said. Wili was embarrassed and went to Prye's office to make amends for her husband. She had wanted to take Prye to dinner that night since Marvin would be with his bowling league, but he had waved that off, with thanks but no thanks. When Wili tried to insist, Prye snapped at her and she'd left offended.

What she didn't know was how on edge he was so soon after Andy's death and Prye's weighing a decision to have Harriet committed temporarily until she came back to her normal self.

One night a few weeks later, Marvin Sykes, when he'd had too much to drink at the bowling alley and fell asleep at the wheel, drove into a power pole, which took out the electricity for a few blocks around Will Rogers Elementary School. When Wili found out that Sykes was to go before Judge Elston P. Gaffney, who had a reputation for limited tolerance for anyone driving under the influence, she went to the police station and pleaded with Prye to intercede.

He told her that on no uncertain terms would he ever try to influence any court decision. Besides, if Marvin was sentenced to lockup for a while it was very likely what he deserved. Wili accused Prye of a spiteful attitude over having been clobbered by her husband and then she stomped out of the station.

Prye had seen Wili a few times in town since then. The first time was months later at the County Stationery cash register. He'd tried to break the ice with her, but if looks were bullets, Prye knew he'd be a dead man. There were two other times he saw Wili, the first one he was relieved that he was driving by in his car. The next time she was on the opposite side of the street by the Sportsman Restaurant. Prye had abruptly turned away to study the bricks on a wall for a few seconds before continuing on his way.

Now he was forced to talk to Wili Sykes and wasn't looking forward to it at all.

There was a knock on his door and Prye looked up to see a

uniformed patrolman.

"They're here, Lieutenant. Those two fellows."

"What two fellows?"

"The ones that came upon that H and R week before last. You said to ask 'em to drop by."

"I figured it'd be after they got off work."

"They're self-employed. Gardeners. Here before their first job of the day."

"Oh." Prye nodded. "Have 'em come in."

The officer seemed hesitant, Pry noticed. "What is it, Pendergrass? You got a question?"

"These gardeners...Something else about 'em…"

"Yeah, what's that?"

"They're Japs, sir."

Roy Kitagawa and Chuck Omani were shown into Prye's office. Prye looked past the two young men taking seats across from his desk and indicated for the officer who'd brought them in to close the door on his way out. Prye looked down at his desk blotter when he first spoke to the men.

"You two…were the first ones to come upon a hit-and-run Thursday night on May twenty-ninth around midnight out on One Twenty-Six?"

"Yeah, a little before midnight," Roy said. "That's why you wanted us to come in. *Back* in, since we came here that night to report it."

Prye barely glanced at them when he got up, crossed to the window, and gazed outside at nothing in particular.

"What did you two see that night?"

"Lieutenant," Chuck said, "Could you plea—"

"At the scene of the accident," Prye interrupted. "Every detail."

"You mean about the guy that got hit?" Roy shook his head solemnly. "He looked messed up bad, *real* bad…man…"

"We know about what shape he was in," Prye snapped, continuing to look out the window. His gaze had become a hard stare. "What else did you see—anything—right when you came on the scene?"

"Well…a pair of taillights driving away."

Chuck said, "Lieutenant, it'd really help if you—"

"What kind of taillights?"

"What kind..? Taillights, Lieutenant. Like on a vehicle."

"Big, small, set high like on a truck, or low on a car. I said every goddam detail, didn't I!?" Prye almost barked as he spun around to glare at them. He moved to his desk, planting his fists on the blotter and leaning toward the two men, looking down at them as he kept standing.

The two other men glanced at each other, then Roy turned to face Prye. "The war's over, Lieutenant."

"What the hell you bring tha—"

"Has been for nearly a couple years now."

"I'll let you know when I need a goddam history lesson."

"You born here, Lieutenant? In this country?" Chuck asked.

" 'Course I was born here. Do I sound like a damn foreigner?"

"No more than us," Chuck said. "We're from here, too. Right here in California, as a matter of fact. Me in Bakersfield…" He looked over at Roy. "…Roy, in some town nobody ever heard of called Lancaster, like that actor guy in *The Killers*."

"*Palmdale*, not Lancaster, I keep tellin' you," Roy said as he elbowed Chuck. They flashed smiles at each other.

"About the hit-and-run…" Prye said, averting his look.

"We can see you have a problem with us, Lieutenant," Roy said.

Prye glanced at the photos of his twin boys on his desk.

"Me and Chuck, we didn't bomb Pearl Harbor."

"No shit. You're off the goddam hook on—"

"And we didn't kill American troops in the Pacific—*other* American troops. Me and him, we were two of the Niseis in the 442nd Regimental Combat Team over in Italy and France. A whole lot of us 'Go for Broke' guys never made it back."

Prye had read about the 442nd, the most decorated American military unit in the war. Mostly all soldiers of Japanese descent.

"There's a reason Chuck was trying to ask you to face us when you were talking." Roy nudged Chuck to get his attention, and he looked at him. "He couldn't read your lips, right, Chuck?"

Chuck nodded, looked at Prye. "German mortar blast near Monte Cassino. Busted the hell outta my ear drums."

Prye had difficulty with what he'd just heard. It didn't set easily. He wondered if it would even with Harriet, in her right mind, with what had happened to their sons.

"We're here to help with your investigation, Lieutenant Prye," Roy said.

Prye sat back down at his desk. He looked at the men briefly, then down at the blotter, cleared his throat. He looked back at the men. "I've, uh…I've thought a certain way for a while. That's just how it's been."

"We all got a lot to put behind us, Lieutenant," Chuck said. He glanced at Roy and they nodded at each other. Chuck looked back at Prye with a wry smile. "Hell, you probably don't resent us as much as some other *slants* do—Chinese and Koreans."

Prye said nothing for a moment. "Getting back to that night on Foothill Road, either of you see anything else besides the taillights driving away?"

"It may not have been tail*lights,* Lieutenant," Chuck said. "Coulda' been more like one taillight."

"You said a *pair* of taillights," Prye said to Roy. Then to Chuck, "You saying the victim was run down by a motorcycle?"

"No, sir. I mighta' said taillights at the time. Roy was driving and he was braking hard to keep from hitting the guy on the road."

"That's right," Roy said. "I was concentrating on not hitting the guy—the body. I didn't notice much about taillights. Chuck did."

"Pardon me if I'm confused here," Prye said with sarcasm.

Chuck said, "We weren't working the next day—Memorial Day. Friday's when we're some of the landscapers that mow the fairways and greens out at Saticoy Country Club. Our biggest job of the week. We weren't gonna be working that day so me and Roy, we had us a few beers in town here before heading back to Santa Paula. That's where we live."

"A few beers…" Prye said.

"Me more than Roy, since he was driving."

"You were maybe a little drunk, then."

"A little, yeah," Chuck said.

Prye shook his head. "Not much of a reliable witness then, are you?"

"Well, seeing that guy sprawled on the road, it sobered me up some."

"But maybe not enough for a court of law."

"We're not *in* court, Lieutenant," Roy said. "Just here telling you what we saw."

"Doesn't make a whole lot of difference. Your buddy doesn't even know how many taillights he saw."

"When I woke up when Roy shouted about somebody lying on the road, I sat up and looked out the windshield, and the line in the middle of the road spread out to two lines." Chuck made a spreading motion with his hands.

"You were seeing double," Prye said.

Chuck nodded. "I'd put away a fair amount of beer."

"So, you were sheets to the wind enough to see two taillights that night when there was probably only one."

"That's about it, Lieutenant. Didn't say about the taillights when we were here to report it that night. Tried to cover up I was pretty drunk."

Chuck and Roy left, with Prye pondering their somewhat shaky testimony about the hit-and-run vehicle having only one working taillight. Even if it was true, it didn't give him much of anything to go on. Then something struck him. When Prye had talked to Hank Elias at his house yesterday, Hank had said, "the call that came in"—not that the two Jap gardeners had come in person to report the incident.

A few minutes later, Prye was talking to two of his men about a bar scuffle they had broken up the night before when he was notified on his intercom that there was someone on the phone for him. When he was told who it was, he realized he should've cancelled the message he'd left earlier. There was no reason to go through an awkward exchange with Wili Sykes, since he now knew there hadn't been any call to the station around midnight before Memorial Day.

For a moment he considered just having the desk say the call he'd put in was no longer needed, but that made him sound indecisive, unsure of what he was doing. So he had the call put through to his office, telling the two officers that they could finish filling him in on the bar fight later. After they walked out, he braced himself and picked up his telephone receiver.

"Hello, Wili," he said, trying to sound as pleasant as he could.

"Nathaniel…" was the cool response.

It was odd, he always thought, that when they had met, she'd told him that she preferred to be called Wili, hating having been stuck with the old-fashioned Wilhemina for a name. This was even though Nathaniel sounded more dignified to her than Nate, she'd told him. She thought his formal given name much better suited Prye's position in the community.

He asked her how she was, just to be polite, and Wili seemed to thaw a bit. She told him that her wayward husband had finally run out of excuses for his behavior and she was ready to cut her losses in her emotional and financial investment in him. She would soon be filing for divorce. Prye expressed his regret about that, not meaning a word of it. Any woman would be better off without a man like Marvin Sykes in her life, but he thought it only decent that he at least pay lip service to the sanctity of marriage. He was glad for this chance to put behind them Wili's ill-feelings toward him, although, as it turned out, he didn't have need to talk to her now.

"Thanks for returning my call, Wili. But the message I left for you, turns out it wasn't about anything," he said on the phone.

"You no longer care about a call that came into the station late the night of May twenty-ninth?"

"Well, it was specifically one that would've come in around midnight. Maybe a little before."

"Yes, I understood that."

"Sorry for the bother, Wili."

"Well, do you want to know or not, Nathaniel?"

"Like I said, it was just that specific time frame I wanted to know about."

"But now you don't care to know."

"There wasn't any call around that time, I know now. What I

was looking for I just found out was reported in person."

"As true as that may be, Nathaniel, there was a call to the station. This was at…" He heard a shuffling of papers on the other end of the line. "…11:56."

"There was? Where from?"

"Outside of town."

"Where outside?"

"On the way to Santa Paula. A residence out on One Twenty-Six."

24

Mig was checking in with the sergeant at the desk when Prye left his office and came into the station entrance area, putting his hat on, ready to head out.

"Hey, Lieutenant, this fellow was here last week."

"I remember, Kesselman," Prye said, then to Mig, "Any new brilliant theories you want to try out on me?"

"Lieutenant, can we go somewhere and talk?"

Prye indicated for Mig to follow him. When they were just outside the door, Prye said, "So why'd you happen to show up this morning?"

" 'Cause I might be in some danger. Put myself there is more like it."

"You don't say."

Prye started walking toward his car, Mig keeping up. "It was in town here. That'd be police business, wouldn't it?"

"Depends. Anyone threaten you?" Prye asked.

"Not so far, but I'm pretty sure it could happen—will happen."

"So will Christmas in about six months."

Prye stopped at his car and opened the driver's side door. "Get in," he said.

"Where we going?"

"It's a free ride. Just get in."

Mig walked around to the passenger side and got into Prye's car.

After the lieutenant backed out of his parking space and turned onto Garden, he glanced over at Mig. "The hit-and-run…what made you suspicious about it?"

Mig explained about Eddie Fulham's strange fear.

"Last week I thought you might have an overactive imagination," Prye said.

"How about this week?"

"Hearing about this moon thing, I'm fairly well convinced."

There was palpable silence for the next block or so from these two men who didn't know what to make of each other.

"Saw you need new tires, Lieutenant. Tread's worn down."

"You're observant, I'll give you that."

"Maybe you brought me along in case you get a flat. Don't have to get your hands dirty. Maybe that's why I'm riding in your car with you."

"Okay…I did a little checking into things—against my better judgement—but I did it, anyway."

"So what did you come up with?"

"At this point it's police business." Prye shook his head, raising his eyebrows, an expression of uncertainty. "Only my own, really, until there's more to go on."

"So you won't talk about it."

"Tell me about this danger you set yourself up for, Mick."

"Mig with a *g*. I dropped a name with Sid Beledayne. Bullshitted him about someone to make him sweat."

"Beledayne? Why him?"

"Because I think he killed Eddie. Or had him killed."

"Jesus, Mary, and goddam Joseph…You know, Earl Stanley Gardner back in the early thirties used to practice law here in

Ventura. Then he started writing crime books, 'cause he knew how to make up a good story."

"You think I'm just making this up?"

"You're chewing on something that isn't too carefully thought out, boy. Going after Sid Beledayne could make you look like a real idiot—and a heartless one at that until his stepdaughter is found, or comes back on her own."

"Well, let me tell you, sir, about what I've found out since we talked last week."

Mig filled him in about the morphine heist and his couple or days down in Los Angeles. All the while, Prye was mainly expressionless, focusing on the road ahead. He would glance over briefly, but Mig couldn't get much of a read from him.

"Okay, Lieutenant, don't you think it's sorta' weird that Eddie Fulham came up here from L. A. just for a bookkeeping job at some used car lot?"

"Oh, yeah. 'Bout the weirdest thing I ever heard."

Just past the high school, Prye turned left and soon they were on Highway One Twenty-Six, heading east out of town.

"If you connect it with everything else—Where we going, anyway?"

"You said you were in danger. Maybe I'm taking you out of harm's way."

"Don't mess with me, Lieutenant."

"Or maybe we're on our way out to Sid Beledayne's place to confront him about all of this." Prye looked at Mig and smiled broadly. "Get to the bottom of things."

Mig sat back and folded his arms, resigned for the time being to not getting a straight answer. For the next half a mile or so neither of them said anything. Then Prye broke the silence. "I think you and Hector Kierney's daughter, what's her name, Louise..?

You two should write crime books. Give ol' Earl Gardner a run for his money."

That was it. Mig looked for barely a heartbeat at the flat, empty landscape ahead. Then he stretched his leg over and stomped his foot down on the brake pedal as he gripped the steering wheel and gave it a hard, sudden turn. Prye's car slid sideways, front and back tires of one side digging in, tires on the other side raising up, almost off the pavement. The car came to a stop, broadsided across both lanes.

Prye's mouth opened and closed, like a netted fish flopping on deck.

Mig glared at the burly cop. "Don't kid around with me, Lieutenant Prye. I came into the station this morning because I didn't know where else to go. On the offchance you'd be some help. But you can go fuck yourself if you think this is all a joke. A guy that picked me up from dying two years ago is dead himself now. Murdered. I'm gonna find out who did it. And I don't need your give-a-shit attitude."

He opened the passenger side door and started to get out. Prye's meaty hand grabbed the back of his collar and jerked Mig back inside like he was almost weightless.

"Calm down, youngblood. You gotta be way off about Sid Beledayne. I got my own suspicions now about the death of your buddy, though."

"Then why didn't you say so?"

" 'Cause I've been a cop too long, that's why. I don't talk much about my business to civilians, especially about current investigations."

Prye turned the car back on the right side of the road and continued in the direction they were heading.

"I'm just fool enough to be a one-man investigation on this."

"Two-man now," Mig said.

"Keep this firmly in mind—*Mig*. You're just along for this one ride, that's all."

"Ride to where, for the third time."

Prye told him where they were going and why, and that he was even more of a fool for allowing a civilian to be with him now. Mig felt a measure of satisfaction. He had an ally on this, sort of. He realized this was only up to the point he'd be shut out. But when Prye indicated the place on the road where Eddie had been killed, it only reinforced Mig's resolve to not be kept out of it by the police.

They turned off the highway onto a macadam driveway leading past a large oak tree to a two-story Queen Anne house and surrounding lawn in the middle of a lemon orchard. Prye parked by the front of the house and he and Mig got out of the car. As they climbed a wide, wooden stairway that needed repainting on their way to the front door, Prye briefed Mig.

"Claude and Ivy Devores. All their kids are grown and moved out now, except for their youngest boy. Nice enough kid, but real slow upstairs." He tapped the side of his head. "He's nineteen or better but more like nine."

He rang the doorbell and looked dead serious at Mig. "Don't ask any questions. Don't say a thing when we're inside, understood?"

"You're the boss, Mister Police Lieutenant, sir."

The door was opened by Claude Devores, a whippet-slender man of about sixty with thinning hair pasted down by Wildroot tonic.

" 'Morning, Claude," Prye said.

Devores gave Mig a curious glance. "Nate…"

"Thanks for letting me come out and talk to you."

"S'alright. You didn't say there'd be anyone with you."

"Hitchhiker I picked up on the way out. Didn't want to leave him in the car, two-way radio in it and all. Hope you don't mind."

"S'alright, I reckon...Coffee?" He questioned to Mig, who just nodded.

"Come on in. I'll tell Ivy to bring in an extra cup."

After ushering Prye and Mig into the living room, he went into the kitchen.

Prye smiled mirthlessly at Mig. "Just like you're doing. Not a word out of you."

Ivy Devores brought a coffee service into the living room, blocking out her husband who followed from the kitchen. The couple reminded Mig of the nursery rhyme about Jack Sprat who ate no fat, his wife who ate no lean. There were pleasantries for a few exchanges, Mig drinking his coffee, remaining silent, anonymous. And then Prye got down to business.

"I understand a phone call was made from here to the station recently. A few minutes before midnight it was."

"Oh, dear," Ivy said. "We never stay up that late."

"We've had no reason to call the police," Claude said. "Not since some tools were missing from the shed out back. That was a few years ago."

"It was a week ago Thursday," Prye said. "Night before Memorial Day."

"That night," Claude said, looking at his wife. "Those young fellows that stopped by, woke us up. Remember, dear?"

"Of course I do," Ivy said. "I stayed in bed while Claude answered the door." She looked at her husband. "One of them wanted to use the telephone, you said."

"Did the young fellow say why?" Prye asked Claude.

"Nothing to do with calling the police station," Claude said.

"Trouble with their truck, he told me. Funny thing is, after he made the call—from the kitchen phone, like I wouldn't hear what he had to say—he went back out and he and his friends drove off. What kind of trouble with their truck could it be if they managed to drive it here?"

Ivy added, "That didn't occur to us, though, till they drove away in it."

"Didn't occur to *me*, dear. You were half asleep."

"Well, we talked about it the next morning, that's what I meant."

"The truck, what did you notice about it?"

"Looked to be white. It was dark and they parked some distance away, but I'd say it was white."

"A white truck," Prye said. "Sure about that? Wasn't a light some other color?"

Mig reacted to a noise from outside. He looked out a window to see a lanky boy of college age mowing the lawn by the side of the house.

Claude pondered. "No..., no, don't think so. Pretty sure it was white."

"What kind of truck? Pickup?"

"No, panel truck. Kind of a high one, it seemed. Hard to tell since they parked it on the other side of the oak tree. Branches mostly blocked out some writing on the side."

"Could you make out what it said?"

"Could tell the letters were big," Claude said, "But that's about all. It was dark."

"The letters, they were different colors, Claude," Ivy said. "Isn't that what you told me?"

"That's right, that's right. And there looked to be some kinda round designs here and there, in different colors, too, but like I said…"

Prye finished Claude's sentence. "…it was dark. Besides the one who came in to use your phone, how many others were there?"

"Two's all I saw. Were outside the truck, shufflin' around like they were nervous. Just two others, back by the oak. Any more'n that I didn't notice."

"The one that came in to use the phone, what did he look like?"

"Pretty ordinary looking. Somewhere in his twenties. Not that fond of haircuts, though. Blond hair kept fallin' in front of his eyes, kept brushin' it back. At least in the few moments I saw him in the kitchen. Not a sort you'd care to have goin' out with your daughter, if you know what I mean."

Prye thought a moment, nodded. "Did you get more of a look at the truck as they were leaving?"

Claude smiled slightly and shook his head. "Noticed one thing wrong with it then, but not something you'd make a call in the middle of the night about."

"What was that?"

"Truck had a taillight out."

Prye thanked them for the coffee, Mig grunted his appreciation. And then Claude showed them to the front door. As they went down the steps, Prye looked disapprovingly at Mig.

" 'Least you coulda thanked 'em properly for the coffee."

"That'd be talking. Promised you not to talk in there," Mig said with a smirk.

"You knew what I meant."

As they stepped off the stairway, Mig peeled off toward the sound of the lawn being mowed by the side of the house.

"Hey, where you going?" Prye called to him.

"Be right back, Lieutenant."

The college-age boy was continuing to mow the side yard. Mig crossed to him.

"Hi, there." The boy stopped mowing. "You Claude and Ivy's son?"

"…Yeah…," he said, as if he had to think about how to respond to this stranger.

"I thought so."

"Your folks are nice people. Real nice."

"…Yeah…"

"I like 'em a lot."

"Never seen you out here before."

"I just met 'em."

The boy just looked blankly at Mig.

"Your folks and me were talking about Memorial Day last week."

"Week before last."

"...You're right."

"I know my days an' weeks."

"Memorial Day, week before last...was there a parade in town?"

"Always is."

"You go see it with your folks?"

"Yeah, always do."

"I get real excited before a big parade day. Have a hard time sleeping the night before. How about you?"

The boy paused to consider. "Sometimes, I guess."

"Where's your bedroom, anyway?"

The boy pointed up to a second floor corner window at the front of the house.

"Why you want to know 'bout my bedroom?"

"Some men came here late the night before Memorial Day.

Thought that might've woken you up…Did it?"

The boy thought for a moment, then nodded.

"Maybe you saw the men."

"Yeah, kinda. Not good, though. Too dark."

"They came in a truck, right?"

He nodded again, and then shook his head. "Didn't make no sense."

"What didn't make sense?"

"The truck."

"Why's that?"

The boy snorted a laugh. "They don't sell no ice cream this far outside town. Sure not at night, neither."

25

Prye had come around the corner of the house in time to see Mig clap the boy on the shoulder and apologize for interrupting his mowing. Despite Mig's limp, he noticed there was a spring in his step as he came up to him.

"Thought I told you to—"

"Keep quiet *inside*, you said. Anybody else have an ice cream truck in town besides Lucius Jefford?"

"*Ice cream truck?*" Prye smiled, chuckled. "That what the kid told you?"

"Think about it, Lieutenant. White panel truck—'kind of a high one;' big lettering on the side in different colors; round designs, also in different colors…"

Prye considered for a moment. "Well…could be painted on balloons, I guess."

"Right. Anybody else have an ice cream truck in Ventura besides Jefford?"

Prye turned and walked toward his car, Mig following him.

"In Ventura, no."

"Then Eddie Fulham was run down by that truck."

"Couldn't be the new one. Luc got it after the hit-and-run. And his old one he said was stolen."

"Then that's it. Whoever stole the old truck killed Eddie."

"It could look that way," Prye said.

"*Could* look that way? Come on, Lieutenant, Jefford's truck, Beledayne one time his brother-in-law..."

They got in the car and Prye started it up but didn't engage a gear yet. "Okay, let's say it's not a coincidence."

"Not likely," Mig said.

"There's too much not known at this point, so don't jump to conclusions."

Mig banged the side of his fist on the door panel. "Oh, for chrissake..."

"Answer me this, Mig...Is Sid Beledayne guilty by association, or might it be that your friend's being killed was set up to look that way, to implicate him?"

Prye saw Mig look overly serious. "Sure," he answered. "By somebody who wants that city council seat *really* bad."

Prye shifted into first and they headed out the driveway. "I'm just throwing out a possibility," he said.

He waited for a passing car and then turned onto the highway back toward town.

"I'll stick with Eddie getting too damn close to whatever's in Beledayne's books, Lieutenant. What nobody's supposed to know about."

Prye nodded as if pensively. "Yeah...An accounting ledger with a note next to a hefty entry stating it was from the sale of military morphine—just as a reminder so Beledayne wouldn't forget." He was pleased with his comeback.

A little ways back toward town, Prye saw Mig look out the window to where he'd had told him the hit-and-run had occurred, fixating on the streak of dark stain on the road as they passed it.

"Goddam ice cream truck," Prye said again as he shook his head. Then he thought for a moment and said, "The *old* truck..."

Prye slowed his car down and pulled to a stop on the shoulder. Another car was coming their way.

"Why we stopping, Lieutenant?"

The other car drove by them.

"Not stopping, turning around."

"Why we turning around then?"

"Just remembered something. Want to check it out, and I could use your help."

He turned his car back the way they'd come.

"Jeez, Lieutenant, help from a civilian?"

"Don't let it go to your head, boy."

Prye stopped on the side of the road by the death scene, and they both got out of the car. Mig looked again at the streak of bloodstain.

"Come on," Prye said, as he trudged up the slight incline toward the open field on one side of the road. When Mig caught up to him, Prye stopped walking.

"We're looking for something red. From a distance away it could look like a little kid's ball."

"Okay. But fill me in, Lieutenant."

Prye continued walking into the field. "Just start looking."

They combed the weeds in one swath for a few minutes, and then Prye had them move over a few feet and inspect another section of the field. Then he turned them back, moving over some more, and they continued looking.

After several minutes, Prye heard Mig call out, "Hey, Lieutenant…Think this could be it?"

Prye looked over and saw Mig holding up a red sphere a few inches in diameter.

The big man hustled over toward Mig, twisting his ankle on a mound by a gopher hole. "Goddam it, anyway…"

When he hobbled up to Mig, Prye took the metal sphere from him and examined it. The ball was hollow with a large machine-made hole in it, torn at the edges. Opposite the hole it was severely dented. Prye bounced it low in his hand. "Unless my guess is way off, this is the clown's nose on—"

"On Lucius Jefford's old ice cream truck," Mig said.

Prye registered surprised. "How'd you know?"

"Guy that owns the café down at the beach, he mentioned it."

"That'd be Daws Salimore."

"Just know him by Sal. Nice guy."

Prye was concerned. "Exactly how much nosing around you been doing?"

"You mean in Ventura?"

"You know that's what I mean," Prye said, irritated.

"No more than I've already told you, Lieutenant."

Prye brushed his fingers on the dent of the ball. "He said in a low voice, "For once, maybe Al Kretzler had a good idea what he was talking about."

"What's that?" Mig asked. "Who's Kretzler?"

"Assistant medical examiner for the county. All too often couldn't tell a turd from a turnip." He examined the metal object. "But this time…Coulda' been about the right height, yeah…" He looked at Mig sternly. "Don't go pumping Sal anymore, hear me?"

"Oh no, just leave everything to you police, right? Without me today where would you be, Lieutenant?"

"Don't get high and mighty with me."

"Not doing that, sir. I'm just saying…"

"You got me started on this, Mig. I'll admit that."

"And, even as a cop, you're alone with it. Isn't that what you said?"

"Got more hunch than evidence still, yeah."

"You got the ice cream truck now," Mig said.

"No. Only *heard* about the truck—word of a *re*tard kid."

Mig indicated the ball in Prye's hand. "And that thing. Important enough for you to come back and search for it, however you knew why to look out in that field."

Prye stared at the ball, turning it in his hand, as he pondered briefly. He shook his head. "Still not hard evidence, not yet…You were wrong about lividity, by the way."

"Wrong how? Don't even know what that is."

"Blood settling at the lowest place on a body. The dark spot on the back of Edward Fulham's neck was a bruise. Bruise from an impact."

Again Prye bounced the ball in his hand a couple of times. "And my guess is, this is what made it."

"So, wouldn't that be evidence, Lieutenant?"

"Sure it would. If any trace of paint from this on the victim wasn't already buried with him."

"Do they ever…you know..?"

"Exume a body? Rarely, and then only with a court order. Guess what that takes."

"Evidence," Mig said.

"Bordering on proof. You'd better believe it."

"You know, I'm wondering about something, Lieutenant. Wondering about whatever it is you know—or have a hunch about—caused you to drive out and question that couple this morning."

"Well, be satisfied with wondering, Mig." He started to walk back across the field, favoring the ankle he'd twisted, Mig limping behind him. "Just don't try acting on whatever goofy idea you come up with."

Mig caught up to him. "Also wondering why you brought

me along today."

"Me, too," Prye said, as he clumsily negotiated his way across the uneven field of high weeds and loose dirt.

They reached Prye's car and got in. Prye started it up, turned around and headed back toward Ventura. He glanced over at Mig to almost see the wheels turning. What tack was this kid going to take now? After a few moments:

"Lieutenant…"

"What?"

"How big is Ventura?"

"Population?"

"Yeah. About how many people would you say?"

"Around fifteen thousand or so."

"That's all, uh?"

Prye smiled. "Maybe you want to know other things about the town. How many square miles, when it was settled, average rainfall, that kinda' stuff."

"With that few people, and you having rank on the police force, you probably have a pretty good handle on who's who in town."

"I know a lot of folks. Know *of* others," Prye said.

"Like the ones that can't seem to stay out of trouble. You'd know who they are."

"Oh, yeah…for the most part."

"You have any idea, for instance, about the guy that used those people's phone? The one that kept brushing his hair back—*blond* hair back?"

Prye shook his head slowly, in mock thoughtfullness. "No idea at all…But if I *did* know, I'd say he's a town low life who's been pretty damn cocksure lately. Like he's gotten away with something."

"Might help me keep safe if *I* knew who he was, Lieutenant."

"I don't think so." He looked at Mig. "You'd just go on the hunt for him…That field off to your right, there: lettuce." He gazed at the road ahead and grinned. "You being so curious about Ventura, I figure you'd want to know what our crops are, too."

Prye wasn't going to reveal any more, and he figured Mig was smart enough to realize that. He was curious about this curious young man.

"What have you been doing since the war, Mig?" Prye asked.

"Putting up with the heat in Arizona. Phoenix, where my mother lives."

"Got a job?"

"Forklift operator in a warehouse. Men's clothes." Mig looked at Prye's rumpled suit. "You could use some of what we got, Lieutenant."

Prye smiled slightly, let that pass. "You like your job?"

"Pays the rent. Boss is a good man."

"And your co-workers?"

"We get along okay. They put up with me, how I can be."

"How's that?"

"Since I got back from overseas, I'm, uh, edgy, sorta'."

"Edgy…" Prye let the word trail for more explanation.

"Quick tempered sometimes."

Prye nodded, considering this. "Bad dreams. Ever get 'em?"

"Sometimes…A lot."

And the shakes?"

"How'd you know, Lieutenant?"

"You're not the only one, Mig. One of my men back from the war was like that. Got the shakes real bad every so often, no matter where he was, or what was going on. We kept telling him it'd get better."

"Was that any help?"

"I don't know. He left the force." Mig turned away. Prye could tell he was uncomfortable with the subject. "You need to give it some time, Mig. You gotta believe it *will* get better."

Mig would go in and out on that viewpoint. He wasn't with it at the moment.

"That's what my mother keeps—You and your wife live here long, Lieutenant? You're married, right?"

Sadness took over Prye. "Sixteen years…sixteen years now for us here."

When they got back to town Prye pulled into his parking spot at the station, but didn't turn the ignition off.

"Okay, out you go," he said.

"This is your place of work, sir. Aren't you going in?"

"Gotta tend to some things first."

"I'd ask if you want company, but I probably already know the answer."

"Mig, maybe you were just being a little—hate to say it—overimaginative when you said you might be in danger."

"Beginning to wonder about that now, too."

"Well, I'm glad to hear you say that."

"I mean how dangerous could three knuckleheads be with a stolen ice cream truck as their weapon of choice? That is, if you pull a surprise on 'em."

"You just won't leave it alone…I'd lock you up if I could. Keep you from getting in your own way."

"If you could."

"But I can't very well on a charge of bullheaded stupidity… Try to wrap whatever you use for a brain around this, boy. Sid Beledayne doesn't need any embarrassment to mix with the sympathy he has right now. And he does have some friends in town, so better watch your step."

"That's the idea. Setting myself up so I'd *have* to do that." Mig opened the car door and got out, leaning down to look at Prye. " 'Bye, Lieutenant. See ya around."

Prye watched him walk to his car and called out to him. "Stay out of this, Mig. It's not your business—civilian business. And you're way off about it."

Then he backed out and turned onto the street.

Mig had gotten Prye to start wondering about Beledayne. He was new in town, not that much was known about him. Still, Beledayne doing in his employee, Edward Fulham, didn't seem to make any real sense. Prye regretted that he'd taken Mig along with him today. It was against his better judgment. With what they'd found out, he'd as good as opened the door for Mig to involve himself that much more in this what seemed to be planned killing.

Prye looked in his rearview mirror and saw a green Chevy coupe following, partially blocked behind another car when he was three blocks away from the station. So the young fellow was tailing him. Prye turned off Main, up Palm, and sure enough, he looked in his rear-view mirror to see that Mig also made the turn, dropping back in an attempt to remain unnoticed, Prye figured. He came to a stopsign and looked back. Mig had pulled over to the curb. Prye smiled.

He made a right onto Poli and speeded up slightly, enough for Mig to wait for a couple of cars to get between them before continuing to follow. The street had some dips and rises, each of the cars being momentarily hidden from the other. So Mig was at a disadvantage unless he stayed close enough to risk being detected. And Prye figured he was clever enough not to do that.

On Encinal Way, a residential street where he'd turned off and pulled to a stop, Prye looked out his back window toward Poli to see Mig's car pass by.

"Nice try, bloodhound," he said. "But you can't count on me to help you digging for a bone in the wrong place."

Before continuing down to Main, Prye made a stop at Strohmeyer's Heating Supply. After learning that it was Buddy Joe Lamont's day off, he drove though the downtown area. He went past the mission for a few blocks, then slowed down and turned right into the Avenue section of town.

Mig gazed ahead on a straight stretch on Poli. Prye's car wasn't in sight. He sped up, but realized within a few more blocks that he'd been ditched. It could be that Prye was looking into some other police business. Mig hoped so. But even if not, he had his own course of action to follow.

He was no cop, but had been a soldier. In battle, procedure quickly gives way to whatever works. Mig had set himself up by claiming knowledge of Lester McPhee to Beledayne—and also by saying that he was staying at Eddie's place at the beach. Nothing was likely to happen in broad daylight. It would be that night, probably late.

He stopped at Floyd J. Hickey's Hardware on East Main and bought some rope. And then he went around to the back of the store and took a long garden tool shipping box from a bunch of trash to be picked up.

In a block in the modest residential area near Irina's apartment, Mig went from one door to the next with the big box, asking housewives if he could collect the same items from under their sinks or back at their incinerators. He used the pretext of being on a scavenger hunt for a friend's birthday party that night.

26

After stopping by Eddie's cottage to drop off what he'd acquired, Mig found a place to park in front of the used book, record, and card store two doors down from SAL'S AT THE BEACH. He walked back to the café and went inside.

A new rendition of "Sentimental Journey" was playing on the jukebox, sung by Ella Fitzgerald in plaintive, silky tones. There was a fair-sized lunch crowd. Sal was doing double duty behind the bar and bringing plates to the tables. Mig took a seat at the bar, had a burger and fries and a tap Acme beer. He downed the last of his brew and signaled to Sal.

" 'Bout ready for a fill-up?" Sal asked as he picked up Mig's glass.

"No thanks, Sal. Got a question for you."

"Shoot."

"Sid Beledayne and this rancher you mentioned last week, Hector Kierney. They don't get along real good, right?"

"Oil and water, like they say."

"Tell me more about that."

"Well, Beledayne's new here, gladhands a lot, wants to be everyone's best friend. Think I told you that."

Mig nodded. "And that doesn't set well with this Kierney."

"Not at all, no. Hector's is one of a network of intermarried ranching families in the county. Irish, Germans, Italians. Old Catholic families. Settled here probably not long after the Franciscans left. They don't care much for carpetbagger types. And they do well enough with their citrus and other crops not to have to care, either."

"Seems odd that Kierney's daughter, Louise, works for Beledayne."

"To spite her father, some folks say."

"Is that why Kierney's so dead set against him?"

"Probably grates him some," Sal said. "But it didn't start with that. I told you Beledayne's trying to set up investment in a housing tract."

"Yeah…"

"The acreage he wants butts right up to the city limits. If he gets on the city council, he thinks he can gain enough influence to get that land annexed to have city services. But first he has to buy it. And that's a problem."

"Because it's Kierney's land," Mig said.

"That's right. And even though it's just lying fallow, old Hector won't sell it to Beledayne. Not a Chinaman's chance."

"Sal, can I borrow your phone book?"

Hector Kierney's ranch was a short distance from the main road on the way to the Ojai Valley. Mig turned off where he'd been instructed and bounced along a heavily rutted dirt section through an orange orchard leading to a rickety barn. He drove around that to a Victorian house. He parked, walked up the steps, and knocked on the front door.

He wasn't confident that Kierney would open up that much. But it was enough for starters that he didn't like Beledayne. Kierney, though, had had dealings with him. Nothing that went anywhere, but maybe Beledayne had revealed to this rancher that he had more to offer for his land than what he made selling prewar cars.

And there was Louise Kierney serving Beledayne his office coffee. Mig didn't know what to make of that, but the connections seemed as if they could amount to more than met the eye.

After several seconds, there was no answer, so he followed the other instruction he'd been given if there was no one in the house. Going back to his car, he leaned in and pressed on the horn for a long blast. Within seconds he heard a motor rev up from somewhere in the orchard. The motor was loud, not muffled, that of a tractor. As he heard it labor slowly toward his location, Mig wandered toward the barn and looked inside.

Nothing much there besides empty livestock stalls lining one wall. Daylight streamed in from all sides and from overhead between weathered wall and roof boards. Off to the side opposite the row of stalls was a pile of old lumber, chicken wire, and what looked to be a wooden flagpole rotted at the base. The top of it had been sawed off. As he heard the tractor approach, Mig noticed something fuzzy stuck in the chicken wire in the dim light. He leaned down closer to see there were feathers captured in the wire. Below most of the pile was something dark. He lifted a 1x4, which raised some of the chicken wire to reveal a length of tarpaper, short roofing nails through its edges. He dropped the board and walked outside when he heard the tractor motor sputter in shutdown.

A slender man in his mid-fifties, Hector Kierney lowered himself down from the tractor. He wore a wide-brimmed straw hat and was dressed in khaki shirt and pants. The shirt was buttoned at the cuffs and collar, which seemed to indicate a stiffness about the man, Mig thought. Or maybe only to shield himself from the sun. Kierney took off his hat, glanced squint-eyed at Mig walking toward him, and then turned his attention to the hat as he slapped the dust from it on his pantleg.

"Mr. Kierney…" Mig put out his hand as he walked up to the rancher, who set his hat back on his head, adjusting it by the brim. "I'm Mig Czerniak. Thanks for taking the time to talk to me."

He felt the man's firm, calloused grasp. When Kierney withdrew his hand, he bent his head back some and looked at Mig, scrutinizing him. "Like I said on the phone, can't be jawin' but for a few minutes. This ranch doesn't run itself."

"I understand, sir."

"You from ranching people?"

"No, but…" Mig panned his look by the dirt furrows and rows of orange trees. "…looks like all this takes a lot of work for one man."

"I got a son. We work the place together. Pick up some *campinseros*—Mexican workers—when we need to fix irrigation, smudge during frosts, whatever."

"You got two kids, then," Mig said.

Kierney frowned. "You know Louise?"

"Met her, yeah."

Kierney looked away, out toward the orchard, and stuffed his hands in his back pockets. "Louise and me…we don't get along too good. Never have." Abruptly, he turned back to Mig. "You said on the phone you wanted to talk about Sid Beledayne."

"Word is, you don't care much for him."

"He's not high on my list. Don't sit well with fast talkers. Slick types coming into the county."

"Even if they offer top dollar for your land?"

Kierney chuckled, which surprised Mig. Humor was something he imagined that didn't come easily to the man. "Where the Sam Hill you hear that?"

"Don't really remember," Mig said. "Did get the idea Beledayne's pretty well-heeled, though."

"That right?" Kierney chuckled again.

"Heard he had some investment or other that paid off in spades," Mig said. "It was when he was still in Los Angeles."

"I wasn't privy to that tall tale. Nosiree. Truth is, that car lot of his barely makes the lease."

This sounded strange to Mig. Why would Beledayne hide the fact that he had a good deal of money? Unless it would bring up questions as to where he got it. And then remembering what Sticks Garrett said about the morphine being long used up, another thought came to him. Could the profits from it be gone, too? But, if so, then why would Eddie have been killed?

"Sounds like you've had him checked out, Mr. Kierney."

Kierney nodded with a sly smile. "That I did. This old fool rancher knows how to look out for himself."

"So, at one time, you must've been thinking about selling him your land. Didn't know that."

"I let the idea simmer a little. Till I could tell all that big talk of his wasn't backed up by real dollars."

"He has some investors, doesn't he?"

"Been claiming to, yup. How much ink's actually been put down on paper, though's, another matter. Then there's his wife."

"His wife? What about her?"

"Claire's got some money. Her husband that passed had an insurance agency in Oxnard. Kinda' man he was, Ben woulda set her and the kids up with more life insurance than most folks ever take out."

"So Beledayne got his wife to invest?"

Kierney smiled again, looked reflective. There was the sound of a vehicle turning off the main road and bouncing on the ruts as it drove toward them.

"Ask her about the night a couple weeks ago they 'just happened' to run into me in the buffet line up here at the country club," Kierney said. "Beledayne insisted I join 'em for dinner. Must've had the idea he could better sweet-talk his wife into investing with me there. But when she got wise to that, well… Claire just fixed a stare on her plate and got graveyard quiet."

A pickup rounded the turn by the barn and came to a stop. The young man driving it turned off the engine and got out, slamming the truck door. He looked something like Hector might've years before. But not much like Louise. Neither father nor son did.

"They were short on three-quarter inch, Pop. Should have more coming in by Friday, they told me."

"Hell. Wanted to finish changing out that pipe today," Kierney said.

The young man indicated Mig, suspiciously it seemed. He stood tall, maybe as if in challenge. "Who's this?"

"Fella came out to ask about Beledayne, Tim."

"That phoney…"

"He knows your sister."

"You don't say." Tim looked at Mig. "Louise still working for the phoney? Or did he lay her off when it finally dawned on him that hiring her wouldn't help him meet the price for our land?"

"As of this morning, she still works for Beledayne," Mig said.

"She's managing to string it out longer than we thought, huh, Pop?"

Tim gave a derisive laugh as his father looked out toward his orchard and slowly shook his head. "Poor Louise…Like an orphan always looking to be taken in." Then Kierney turned to Mig. "You want to find out about Sid Beledayne, try where he sleeps at night. Maybe it's not still on the couch by this time."

When he left, Mig tried to size up Hector Kierney. He was a sly one, in his way, giving Mig the impression that he only gave out so much but knew more.

His son Tim, Mig found to be sort of mean-spirited. Could he have been the one who'd stolen Lucius Jefford's old ice cream truck and with the blond-haired guy and one other man run down Eddie with it? Mig remembered what Prye had said about the outside possibility of someone stealing the truck and using it to implicate Beledayne in Eddie Fulham's death. There was the connection of Beledayne both to Lucius Jefford as ex-relative by marriage and Eddie as employee. But could the two Kierney men want Sid Beledayne out of their lives badly enough to frame Beledayne for murder? The idea to Mig seemed a little hard to believe. Unless, of course, there was more to the story about them and Sid Beledayne that Hector and Tim weren't letting on.

But Mig still pegged the used car dealer as perpetrator, not victim.

27

As Mig drove back toward town, he tried to think of some way to question Beledayne's wife without coming off as insulting to her husband. Beledayne had tried and failed to have her invest in his housing tract plans. This had angered her in the process, according to Hector Kierney. But that wouldn't necessarily mean she didn't still have loyalty to the man she was married to.

Mig knew he needed to approach her in a non-threatening way to try to find out if Beledayne was struggling financially. A delicate subject. And Mig was all too aware of his not coming across that delicately these days. Considering that he was trying to nail her husband for murder, he needed to be convincing in a whole other direction.

"Bobby Lanyon's my best friend, Mrs. Beledayne. What he makes as a movie projectionist isn't much. I just want to make sure it'll be a good move for him investing in that land is all."

Claire Beledayne had invited him into her living room. She nodded and said, "I see." Then she looked away as if in thought. "Your friend probably shouldn't rush into anything too quickly."

Claire was an attractive woman in a worn sort of way. She gave Mig the impression that any good years she had were behind her and life ahead was something to get through as best she could with limited expectations.

After Mig had introduced himself he'd followed immediately with expressing concern about her missing daughter. The woman sighed at that and appeared weary.

"She's an exceptionally bright child. Older than her years and quite manipulative. I've been unable to keep up with her for some time. She's taken off before. Taken the bus to her older, bohemian cousin's in Los Angeles. Then they'll go on some excursion. A couple of days later she'll call for us to drive down and pick her up. She'll come home sunburned and exhausted…" The woman looked almost bitter. "…not even the least bit sorry for what she's put us through."

The woman seemed to not care much for her own daughter, missing or otherwise. Still, he felt he should be reassuring.

"I'm sure Peggy will come back soon, Mrs. Beledayne." Mig sounded foolish to himself. What did soon mean?

Claire didn't have much to say about Mig's "friend" investing in her husband's proposed land development, except that even now, when times finally look good, she thought that people should be financially cautious.

"I'm the wrong person to ask about Sid's investments. But, I'd advise your friend to be careful with his money. Especially these days when there's so much…wishful speculation that's taken hold."

"I don't mean to put you on a spot, Mrs. Beledayne."

"You're not. It's just that I really don't know much about these matters. I've been able to have some faith again in banks, but other than that…" She shook her head slowly. "…I really don't know."

There were footsteps on the hardwood floor coming from the hallway toward the living room.

Mig figured she had nothing for him, and felt uncomfortable

being here. "Thank you for your time, Mrs. Beledayne. I'll tell Bobby what you advised. And I hope that your daughter…"

"Mom…" a boy's voice called out.

"I'm not worried," Claire said.

"*Mom…*"

"Even at her age, she's quite capable of taking care of herself. Mary Marg—What is it, Doug?"

Two boys of about thirteen or fourteen stood in the living room entrance. Mig recognized one of them as the scared seeming kid he'd seen last Wednesday outside the police station when he'd first arrived in Ventura. The boy looked away from Mig, it seemed furtively.

"Okay if Lon and me hike up the barranca?"

"It's close to dinnertime," Claire said, glancing at her wristwatch. "Not today."

The boy named Lon added nervously, "I should be goin' home, anyway."

Claire's son looked strangely at Lon. "It was *your* idea."

"I should go home," Lon said.

"It's close to Lon's dinnertime, too, Doug. You boys can go for a hike tomorrow."

Lon walked quickly to the front door.

" 'Bye, Doug, Mrs. Beledayne," Lon said on the way out. He'd closed the door behind him before there was chance for response.

Doug shook his head. "He's really weird lately."

"Even though it's the last week of school, I'm sure you have some homework to do, honey."

"Yeah, okay…" Doug said. He walked back down the hallway toward his room.

Mig thanked Claire Beledayne again and left. As he got in his car, he wondered why he'd even bothered coming here. Of course the man's wife wasn't going to offer much of anything about her husband's business to a stranger like him. She might've been playing ignorant, but Mig doubted it. The time she'd shown displeasure toward Beledayne in that country club, it only sounded as if she'd objected to his attempt to influence her against her habit of being careful with finances.

Mig's impression from having just talked to the woman was that she really didn't know much of anything about her husband's business affairs, nor did she care to. She only wanted to safeguard what money she had, and wasn't to be lured onto any postwar investment bandwagon.

He started his car and drove back down the street. The chimes on the community church at the junction of Barnard Way and Poli were ringing the hour, five o'clock. He saw the boy Lon crossing the front yard of the last house on the street, next to the church, heading to go inside. Mig pulled to the curb, leaned over to roll down the passenger side window just as the boy was getting to his front door.

"Hey, Lon…"

The boy stopped and turned around.

"That's your name, right? Lon?"

The boy nodded, it seemed nervously.

"Come here a minute," Mig said.

Reluctantly, Lon came about half the way to Mig's car.

"I'm not gonna hurt you. Come over here."

Lon walked the rest of the way to the car. "What'chu want?"

"Saw you last week at the police station. Right outside of it."

"Maybe…"

"It seemed to bother you just now at the Beledayne's house that I did see you there. Like you were worried that I'd say something about it. How come?"

Lon didn't say anything, just looked away.

"Hey, look at me," Mig said in a friendly tone.

The boy looked at Mig, apprehensively.

"You know, I had some experience with the cops when I was about your age." He smiled. "Run-ins, is more like it. But you don't look like any lawbreaker."

"I didn't do nothin'." Lon said it rushed.

"Didn't think so," Mig said. It did seem like you had something to say to the police, though."

"It was a mistake, that's all."

"Okay…But if you change your mind, I know someone you can talk to. It wouldn't hurt if I give you his name, would it?"

Lon didn't respond.

"Lieutenant Prye. He's a—he's been a father, so he'd be easy to talk to. The lieutenant's really an okay guy."

Lon just stood there, his eyes darting from Mig to anywhere else.

"Remember his name. Lieutenant Nathaniel Prye. Want to get something off your chest, he'd be a good man to talk to."

Mig watched Lon turn away and go into his house. The kid had been holding something in for days, was scared to talk to the authorities about it. It brought Mig to mind of himself and the police when he was about Lon's age, not much older. The trouble he'd gotten in wasn't that serious, mostly for fighting and disorderly conduct. His anger had a way of getting the better of him.

Carmen feared that he might get into gang activity, as had some of the other boys in their neighborhood. And there had been the incident with the drunken old boxer Paddy Burkette that was upsetting for her and Mig. So she thought a change of venue would be good for them both. She applied for several registered nursing positions, accepting one in far away Arizona.

Mig had three stops to make to get ready for that night. He went back to Korb's in Montalvo, then to Kennedy-Gillette Sporting Goods on Main. What he wanted to buy he would have to wait twenty-four hours to pick up, so he made do with a substitute purchase. He figured it would be good enough for what he needed.

At a Safeway he took three large bottles of Wesson Oil off a shelf. Passing the meat counter on his way to the cash register, he stopped and looked at the mostly expended roll of butcher paper hanging in the middle of the meat section. He could have it, the head butcher told him when Mig asked to buy it. "Naw, that's okay," the butcher said as he took down the roll. "Tell 'em up front I said no charge. We got plenty of the stuff. What are you gonna do with it?" Mig told him he was painting a ceiling. The paper would work as a drop cloth.

Now he'd get something to eat at Sal's, with coffee instead of beer, before going back to the beach cottage to set up for late that night or early enough in the morning when it would still be dark. Mig's concern for having to keep awake was uncommon. His being able to sleep was usually the problem.

28

It was well after six, past the time Nate Prye usually left the office. But he'd gotten a phone call a short while before. The eager response to a note he'd taped to a front door kept him at his desk. He heard footsteps coming brisky down the hall toward his office. Then a quick couple of soft knocks on his open door.

"Hi. Lieutenant."

Prye looked up to see Hank Elias standing in the doorway. He was neatly dressed in street clothes and smiling broadly.

"Come on in, Hank."

Hank came into the office, up just behind one of the chairs on the other side of Prye's desk. He was not offered a seat.

"Your note said you wanted to see me, sir."

"I'm taking you off probation."

Hank cocked his head slightly in a humble gesture and smiled. "I was hoping that was the…Had my hopes."

"I'm sure you did. You know, Hank, I had you figured all wrong."

"How do you mean, Lieutenant?"

"Never was around you much until last Thursday when you and me went out to that H and R site. And then I thought you were just plain dumb."

Hank frowned at that.

Two uniformed officers appeared at the doorway. Prye looked past Hank to them.

"Be just a minute here, men."

When the officers backed away into the hall, Prye returned his look to Hank, who now seemed concerned about the other two cops overhearing.

"But you're brighter than I thought."

Hank relaxed at bit, seemed relieved.

"Maybe bright enough to even be considered for promotion," Prye said.

"Wow, sir, that's more than I…Wow."

"Maybe considered for promotion—except for what you did." Hank's expression faded. "You played me, Hank. I don't appreciate that."

"Whadayou…I—I don't get what you're saying, sir."

Prye leaned to the side and opened the bottom drawer of his desk. He took out the red ball with the hole in it that Mig had found in the field and set it on his desk, tapping the metal with his fingernail.

Now Hank started to sweat.

" 'Some kid's ball,' you said that day out there, right? Before you threw it out into that field where you thought it wouldn't be found."

"That's not it." Hank's words came out rushed. "That's not what I threw. It was a kid's ball. Rub—rubber ball."

Prye ignored this. "You did your best to keep me off-track out on the highway that day. Your level best."

"Sir, that's not what I—"

"To cover up what happened late the night before Memorial Day, when your cousin Buddy Joe Lamont and two other scumrats ran down—murdered—a young man by the name of Edward

Fulham."

Hank's words almost tumbled over each other. "I don't know anything about any a' that. I don't know anything."

"Maybe not all of it, Hank. The sickening details. In case not, I'll fill you in."

Prye again leaned over to his open bottom drawer and took out the length of duct tape that he'd found by the roadside ditch culvert. "There's plenty of this at Strohmeyer's Heating, where Buddy Joe works."

"I don't know what Buddy Joe does when he's—Don't know shit abou—"

Prye held up his hand to stop him.

"We haven't found Buddy Joe yet. But we will soon enough. By tomorrow, I expect. And then get it all out of him…Here's the way I see what happened. They held Edward Fulham by his wrists on each side by this length of tape and another one that'll probably never be found. Two of 'em held him, his arms stretched out in the middle of the road, while the third—"

"I don't want to hear this!" Hank waved his hands in front of him to dispel the words coming at him like darts.

Prye looked at him hard.

"I'm sure you don't, Hank. It's ugly. But you're gonna hear it—goddamn right you are…They held Edward Fulham standing, arms stretched out in the middle of the road while the third one ran him down with the ice cream truck they stole from Lucius Jefford. Just ran him down like a…" Prye shook his head in disgust.

"Lieutenant, I don' know anyth—"

"Shut the fuck up, Hank…Then they got nervous about what they'd done. Scared. Stopped at the nearest house and—here's the part that you *do* know about. Buddy Joe phoned you—his loyal cousin—who was on the desk that night, to get out there quick as you could and cover up any evidence under the pretext of a routine police investigation."

"Lieutenant, shit, I don't—"

"After you did that, you came back and wrote a report. To make it seem like you never left the desk, you tore up Joe Lefebvre's report about the two Jap gardeners who were on the scene right after the victim was run down. To keep the handwriting consistent you wrote your own report about that, too, mistakenly stating that the two almost witnesses *called* in—not *came* in, as they did….It was just an H and R., right, Hank? Besides, the victim wasn't much known in the county. Whole thing'd never bring any attention…Now, you got anything to say about all this?"

Hank's lips tightened. He just stared at the floor as if it contained some answer to his predicament.

"No guarantees, Hank, but it might go easier on you if—"

"You said you were taking me off probation. You lied!"

Prye shook his head. "I didn't lie, Hank. Only makes sense to take you off probation before putting you under arrest."

"Under *arrest?* It was those oth—I didn't do anything! Didn't do a damn thing!"

"Charge of accessory after the fact. Sometimes family loyalty's not such a good idea." Prye looked to the two cops out in the hall. "Come on in, gentlemen. And take former Patrolman Elias to his new quarters."

Hank sagged a bit as the officers took him by each arm.

"Not a damn thing…" he weakly maintained.

"Dinner'll be served soon, Hank," Prye said. "And I'll make sure they bring you in a phone book. You're advised to call an attorney."

After the two officers left with Hank Elias, Prye sat at his desk, troubled for a time. He took no satisfaction in what had just happened. Only had a sour taste about it. One of his officers had gone bad. Over the years he'd had a few men leave the force for one head-downcast reason or another, but never for involvement in a serious crime.

And he was left wondering about something. It was something that Hank might not know anything about. Prye got up from his desk and snatched his hat off the rack on his way out of the office. He'd check it out.

A veteran's coffee social was breaking up at The American Legion Hall when Prye walked in. He stood just inside the door and watched young men getting up from their folding chairs, conversing in pairs and small groups, some using their empty cups as ashtrays. He got wistful looking at former servicemen talking and joking around, wondering for the thousandth time how could it be that Greg and Andy were gone. He found himself almost trying to spot them among these others.

When the last of the veterans were leaving, Prye approached a beaming middle-aged man in a Legion cap, waving goodbye to the departing vets. He lowered his hand and looked at Prye with a puzzled expression.

"Nate…Didn't expect to see you here." He paused, considering what he'd said, Prye could tell. "I mean—Don't know what I mean," he said with a renewed smile.

"Good meeting tonight, Burl?"

"As always, uh-huh. Can I help you with anything?"

Prye surveyed groupings of framed photographs on one of the walls, mostly of servicemen in uniform posing for the camera, hands over shoulders with older civilian men wearing American Legion caps. He turned to the other man. "New ones up yet? From Memorial Day?"

"The parade and picnic? Not yet. Should be developed and printed by this week."

"I see. Which lab you use?"

The Legion booster shook his head. "They work in doing our film at the paper, Nate. Free of charge for vet stuff. Have to wait a few days longer is all."

Prye stopped for a New York steak, blood rare, at The Sidecar. Then he drove to the *Star Free Press* building. Dusk was just starting to give way to night. He knocked on the front door and waited. After several seconds the door opened just enough to reveal a nervous looking, slightly built man. He looked at Prye with suspicion, or simply not wanting to be bothered.

"What do you want?" was his greeting.

Prye turned the right side of his coat out to show his badge pinned there. The man inspected it.

"There's been no trouble here, officer. And there's nothing illegal going on. We don't engage in illegal matters—never."

Prye blinked slowly with forbearance as he closed his coat back up. "Relax. I know you 'don't engage in illegal matters.' You're the newpaper, for God's sake. I'm Lieutenant Nathaniel Prye and I'm just here to look at some photos."

The man's mouth twitched, eyes widened.

"Photos? What photos would that be, Lieutenant?"

"The ones the *Star* printed of the Memorial Day Parade. Can I please come in?"

"Oh—Oh, certainly, yes."

He opened the door wide enough for Prye to enter. Once inside the outer office, the man closed the door, hesitated, then turned to Prye with a nervous smile.

"Those pictures, they were in the paper, you know. They

would've been in the next afternoon's edition."

"Not every one taken. I want to see 'em all. Prints and contact sheets."

"Anything specifically you'd be looking for, Lieutenant?"

Prye looked toward the ceiling and spoke with impatience. "What's your name?"

The man hesitated, seeming trapped by the question. "My name?"

Prye brought his gaze down to the man. "Your parents must've given you one. What is it?"

"Uh, Earl Terwilliger."

"Okay, Earl, will you kindly show me where you keep copies of all photographs? I'd be really grateful."

Oh, yes, yes," he said, as if needing to be reminded.

He led Prye down a hall.

"I'm the night man—just got hired—and what they want me to do is, uh, just keep an eye on things, you know. Make sure the personnel can work in the back without being disturbed. That's what I'm to do."

"Not supposed to let anybody in."

"That…That's my understanding, yes."

"Then we'll keep this just between you and me, Earl."

Terwilliger took him into the file room, approached a pair of filing cabinets, and squinted at the labels on the drawers. He pulled out one of the drawers an inch or two and stood aside.

"This is last month's. Whatever you're looking for would be on the second to last day of May, Lieutenant."

"Thanks."

Prye pulled the drawer out all the way.

"They showed me this room when I got hired, but I didn't think I'd ever have much reason to be in it."

As Prye took out three filled Manila folders from the drawer, "Ain't life full of surprises. Earl?" He carried the folders over to a table and sat down to look through their contents.

"I'll need to stay in here with you, Lieutenant. I hope you're not offended."

"You babysit the place at night, so whatever you gotta do."

While Prye looked through the photographs, every several seconds Terwilliger rushed from the room to check out in front, then scurried back in. On his fourth return he saw Prye stacking the files back into the drawer. Terwilliger smiled.

"All done here, Lieutenant?" he said brightly, seeming relieved, Prye thought, at the bothersome interruption being over.

"Now I'd like to see the ones from last year's parade."

The man's relief faded quicker than a politician's promise. "That would be in, uh, archives. The archives."

"Okay. Where's that?"

"I've never been in there."

"Well, bet you can find it for me, Earl."

29

There was one last stop that Mig made. He remembered that Korb's Trading Post out in Montalvo, where he'd bought clothes last week, was an Army surplus store. And from a time during the war about a week before he got wounded, when his decimated platoon was on the move and needed every man, he remembered that a pup tent could have more than one use.

After he'd gotten back to what had been Eddie's place and made his preparations, Mig had second thoughts about what he'd set up. Maybe he should've told Lieutenant Prye about his plan. Of course, Prye would only try to shoot it down. Besides, evidence of even one cop around here risked spooking the whole thing. He needed to be vulnerable. But just hoped he wasn't overreaching his capabilities by trying to trap what he expected to be three guys coming for him.

Crouched in the hallway of the cottage, Mig now looked at his preparations and shook his head slowly. Was he up to this? He turned off the lights, scooted deeper into the hallway, sat next to the pistol he'd bought that day. And then he waited for what seemed like forever.

It was just before dawn when they came.

He heard the front door creak open, hushed male voices, then, after a moment, the clattering of the cans that he'd gotten from the undersink trash and backyard incinerators of all those housewives. Mig flipped on the living room light to see three young men, two of them slipping on the rows of Wesson Oil-slathered butcher paper and falling on their butts. The third one was just inside the door, peering surprised through strands of greasy blond hair, and gripping a tire iron. He turned and bolted out.

Mig pointed the pistol at the first man, then to the second one. "Just hold it right there, shitheads."

The first man said loud, *"It's only a damn pellet gun!"*

Moving up to him, Mig knelt down and grabbed him by the back of the neck. There was the sound of a car starting up and revving high down the street. Mig put the muzzle against the man's eye socket. "That's right, asshole, only a pellet gun. So if I pull the trigger, it'll only shoot through your eyeball, and not that far into your brain."

Mig froze at the remembered sound of a rifle shot—his approach to a fallen German soldier—the man shot through the cheekbone, just below his eye.

With Mig's hesitation, the second man yanked the length of butcher paper Mig was on and he tumbled, pistol still in hand. The man jumped him. They grappled briefly as the first man kept slipping on the oil-slicked paper, trying to position himself to get into the fray. Mig slammed the second man hard on the nose with the pistol butt.

The man cupped his hands protectively over his nose, blood coursing out between his fingers. *"My fuckin' nose! You busted it!"*

"Hope so," Mig said. "Make you even uglier than—"

The first man wrapped his arm around Mig's neck in a chokehold and grabbed at Mig's wrist, trying to get to the pellet pistol. Mig wrenched his arm free and shot him in the calf. The man yelled out in pain, reaching for his wounded leg.

Slipping in the oil some himself, Mig got to his feet, aiming the pistol from one injured man to the other.

"Lie down on your backs, next to each other."

The two men only fixated on their injuries.

"*Do it!*"

The men painfully complied.

Mig stuffed the pistol into his waist of his pants. He bent down to pick up a crumpled army surplus pup tent at the side of the living room and spread it out next to the men. He took the pistol back out and hunkered down on the opened tent, close to the second man.

"A week ago Thursday night—who put you up to running a man down?"

The man spoke through his hands covering his nose. "Don't know what the hell you're talking ab—"

Mig raised the pistol over the man's hands.

"Don't, *don't!*"

He tapped the pistol lightly on the man's knuckles guarding his broken nose. "Who put you up to it?"

"Jesus, man, what's with you?!" his now nasally voice said.

"I'm just one mean bastard," Mig said calmly. "You," he said to the first man, "Tell me about that night…"

"I don't remember," he said, agonized, through clenched teeth.

"…before I put another one into you."

"*Nothing!* I don't remember shit about nothing."

How bad was he going to have to hurt one or the other of them to get a confession of murder, Mig wondered. Mig wasn't quite mean bastard enough. He stood up.

"Okay, you first," nudging the second man with his foot. "Roll onto this tent. To the middle of it." The man did as he was told. "Now you," Mig said to the first man. "Roll right next to the other fuckhead, like the the two of you are going steady."

After he complied, Mig flapped one side of the tent over the other, then rolled both men up in it, as he had the time his point squad was on the move and couldn't be slowed down by having three German prisoners with them. They'd rolled them in a tent, tied them in it, and suspended them from a tree branch to be found by the rest of the platoon following.

Mig picked up the rope he'd bought and started to wrap it around the tent when there was a loud knock on the door, followed by a command from outside.

"Open up. It's Ventura Police—the police."

Mig opened the door to admit in a pair of uniformed officers. They introduced themselves as patrolmen Trask and Ducommen.

"Neighbor across the street—milkman about ready to leave his house to do his deliveries—saw three guys park next door to here, then sneak up and into your house," Trask said.

"I'll appreciate milk more from now on," Mig said. "One got away. The other two…" indicating the rolled up tent, "…are all wrapped up."

"I'll be go to hell," Ducommen said, shaking his head. The two policemen shared a smile. They started into the room, but Mig stopped them.

"Hold it, fellas. You're liable to break your butts."

He cleared away enough of the oiled butcher paper to make a clear path to the tent. The officers unrolled it and got the two young thugs to their feet. One of the men worked to keep his balance on his good leg. The other one spit out some blood that had coursed from his nose into his mouth.

"Well, well…Max Overton and Ronnie Cathcart," Ducommen said.

Trask followed up with, "You two really need to find some other line of work. Couldn't be any worse at this one."

The cops handcuffed them.

"The third one, he had sort of greasy looking blond hair," Mig said. "Some of it over his eyes."

The cops looked at each other and nodded.

"Sounds like Buddy Joe Lamont," Trask said. "He'd be the half a brain running the show." He said to the two prisoners, "Buddy Joe winding you two up again now that he's out of the big house?"

Cathcart and Overton said nothing, just looked sullen.

Ducommen turned to Mig and asked, "You know the way to the station?"

"I've been there."

"Can you follow us down there? We'll want to type your statement on a breaking and entering report."

"Sure," Mig said. "But if you sweat 'em for a while, I think you'll come up with a bigger charge than that."

There was an early morning rucus at the police station, causing some wait time before Mig could give his statement. Two cousins had gotten into a donneybrook over one making a pass at the other's wife. The police, who'd been called to break up the fight, couldn't stop the threats and invectives that had woken up the adjacent households. So they brought the men to the station to talk them down in a last ditch attempt not to have to book them. The wife followed in her car, only intensifying the venting of anger.

During this delay Mig found out that Cathcart had worked for Lucius Jefford occasionally, taking the afterschool ice cream truck route when Jefford had other appointments. Jefford had fired Cathcart a few weeks before, which could mean that he came up with the idea of using the truck—smashing it up in killing Eddie—to get back at Jefford. The vehicle was convenient since

Cathcart had made his own key to it.

Cathcart and Overton were clammed up tight, probably, the police told Mig, until one thought he could make a deal by giving up the others. On something this big, it could take hours or even days. And Mig knew that until one of them cracked there'd be no connection between the three killers and Sid Beledayne.

A short while after daybreak, in the courtyard of an apartment house on Ramona Street in the Avenue, a few police, plainclothes and uniforms, watched the county coroner who was on his knees, doing his work. Most of the policemen weren't needed here, showing up because so little was happening early this Tuesday morning. Small town cop curiosity.

They stood well back, giving the coroner room as he examined the lifeless form of Buddy Joe Lamont. The coroner lifted one of the corpse's pantlegs, felt the lower leg, and then pulled down the pantleg. He pulled up the other one, felt the calf from ankle to knee, and lowered that pantleg. Lieutenant Prye, who did have reason to be here, was impatient as he leaned down next to the coroner.

"So, what do you got, Sherm?"

"Hold on, Nate. Don't rush me."

The coroner held Buddy Joe's head an inch or so off the ground and turned it slightly one way, then the other. He then set the head back on the bricks, almost as if respectfully. He surveyed the body as he made a clucking sound with his tongue. And then he stood up, facing Prye.

"Well..?"

"Came out of that window, be my guess," the coroner said, indicating an open second floor window.

"Kinda looks that way," Prye said, shaking his head.

"Landed on his feet. One shoe came off. That happens

sometimes when they land on their feet."

"Guess you'd know, Sherm."

"Usually break something, too. One ankle or the other, tibs, fibs…something. 'Cause they brace themselves in the fall. Bracing's a natural reaction."

"Uh-huh, right," Prye said.

"No lower extremity fractures with this one, though."

"Nothing broken. What does that tell you?"

"I didn't say that. Just no lower extremities."

The coroner crouched down and moved a finger along Buddy Joe's neckline.

"Neck's broken. Not from the fall, the way he landed…Was he one of our local bad boys, Nate?"

"Oh, yeah."

"I'd say he overstepped his bounds with somebody."

Prye gazed down at the body. "That genius up at San Quentin you told me about, Buddy Joe…The one you were smarter than… He's probably sitting down to breakfast about now."

30

It was close to nine o'clock by the time Mig's statement had been transcribed into the police report and he'd read it over for accuracy as he'd been asked to do.

Leaving the station, he drove to Beledayne's used car lot and saw that the owner's Cadillac wasn't there yet. Mig parked by the curb near the entrance, got out of his car, and walked into the lot.

While the salesman who'd tried to corner him the day before was turned away to engage a potential customer, Mig concealed himself between two cars for sale on the edge of the lot and waited until he saw Beledayne's Cadillac slow down on Thompson and start to make the turn in. He stepped to the side of the car and pounded his fist once on the fender. Beledayne braked, and then stuck his head out of the window, looking more than exasperated.

"You again…"

Mig strode up to him. "Yeah, just like a bad penny. As you can see, things didn't quite work out as you planned."

"I have no idea what you're—"

"Two of the goons you sent to shut me up, the police have 'em in custody. It's only a matter of time before they'll spill everything they know."

Beledayne narrowed his eyes with an incredulous look. "You're accusing me of having two—"

"Three not so tough guys. The one with the tire iron got away. But not for long. The police know who he is." Mig leaned in closer to Beledayne. "Buddy Joe Lamont."

"Never heard of him."

"Yeah, sure. You also got amnesia about sending those guys out to get Eddie Fulham. Silence him for good about the hijacked morphine."

Beledayne jabbed a finger at Mig. "Listen, young fellow, I don't know if you're just plain loony or what. But I'm telling you, get off my property and stay well away from me and my family."

Beledayne stepped on the accelerator and his Caddie bolted into the lot and screeched to a stop by the office. Mig watched him get out, slam his car door, and pound up the steps into his office.

"Not getting on the city council is gonna be the least of your problems, you son of a bitch," Mig said low.

After he got back to the beach cottage, Mig cleaned up the empty food cans and butcher paper, putting as much as would fit into the incinerator in back, and the rest in a trash bin. When that was done, the events of the past few hours and lack of sleep started to catch up with him. He went inside, shut the bedroom curtains, and flopped on the bed, not bothering to undress or even cover himself with the bedspread. He'd catch a little shuteye for an hour or so, before checking back with the police to find out whether they'd gotten anywhere with Overton and Cathcart.

He was awakened by a woman's loud voice from outside. She was calling out to her friend that she'd better hurry up before they stopped serving lunch up at The Pierpont Inn. Mig realized he'd slept into the afternoon.

He got up and showered. Under the spray of hot water, he was thinking that by confronting Beledayne about his hired killers now being in police custody, the man would begin to come apart and do something to reveal himself. Mig only wished that he could be there when it happened. But if he didn't witness Beledayne's actual takedown, it would have to be enough just to know that he'd rattled him sufficiently to start his fall in motion. That shouldn't be long in coming.

After drying off, he put on some clean skivvies, socks, and pants. While deciding which of his two shirts he'd wear that he'd hung in the closet, Mig thought of his mother. If Carmen were to know about what had gone on during the past few days, what would she think? The boy still part of him would want her approval. He imagined one of her proud looks and her saying something like, "You have done well, Angel Miguel."

Then a realization —Angel Miguel…

As with him, nickname from middle name. When she was interrupted by her son and his friend Lon the day before, Claire Beledayne had started saying the given names of her missing daughter—Mary Margaret! He thought about the likelihood of Eddie having known Peggy, working as he did for Sid Beledayne. And then Mig reached up to the shelf and took down the jewelry box. He looked at the initials on the locket, *M.M.R.*, turning the locket over to read, *Remember.*

Sal was wiping down the bar with a towel when Mig rushed in. There were only a few customers having a late lunch.

"Hey there, Mig…"

Mig leaned across the bar. "Peggy Beledayne's real father. Hector Kierney said his name was Ben—Ben what?"

Sal looked wistful. "Great guy. Had a heart attack playing tennis before he was even forty-five."

"His last name. Sal. What was it?"

"Reineke. Ben Reineke."

The initials were too much for coincidence. What had been Eddie's connection to this child? Somehow, it had to matter. And the jeweler who had made the engravings. What might Eddie have said to him? That was such a long shot, Mig knew. But he had to follow up on it.

"Steller's Jewelry. Where is it?"

"Downtown on Main. Where most things are."

The only clerk working at Steller's was busy with a young woman and her friend, showing them wedding bands. Mig paced impatiently as the two women took their time in near reverie looking at the store's selection of rings. Finally, they left the store and Mig took the locket out of its box and approached the clerk.

"Who does your engraving?"

The clerk didn't have to look at the locket. "Gus Lydecker. He's been doing our special order work for years."

"Is he in the back?"

"Not at the moment. Gus took lunch a little late. He should be back any…" The clerk looked from Mig to the door. "Oh, here he comes now."

A man a good ten years past retirement age holding a restaurant "doggie bag" box was crossing Main toward the store at glacial speed. Traffic was stopped both ways to let him pass. He eased his way into the store and proferred the box to the clerk.

"Half a club sandwich, Jimmy. I went too heavy on the French fries."

"Oh, no thanks, Gus. Just ate a couple hours ago." He indicated Mig. "This gentleman wants to talk to you about some engraving."

Lydecker looked pleasantly at Mig, who thought that he

somewhat resembled the actor playing Santa Claus in the movie poster Mig had seen at Twentieth Century Fox.

"Whatever you want work on, as long as it's not the Gettysburg Address on the inside of a ring." He chuckled with a gravelly purr.

"Want to ask you about something you already did," Mig said, holding the locket up for the engraver to see closely.

Lydecker took the locket and looked at it sadly before giving it back to Mig.

"I did this for Mr. Edward Fulham." He shook his head slowly in regret. "Terrible thing that happened. Read about it in the *Star.* Such a nice young man…"

Mig introduced himself, asked if they could talk in private.

"Come on back where I work." Lydecker held up the small restaurant box. "Want the rest of this sandwich?"

Mig accepted the box. "Thanks. It'll be my breakfast."

On their way back to Gus Lydecker's workstation, Mig ate the half a sandwich. Lydecker pulled up a chair for him and sat in his own at his worktable. By the light of a gooseneck task lamp over the table, Mig saw the man's engraving hand tools lined up with near exactitude. A jeweler's loupe was set almost in the precise center of a square of black velvet. And the engraver had only been gone for lunch. Old Gus Lydecker was a man of careful measure.

"You must've been a friend of Mr. Fulham."

"He was a better friend to me." Mig didn't want to say more.

"I take it he didn't have a chance to give…" Lydecker indicated the locket in Mig's hand.

Mig shook his head no.

"What do you want to know, Mr. Czerniak, about the locket?"

"Just what Eddie—what he might've said about it."

"It was for a young girl he knew. Still a child, it seemed."

This removed any doubt. The locket had been for Peggy

Beledayne. But Mig was almost certain that the man he was talking with wouldn't know much more. He was trying to find out he didn't know what.

"Don't suppose you remember anything else, Mr. Lydecker. I'm sure with all the customers here…"

The old man looked thoughtful as Mig hoped against hope for something useful from him.

"What I do back here, Mr. Czerniak, is lonely work. Fit for a hermit, you might say. Jimmy and Bert up front, I talk with them some. But, except for every now and then during slow times, they're usually busy with customers. So I spend most of my time back here alone. But I'm not much of a hermit by nature. Not really. I like to chat with those I do work for. I find satisfaction in learning the reasons behind whatever they want me to inscribe. There's often interesting personal stories." Then he smiled. "Besides, I'm nosy."

"Eddie Fulham, did he say anything?"

"I had a chat with Mr. Fulham. Enough of one to know that his passing had to be quite a loss indeed for those he left behind." Then Lydecker looked troubled.

"What, Mr. Lydecker? What do you remember?"

"Our talk, it was disturbing."

"Disturbing how?"

"He told me that he'd come to Ventura too late for his original purpose, without mentioning what that purpose was."

Maybe by this time, Mig was thinking, the profit from the stolen morphine was used up, not even traceable. Eddie had been too late, but still he was killed. Why?

"And that's what bothered him? That his purpose…"

"No, no. I mean, I can't say for sure about that, but…what disturbed him had to do with the girl, the young girl."

"What about her?"

"Mr. Fuham was very concerned about her. Deeply worried."

"Why?"

"He said she was being…terribly mistreated." He frowned and slowly shook his head. "In a way that decent people don't even want to think about….Mr. Fulham wanted to give her the locket for her to put her father's picture in it. Not her stepfather. But a picture of her real father, who had been good to her."

"Her real father..." Mig said.

Lydecker further recalled, "Who'd passed away."

"To remember him by."

"Yes. The one word inscription."

Now Mig realized the real reason that Eddie had been a threat to Beledayne. He'd found out an ugly family secret that could destroy him.

"Mistreated by the stepfather," he said as he stood up to leave. "Thank you for the information, Mr. Lydecker."

The man put his hand out in a gesture to stop Mig. "No, Mr. Czerniak, not the stepfather. Not *him.*"

31

Behind the ice house near the south end of town was an alley that provided access to a loading dock. Mig turned into the alley and saw Lucius Jefford by his new ice cream truck. He was beaming down at a girl of maybe ten or eleven years old, licking a frozen fruit bar. His hand was caressing her back. Jefford looked up as Mig braked hard to a stop. The girl was startled. Jefford looked away from Mig and back down to her, continuing to stroke the length of her spine gently with splayed fingers. Mig got out of his car and approached them, suppressing his rage.

He spoke gently, to not frighten the girl. "Go home to your mother, honey."

"Laurie's enjoying the treat I gave her," Jefford said with a smile.

Mig kept focusing on the girl. "Go on home," he said.

The girl pulled away slightly from Jefford, looking from one man to the other.

Jefford took in Mig for a moment, his barely contained anger, and then looked down at the girl. "Maybe it's better if you do go, Laurie," he said, winking at her. "We can meet again tomorrow."

The girl nodded dubiously as she licked her fruit bar. She backed away, then turned and skipped down the alley. Mig watched her go. As he swung around to confront Jefford, he saw him jump up on the loading dock, stuffing a pair of work gloves in his back pocket. He went through a mandoor next to the closed freight roll-up door into the back of the icehouse. Mig followed.

Inside the deeply shadowed room, pools of illumination from high industrial lights revealed blocks of ice stacked against the walls between strips of canvas to keep them from freezing together. There were a few loose blocks on the floor. Between the stacks in a cleared area, Jefford, his hands spread wide as if welcomingly, faced Mig, who turned away briefly to close and lock the door.

"This place is only open Wednesday through Saturday these days," Jefford said. "So we've got it all to ours—"

Mig lunged at Jefford, slugged him hard, and he slid on his back for a few feet. He sat up, rubbing his jaw. "You pack a not bad punch."

" Get up, you piece of shit."

Jefford got to his feet, reaching in his back pocket for his work gloves. He put them on, pushing the fingers of each hand into the rough leather gloves. "Like I said, pretty good punch—lucky punch. But do you know anything about how to box?" He smiled, it seemed with confidence. "This'll be more satisfying if you do."

Mig welcomed the challenge. As they began circling each other Mig started to size up the other man's skill level. But anger took over whatever he remembered about boxing. He moved in and swung a wild roundhouse, which Jefford neatly sidesteped.

"Oh, that was sloppy. Would never do in the Golden Gloves. Not to make the state semi-finals like I once did."

He gave Mig two staccato jabs to the face. Mig threw a left, barely scraping Jefford's cheek.

"That'll probably show," Jefford said. "Need something to show if it's gonna look anything like self-defense. I'll have to let you get in a few good pops."

Mig began to realize that he was outmatched. So he set himself more defensively. The two men paced in arcs, studying for advantage, Jefford light-stepping, Mig shuffling solid on his feet.

"That limp you've got, soldier...too bad."

They kept slowly circling each other, Jefford with more grace.

"Not too quick on your feet."

He dodged in and gave Mig a gut shot. He doubled over, then recovered, got back to a fighting stance.

"You've become a pain, Czerniak. Coming to Ventura to find out what happened to your friend."

Mig got in a glancing shot to Jefford's chin.

"Let you have that one…First, your buddy, then you, traced the dough from the morphine to Sid's car lot in L.A. But it wasn't to Sid, like you both thought." Jefford shook his head. "Straight-arrow Sid…Never looked too hard at where the money came from that's kept him in business…It'll serve *me* to keep him in business."

Jefford feinted a jab, seemingly toying with his opponent. Then he landed a solid punch to Mig's cheek, twisting his fist on impact so the glove's rough leather tore skin, and Mig started to bleed.

"But you caught up to current events—like Eddie Fulham did—things you had no business knowing about. Nooo damn business in the world." He faked a left hook, then shot lightening fast with a right to Mig's face.

Mig, his face now cut, left eye quickly swelling, moved in for a good hit to the gut. Jefford staggered back a couple of steps.

"Nice one…"

Jefford rallied with another left, ducked low and followed by a hard right to Mig's kidney area. He gritted his teeth against stabbing pain.

"Ooo, tender there, uh?"

He danced in place as Mig recovered from the blow. Then Mig stepped in, faked a right jab, and then just missed Jefford's jaw with a left hook. Jefford took another quick shot at Mig's kidney area. He stopped in his tracks, winced in agony.

"You're maybe wounded there, seems like...Those two clowns in lockup...they only know Buddy Joe Lamont brought 'em in for some fun that night...Word is, Buddy Joe somehow fell out his apartment window—careless of him."

Mig moved in, tried a left jab, tapped in a second one, then grazed Jefford's cheek with a right cross. Jefford backed away, crouched, and moved in, giving Mig another blow to his kidney, a hard punch.

"Better block that area, soldier boy. Seems to hurt you there bad, a real soft spot...Their using my old truck for the job..." Jefford shook his head in disbelief. "...That was lamebrained."

Mig was beginning to wear out. Blood from a cut above his now swollen shut eye had started to spread down one side of his face.

"I got a sure thing investment. It's just a matter of time," Jefford said. "Sid's getting on the city council will be good for me and him both...For right now, though, my one truck will do."

Mig threw a wide, desperate right, which Jefford easily ducked.

"Oh, that was a sorry try...By and by, with help from Sid's housing development, I'll have trucks in other towns in the county...and I'll take over from my drivers every so often, to make young friends in Oxnard...Santa Paula...Moorpark....Simi..."

He moved in for a flurry of punches to the gut and face. Mig couldn't block most of them. He reeled back, staggering.

Jefford danced around him as Mig slowly recovered, "But there's my little Peggy. I miss her so much…all those damn dolls she's made me buy her…" He took on a look of concern. "She's always come back sooner than this. I'm worried about her. I really am."

He gave Mig a fast one to the gut, and he doubled over. Jefford waited for him to stand back up before landing a solid punch to the jaw. Mig dropped to his knees. Jefford paced around him, watching as Mig tried, and then failed to get back on his feet.

""Hey, don't quit on me just yet, war hero. Not when this has gotten to be so much fun."

He shoved Mig with his foot and he fell over. Jefford stood over him for a moment and grinned. "Ding, ding, ding—that's Round One." He hunkered down to look more closely at Mig. "I don't think you're gonna make it through Round Two. You're not looking too good."

Mig glared up at him with the one eye he could still see through. His words came out slurred, through labored breathing. "Fuck you…Jeffor..."

"Knowing you're gonna die makes you mad." Jefford shrugged. "Yeah, guess it would." He paused before saying, "But look at it this way. You must've killed other guys in the war, right? And now you're paying for the ones you killed." He smiled, his eyes expressionless. "Me, I'm only delivering the justice you deserve."

Mig looked up at him with hate.

"What happened in here today," Jefford said, "it's gonna take some explaining." He stood up. "Let's see… I was loading my truck up with ice…" He started pacing back and forth. "…and then you bust in making the damdest accusations. Lock us both in here and threaten me. Then you haul off and hit me."

Mig pulled himself up to one elbow, blood streaming down his face.

Jefford looked down at his victim. "That's about right so far….I tried to talk some sense into you, but it wasn't any use. You kept coming at me, yelling and swinging. You just went out of your mind. War'll do that to some guys." He leaned down close to Mig. "Won't it, soldier boy?"

Jefford walked away a few steps, folding his arms and looking away to gather his thoughts. "I was starting to get pummeled, when luckily I remembered some defensive moves from my old boxing days."

Mig managed to scoot himself up to a loose block of ice as Jefford continued voicing his scenario.

" At first, I tried as well as I could to fend off your punches, keep you from hitting me. Just did what I could to try to hold you at bay…"

Mig drew his knees to his chest and placed his feet on the block of ice.

"…but you kept coming at me. I was left with no choice. I had to do something. Go on the attack to defend myself."

With whatever strength he had left, Mig shoved the block toward Jefford, who started to turn back to Mig when he heard the sliding sound. The block impacted into his lower legs, and Jefford fell hard. His head struck the corner of another loose block of ice. He rolled on his back, and was still.

Mig tried to stand but couldn't. He crawled toward Jefford as the other man began to sit up and shake off the effects of his injury. He reached out and grabbed Mig's foot. Barely able to summon the energy, Mig swung his other foot, making a solid impact on the side of Jefford's head. He wavered for a second or two, stunned, before going down.

Mig crawled close to him. Raising his fist to pound Jefford's face into the floor, he saw that his eyes were open, staring into infinity. Blood had begun to spread in a widening pool around his head. Mig backed away from him a few feet and collapsed. His eyelids fluttered weakly and then closed.

When he became conscious, Mig was shivering from the coldness of the room. He saw a wide sliver of daylight, blindingly bright as it expanded higher with the creaking gear sound of the freight door being rolled up. There were silhouetted figures entering. Two of them framed a broader silhouette that moved from side to side, sort of like an advancing metronome.

Prye knelt next to Mig and cradled his head in his big hands. Mig looked up at him and tried to smile. "Lieute…gla…sure glad…see you."

"Can't say the same, Mig. Goddam, you're a mess."

One of the uniformed cops who'd come in with him, called over to Prye. "No pulse on this one, sir. Uncle Luc's outta business for good."

Prye gently started to pull Mig to his feet. The other cop came over.

"Let me help you, Lieutenant."

"I got him, I got him. Just open my car door."

Prye lowered his head to put Mig's arm around his shoulder. Holding him around the waist with his other hand, he started to walk outside with Mig, who was pretty much a man-sized rag doll.

"Easy does it, son. I'm taking you in to get looked at."

32

When Prye brought Mig into emergency at Foster Hospital, he was told it was probably best that the young man stay the night for observation. He agreed, and then left, driving back toward the station.

When he got there, he'd just parked and was getting out of his car, when an officer came out the front door with the boy Lon Torgen. The officer told Prye that the kid had come in right after school, but wouldn't talk to anyone but Lieutenant Prye. That was the one the guy in the green Chevrolet said he could trust. Prye was appreciative of Mig's good word. He asked Lon what he had to tell him, but he wouldn't say. The boy was plainly scared and started to break down.

"I gotta show you, sir. I gotta show you."

Prye patted the boy on the shoulder. "Okay, lad. It's okay. Where is it what you need to show me?"

"My house…Behind my house."

Lon told Prye where he lived and they drove to his house on Barnard Way, next to the Community Church. Prye parked in front of the stucco house with two thick posts on either side of a paver-tiled front porch. They got out of the car and Prye followed Lon down his driveway. Back several feet before the garage Lon led him to a brick walkway next to a tall picket fence.

"Excuse me…"

A woman had come out the back door, wiping her hands on a dishtowel.

"May I ask who are you and why you're with my son?"

Prye showed her his badge, only saying that Lon had something he needed to show him in back, but he didn't know what it was. As she asked if Lon had gotten into some kind of trouble, Prye looked through the high pickets to see the back yard paved in brick. There was a wide round well about four feet high with a brick facia. It had a heavy wooden cover. On the other side of the yard was another house made of mortared rock.

"He's not in any trouble, ma'am. But he needs to show me something."

"Well, then I'm coming, too."

"*No, Mom! No!* I'm just showin' Lieutenant Prye."

Prye put his hand on Lon's shoulder with a gentle squeeze. "Wait here, if you would, ma'am. Please."

Lon's mother pursed her lips, looking indignant, but, as asked, she remained where she stood as Prye followed Lon down the brick walkway and through a high wooden gate.

There was another part of the backyard, also bricked in, with two low tiers stepped up on the right side to another door of the rock house. On the left was a work shed built off the back of the garage. In front of that was a cement fishpond in the middle of a patch of flower garden strewn with leaves from a tall eucalyptus tree near the middle of this section of the yard. Prye was surprised to see yet two more houses, a cottage on the other side of the fishpond, and a smaller building, maybe for storage, up on the top tier against a wall bordering the property. Each of the structures was sturdily built of concrete chunks and river rock. It was the most intriguing backyard—double backyard—Prye had ever seen.

Lon took him through another gate and they stood at the top of a wide, deep ravine with thick brush and stands of trees, mostly eucalyptus. Off to the side of where they stood was an incinerator. Lon pointed to the bottom of the ravine and began to cry again. "Down there in the barranca….I covered it up."

Prye held to handfulls of brush and tree trunks as Lon led them down the side of what he'd called the barranca. When they'd reached the bottom, he sobbed even more openly as he cleared brush away to reveal a family-sized icebox. Through one edge of its closed door was a fragment of blue and white gingham, the hem of a girl's party dress.

When Prye was able to calm him down, Lon explained that his best friend Doug up the street had had a birthday party a week ago Sunday. His parents had given him a new wristwatch, which was in the pile of presents.

After everyone but Lon had gone home, Doug had discovered that the watch was missing, and he guessed that his sister Peggy had taken it. She'd stolen things from him before. Lon was with Doug and they both saw Peggy's secretive reaction when Doug shouted an accusation at her from across the yard. She ran away down the barranca and the two boys chased after her. But she managed to evade them, and after a while they gave up looking for her.

The next day, when Lon went back to his family's incinerator with a bag of trash, he wondered where their discarded icebox was. They'd gotten a refrigerator a few days before, and Lon's father had taken their old icebox out to be picked up with their unburnables. Lon found the icebox with the bit of cloth sticking out at the bottom of the barranca. He opened the icebox to see Peggy dead inside, her gray fingers clutching Doug's new watch.

Prye figured that Peggy had gotten inside the icebox to hide from her brother and Lon, and soon found that breathing became difficult and that the door didn't open from inside. She'd panicked, struggling hard enough for the icebox to tip over and slide down the barranca's embankment.

Lon had been carrying this for over a week, needing desperately to tell the authorities, but at the same time, conflicted with not wanting his best friend to have to live with what had happened to his sister, to be devastated by that as Lon was.

Mig had been thoroughly examined by more than one doctor. He ached all over, but was found to have no lasting damage. Prye came to pick him up the next morning, explaining what had happened to Peggy Beledayne. Through his one unswollen eye, Mig kept looking at the large paper bag in Prye's hand. Finally, his curiosity forced him to ask what it was. Prye reached into the bag and took out a broad-brimmed Stetson.

"Hope it fits. Didn't know your size."

"Thanks, Lieutenant, but I don't wear hats."

"Do everyone around you a favor and wear this one." He set the hat on Mig's head. It almost wasn't too big. " At least till you start looking human again."

Over breakfast at the Hob Nob Cafe, Mig asked Prye what had brought him and his men to the ice house, how he'd come to suspect Jefford.

"Should've started my wheels turning day before yesterday," Prye said, "When you pegged his old ice cream truck."

"How so, Lieutenant?"

"When you first arrived here last week, when Jefford came into the station with blood in his eye, thinking that poor Russian fellow abducted Peggy…"

"Yeah…"

"He said it was the day after she was reported missing that his truck was stolen. That would've been a week ago Monday." He chopped his arm at the table. "But the truck was gone the Thursday night before."

"Right, sir, but how did you know his truck wasn't taken that night and brought back so Jefford wouldn't ever—Oh, yeah, the front end."

Prye went on to explain that the damage to the truck wouldn't have mattered. It still could have been in Friday's Memorial Day parade, the Kiwanas banner across the front of the truck as it had been the year before, as Prye had seen in photographs. But He'd looked at all the parade photos from this year and the truck wasn't in any of them.

"I found out that early Memorial Day morning," Prye said, "Jefford called Bo Nellins, the Kiwanas Club president, about some mechanical problem why his truck couldn't be in the parade…. Only thing we don't know, not that it bears any real importance, is where they dumped that old ice cream truck."

"Suppose it'll turn up eventually," Mig said.

Prye stuffed the last of his waffle into his mouth, chewed and swallowed it.

"Sooner or later."

They argued over the check, Mig giving in to an insistent Prye. Out in the parking lot they shook hands and said goodbye. Prye headed to the station, Mig to the beach house to pack up the rest of Eddie's things and his own.

After he'd done that, he dropped in at Sal's to bid him farewell, joking, when Sal expressed shock at his beat-up face, that it only hurt when he laughed. Sal hoped Mig would come back "real soon to our fair seaside town." Mig said he probably would, but knew his chances of returning were slight, if any.

There was one stop he needed to make before he left Ventura. He turned onto Thompson from Seaward and drove the few blocks to Beledayne's used car lot. Mig didn't expect to see the owner's car there, and it wasn't. Sid Beledayne was no doubt home, being of comfort to his wife and stepson today.

Louise Kierney was filing paperwork when Mig walked into the office. It was obvious she wasn't glad to see him. She didn't question his appearance, evidently knowing what had happened the day before.

"What are you doing here?" she said.

"That must be your standard greeting, Louise."

"I found out you talked to my father. I have nothing to say to you."

"That's okay, I'll do the talking…Fellow I met recently told me to pay attention to the what is. I'm gonna go over the what is about you, Louise…You sent me on a wild goose chase down to Los Angeles to find out about morphine profit you knew was long used up."

She turned away, busying herself with filing.

"But I'm not here to rub your nose in that…You were in love with Eddie Fulham. Understandable. He was everything your old man and brother aren't. Kind…sweet…a loving sorta' guy."

He moved to better see her, the pain on her face.

"But as nice as he was to you, he didn't love you back. The man of your dreams you could touch but not reach…And for that you resented the hell out of him."

"Don't…"

"You had me go away to keep from finding out the real truth."

"Stop with this," she said. It sounded less demanding than

pleading.

"You went to Lucius Jefford with what Eddie told you. What he'd found out about Jefford and Peggy. You thought it sounded too sick, couldn't be true. But a good reason, you figured, for Jefford to do something bad to Eddie. To hurt him."

"That's ridiculous."

Mig shook his head. "That's the what is, Louise. Or the what was."

"Except for Luc coming in here for coffee sometimes, I never even knew him that well."

"I saw a flagpole in a pile of old lumber out at the ranch, your father's ranch. The top was sawed off. The part with the metal ball. Good at crafts as you are, I think you used it for the clown's nose on Jefford's old ice cream truck."

"That doesn't mean anything."

"Only that you two were good enough friends that you did that for him. Good enough friends that you could probably get Jefford to do something to Eddie."

"Louise turned to face Mig. She looked stricken. Then she blurted out, "Not to kill him!"

"Maybe not. Maybe only for Jefford to mess Eddie up enough that he'd leave town. Be out of your sight forever."

"I didn't commit any crime," she said weakly.

"Crime...that'd be hard to prove. But you'll have the rest of your life to think about what you caused, Louise. The rest of your sorry life."

When he got to L.A., Mig was relieved to find that the Fulhams weren't home. He didn't want to have to go into why he looked so wrecked, and that lead to explanation of the circumstances behind Eddie's death. He'd write them in time about all of it. But they didn't need to know this soon after their son's passing. Being in mourning was enough for them to have to deal with for the time being. He set the boxes of Eddie's belongings on the porch and left. It was just easier that way.

Driving away, he thought about Eddie's fear of night and the moon and how knowing the secret of that had gotten Mig involved. That last time he saw Eddie, in the field hospital at Mannheim, he had explained about it. One time when he was little, Eddie was out by himself a few minutes after dark. His mother was in a panic, and when he got home she told him that the moon goes looking for people at night. And when the moon found anyone alone, as he had been, it would do something bad to him.

When Eddie was beginning to be old enough to know that the moon story was only made-up, he and a neighbor kid his age were on a weekend camping trip with the other boy's family. Eddie and his friend were on a hike late in the afternoon. By the time it was dusk, Eddie decided to head back for camp, but his friend was determined to keep hiking for a little while longer. When it became night, a clear moonlit one, Eddie's friend stepped on what might've seemed to be a wide shadow. But it was a crevice several feet deep, and he was smashed to death in the fall. That was what had locked in Eddie Fulham's strange fear.

Mig stopped at a coffee shop near downtown L.A. before starting the long drive back to Phoenix. He wasn't hungry, told the waitress who came to his booth that he only wanted coffee.

He thought about what had happened over the past few days. About the hidden evil of Lucius Jefford…his use of Sid Beledayne…the finding of Peggy's body and what she had been a part of…Louise Kierney, the guilt she'd always carry…and Eddie. How his murder led to making things right. That was Eddie, sure enough, the way he was.

Mig's thoughts were taken over by the memories of it all.

"Who's that, mister? In the pit'cher?"

A little boy was standing next to Mig's booth. He looked up at the boy from under the broad brim of the hat Prye had given him.

"Wow! What happened to your face?"

"Ran into a wall," Mig said, then looked down and reflected. *Through* a wall? He wasn't sure about that. He saw the nearly empty cup on the table in front of him. He didn't remember being served the coffee. He had been lost in his thoughts and realized that he'd taken out his money. There was a dollar for the waitress next to the cup.

"Who's pit'cher you lookin' at?" the boy asked again.

He didn't look back at the boy, only gazed at the snapshot in his open billfold that he was holding.

"…My father," Mig said. "He's my father."

A young man, dressed day-off-work casual, followed closely by his concerned looking wife, rushed up to the booth.

"Come on, Kenny," the man said. "We've told you so many times not to talk to stran—"

"People you don't know," the young woman interrupted. Sighing, she looked down at Mig, gasping slightly at his appearance, and then saying, "We apologize. He just goes up to anyone and…" She shook her head, a gesture of mild embarrassment.

"Yeah, he can really be a bother. Sorry," the man said. Then to the boy, "Now, let's go, Kenny, and leave this gentleman in peace."

Mig watched the family walk toward the coffee shop's exit, their son between them, the father tousling the boy's hair as they left.

Then he looked back at the photo in his billfold of the other young man. The pale eyes like his. The face that bore some resemblance to the one Mig would see in a mirror.

"Hey, Aaron…" he whispered, as if wishing for response.

He'd never before spoken to the photograph. And Mig had never before looked at it through tears.

After a few moments, he put the billfold back in his pocket. He got up from the booth, grabbed his leather jacket, and headed for the public phone in the back of the coffee shop to call Carmen and let her know he was on his way home.

She advised him to sleep over on the way since it was a long drive to Phoenix. Starting when he was, and with the rest stops she knew he would need to make because of his shrapnel wounds, he'd be on the road most of the night. He told her that he'd think about it, but was anxious to get back. There was something in his voice that made her ask if he was all right.

"I'm okay, yeah. But I gotta warn you."

"*Have* to warn me about what, *hijo?*"

"Right now my face looks like something from a Lon Chaney Junior movie."

"Were you in an accident?"

"Not much accidental about it, Mama. Tell you when I get back."

After

When Mig returned to Phoenix and recounted to his mother what had happened in the nine days that he'd been gone, she said that God had certainly been with him. She'd hold to her belief in divine intervention. As Mig saw it, he'd just been incredibly lucky.

Bernie was glad to have him working in the warehouse again. The other guys seemed to be, too. Carl and Leroy took him out for beers and to shoot pool his first day back. Over the next week there was kidding about how the bruises he had were changing shape and traveling around his face as they began to fade.

Mig took up again with Dominic's widowed sister. But that was short-lived. They ended their relationship with a blowout over his unavailability three nights a week. Mondays, Tuesdays, and Thursdays, without compromise, Mig was tied up—boxing lessons.

Every day, when the sun was beginning its descent over Camelback Mountain, he walked in the desert, working on losing his limp. Within weeks, he was able to do some slow running for short distances. He had to heal, had to get stronger.

Carmen expressed her wish that he'd return to Maricopa J.C for the fall semester. Mig told her that he'd take a couple of classes. He owed her at least that much.

He started getting through more nights without troubling dreams. Bouts of the shakes were a little less frequent. He wasn't all the way out from the cold, dark place of the war, but doing for Eddie had given him something to build on. He had to believe that.

Jack Tolafsen and Carmen were going out to dinner one evening and asked Mig to meet them at the steakhouse they liked. When he got to the restaurant, his mother and Jack were already there, looking a little…he didn't know what. Happy in a kind of private way. When he asked them about it, Carmen brought her left hand up from her lap to the table. Mig looked at her ring finger and beamed. "Hey, no shi—no kidding? You two are really gonna do it?"

They told him they hadn't made any wedding plans yet, but wanted to wait until Jack's lettuce harvest was in so they could take a long honeymoon. Mig gave his mother a tight hug and then shook Jack's hand in both of his.

He offered to make them dinner in his apartment the next Wednesday. No boxing that night. All the cooking he'd ever done was just for himself, out of cans. But that wouldn't be good enough for the occasion. He decided on spaghetti, thinking he could handle that. And he had Bernie's reassurance. "Simmer the sauce real slow, don't'a overcook the pasta, and even a no-cook like'a you won't'a fuck it up, Mig."

They came over shortly after seven. Jack walked in with a bottle of Chianti and Carmen had mixed a bowl of salad. Mig wished that he had thought of these, but at least he'd remembered candles for the table setting.

After a few minutes of conversation, Mig excused himself to set the spaghetti to cook. His mother asked if she could help but he told her to just relax, he had everything under control. Jack turned on the radio to a new crime program, *The Big Story,* and he and Carmen sat together on the couch to listen to it.

As Mig was dumping the noodles into boiling water, the phone rang. He left the kitchen to answer it, and was surprised to hear Nate Prye on the other end of the line.

"Oh, Hi, Lieutenant. How things goin'?"

"Not too bad, can't complain. Just calling to bring you up to date." He said that Overton and Cathcart were still awaiting trial. Even if they didn't get the hot seat, they'd be locked up till the first rocket ship to the moon.

Mig expressed regret that he'd never made things right with Sid Beledayne. Prye said it was too late for that. "He sold his car lot and the house. Rumor is, Beledayne and family moved to somewhere up in Oregon….And get this: When they were cleaning out the house, in the basement they found all these dolls Peggy had hoarded. I mean at least a couple hundred dollars worth. It seems that bright little girl was using whatever she had over Luc Jefford for as much as she could get."

Mig thought of that old man, the one he'd met on the road to Ventura. What he'd said about opportunity becoming greed. Mig was beginning to see it in people all around him. It was even true with this now dead child who'd squeezed from Jefford as much payment as she could, even as he had so vilely used her. They'd played one other, each in their own greedy way.

"Oh, you remember that Russian woman, Irina Temiarov? The sister of the poor fellow that—"

"Yeah, I remember her."

"It turns out the Displaced Persons program hasn't reached the States yet. She managed to dodge around that for her and her brother. But Irina got deported."

"Too bad." Mig said, saddened. "That's really too bad."

"Oh, I bet she'll somehow work her way back. Somewhere

over here, if not to Ventura… You know, Mig, you saw this town with June gloom and all. Looks a lot better when the sun's out, as it is pretty much every day now."

Mig found it odd Prye mentioning that. "So, Lieutenant, you want a weather report back from here?"

The chuckle on the other end sounded a bit forced to Mig. Like Prye didn't quite know how to say why he had made this call.

"Sir, pretend there's no escape from, uh, the Empire State Building about to fall on us. You got ten seconds to tell me whatever you want before we're both flattened."

Prye told him that he and the chief of police had been discussing how they could use another young patrolman since the replacement for Hank Elias had decided to go into his uncle's radio and small appliance repair business. Then he seemed to wait for Mig to say something. When he didn't, Prye cleared his throat and continued in a businesslike tone, "Unless you've got firm plans for your future, Mig, it's something you might want to consider."

"Is that why you called, Lieutenant?"

"It's been on my mind."

Mig looked over at Carmen and Jack on the couch, listening to the crime show on the radio. They were holding hands, and he smiled at that.

"Like I said, just something for you to think about…"

Mig continued watching his mother and Jack, didn't respond right away.

Not for a few moments.

Acknowledgments

Probably no less than a few thousand authors have stated on like pages their versions of the thought that although writing a novel is a long, lonely task, ultimately it's not done without input, feedback, research assistance, encouragement from others.

This makes it a few thousand and one.

I'd fear being unfair with any ranking in importance or function in giving my appreciation to those who have generously offered their time and effort to me in fine tuning this book, so just listed alphabetically:

Steve August, Moira Brennan, Kimberly Cameron, Angel Cuevas, Don Ellis, Shannon Fee, Steve Ganz, Charles Johnson of the Museum of Ventura County, Tatyana Kurtulan, Adam Marsh, Maureen McRae, Zac Rymland and Jeffrey Reynolds of Liquid Pictures, the Staff of Ventura's Main Street Library, Corey Tyrell, and, unaware as he is of his considerable help, Jimmy Wales. My apologies to anyone I may have forgotten to mention.

The one exception to the above alphabetizing is my wife, helpmate, and best friend Elise. I felt her love and support all the way through.

Paul Samuelson grew up in Ventura, California. After attending UC Berkeley, he served in the 82nd Airborne Division as a news writer. Since working in the L.A. film industry for several years, he's been a freelance editor. He lives in the San Francisco Bay Area with his wife and two dogs. This is his first novel.

paul@storywrangler.com